GALAXY'S EDGE

EDGE

TURNING POINT

JASON NICK
ANSPACH COLE

Galaxy's Edge: TURNING POINT

By Jason Anspach & Nick Cole

Edited by David Gatewood
Published by Galaxy's Edge, LLC

Cover Art: Fabian Saravia
Cover Design: Beaulistic Book Services
Interior Formatting: Kevin G. Summers

For more information:

Website: GalacticOutlaws.com
Facebook: facebook.com/atgalaxysedge
Newsletter: InTheLegion.com

HISTORY OF THE GALAXY

IMPERATOR

0	The Pilgrimage
98	The Exploration
501	Savage Wars Begin
2000	Savage Wars Officially Declared Over
2047	Battle of Kublar

LEGIONNAIRE

| 2049 | Operation Ghost Hunter |

KILL TEAM

| 2054 | The Hunt for Goth Sullus |

GALACTIC OUTLAWS

| 2055 | Last War of the Republic |

ATTACK OF SHADOWS

SWORD OF THE LEGION

PRISONERS OF DARKNESS

TURNING POINT

01

Captain Keel looked from shock trooper to shock trooper, his blaster pistol leveled at the tall, deep-voiced soldier in front of him. The troopers kept Keel and Ravi in their sights despite Exo's best efforts to defuse the situation.

"Everyone, calm down." Exo lowered his palms in a soothing fashion, his blaster rifle slung over his shoulder. "If this had been anyone else, I'd say dust 'em. But Captain Ford is one of the best the Legion ever produced. Call sign was Wraith. He was on Kublar with me."

The big shock trooper, who seemed to be the team leader, looked casually to Exo. "Then tell him to drop his weapon."

"Drop your own weapons," retorted Keel. "Exo here bought you a few extra breaths, but those won't last forever, pal."

"Be cool, Wraith," urged Exo. He nodded back at the open grave of Kael Maydoon. "We weren't coming for you. We were coming for him."

Keel gave a sardonic grin. "So drop your weapons and go see him. He's waiting patiently enough."

The shock trooper standing before Keel flipped up his bucket's front plate, revealing a stern, dark face with expressive brown eyes. "It is not so simple as that. You're here. That raises questions my team will need answered. Why are you here, digging?"

"I'm an archaeologist," Keel shot back. "Looking for potsherds and found a body. Happens all the time. My friend here is a professor at the University of Utopion."

Ravi nodded. "Eighty-three percent."

Keel knew that Ravi was relaying Keel's chances of taking down every shock trooper with the *Indelible VI*'s guns. Eighty-three percent—those were odds Keel would take any day of the week.

Exo attempted to settle down the situation again. "Wraith, this is Bombassa, our team leader."

Keel gave a nod that morphed into a disapproving shake of his head. "Great. Nice to meet you. I don't care. We're leaving now. Ravi, if they twitch, have the *Six* open up on 'em."

Fearlessly, Keel turned to leave.

"Do not toy with me," warned Bombassa. "We hold your life in our hands."

Without breaking stride, Keel said, "Ravi?"

At once the *Six* spewed forth a blistering barrage of fire, knocking the unprepared shock troopers to the parched ground and sending their repulsor bikes up in flames. Keel was nearly hurled off his feet, but he steadied himself enough to keep his blaster aimed at the floored soldiers covering their heads. The dust and sand spewed up around them and rained down on their gleaming black armor.

Keel held up a hand, and the blaster fire stopped. "You can all thank Exo you're still alive. Have a nice walk back to your ship."

Exo coughed and spit sand from his mouth. He pushed himself to his feet and held out his hands.

Keel squinted to see what the shock trooper was holding. In one hand was a fragger; in the other hand was... a hand.

Maydoon's hand.

"Not cool, Wraith," Exo said between coughs.

The team leader, Bombassa, had been knocked out, and the rest of the shock troopers seemed too afraid to move. Or maybe they were dead. Keel was fine with either possibility.

"Don't be stupid with that fragger," Keel warned Exo.

Exo shook his head. "Not for you. Don't worry." He tossed the grenade casually over his shoulder, dropping it into the bottom of Maydoon's grave.

The ordnance erupted into a plume of white-hot flame so intense it seemed like it would turn the sand at the lip of the grave into glass. A burner. Kill teams used these to erase evidence before it could be compromised, or to destroy weapons caches. There wouldn't be anything left of Maydoon beyond carbon ash.

Exo held up the severed hand. "It's not hard to figure out what you were doing here. Same thing as us. The fleet. We're not the bad guys, Wraith. You know me. This is disruption to the status quo. This is opening eyes, man. It's what needs to happen to save the Legion from itself and a corrupt Republic that's poisoning it from the inside."

Keel held out an open hand. "No. Give it to me."

Exo pulled the severed appendage close. "You'll have to shoot me to take it, Wraith."

"Fine."

Keel aimed his blaster, but didn't shoot. Exo didn't crack. Finally, Keel shook the barrel of the weapon up and down and holstered the weapon.

"So how's this gonna work?"

"Guess that depends on who you're working for," Exo said.

Keel pushed a thumb into his chest. "I'm working for me and have been for years. I need that hand to rescue a crewmember of mine that Nether Ops kidnapped."

"The girl?" Exo asked.

Keel hid his surprise that Exo knew about Prisma. "Yeah. The girl. And a couple others."

"Good," said Exo. "That's good. We'll help you rescue your crew from them psychopaths at Nether Ops. And we'll get the ships. And the galaxy will be a better place for it."

Keel didn't like this, but he didn't know what better play he might have. He looked to Ravi, who only shrugged in reply. "Okay. You can come with me."

"What about the rest of the team?"

"Who cares?"

"Wraith, *I* care. You don't let down your squad."

"Fine. You got planetary comm capabilities in that helmet of yours?"

Exo nodded.

Keel gave a slight frown. He knew all this, but he wasn't going to tip his hand. Not until he felt he'd fully vetted Exo. "We'll tell them where to find us after we're in the air. Anything else?"

"Bombassa comes with us. He's not gonna be happy when he wakes up, and I'll need to be there to let him know there's been a change of plans."

Looking down at the unconscious trooper lying prone in the sand, Keel pulled down on his chin with the palm of his hand. "Fine. But he'd better behave himself on my ship or I'll send him out an airlock."

"It'll be fine," Exo promised.

"Okay." Keel moved toward the ship without turning his back on Exo. "I'll let you get him on board." To the shock troopers he said, "Enjoy the walk back home!"

***

Exo chewed on his glove as he watched Bombassa's vital signs on the medical bunk's holoscreen.

Better than my nails, he thought. He'd chewed those down to the point of bleeding over the past several weeks. He was on edge—had *been* on edge for a while now. Part of it had been the jitters of going up against the Legion in a head-on fight. That was daunting, but they'd gotten it done. They'd shocked the galaxy with a victory at Tarrago.

But the rest of it, what was causing him turmoil now, was twofold. Goth Sullus was not... normal. Exo had seen the way he just... manipulated things. Made them move of their own accord, like some kind of armored space wizard. Up to the point when he fought at Sullus's side on Tarrago Moon, Exo had figured the enigmatic leader of the Black Fleet was just a sound strategist. A former leej who, like Exo, was tired of the galaxy's best dying in droves for a government that didn't care. But clearly he was something more.

For Exo, this unknown caused worry.

Wraith was the other concern. Not the man specifically, but what he represented. Wraith was Exo's first former comrade to have seen Exo in his new skin: the black shining armor of a shock trooper. If Wraith held it against him, it didn't show. Then again, Captain Ford seemed done with the Legion himself, content to live a life in open space.

But would his reaction be typical? If Exo ever ran into Chhun or Masters… what would they say? Exo had a speech all planned out, but would it matter? Would they understand that he was doing what he was doing in order to save the Legion from extinction?

Bombassa moaned but didn't open his eyes. Exo watched the shock trooper for a moment, then looked again at the vitals on the screen. He had no idea if they were good or not. He had never been a medic, had never moved much past applying skinpacks or giving out pain nullifiers. Combat stuff. Bombassa had been unconscious for a while now, and Exo remembered reading somewhere that long stretches like that were a bad thing. Like, the longer you were out, the more damage might be done. Something like that.

"Hey, man." Exo gently smacked Bombassa on the face, which probably wasn't good for him either. "You okay? Wake up, Bombassa. You okay?"

Bombassa stirred and let out a groan. He opened his eyes and blinked at the bright lights shining down on him.

"Dim lights," Exo called.

The ship responded, and Bombassa looked around, clearly confused by his surroundings. "Where—" He began to sit up.

Exo pushed him back down, gently. "Take it easy, bro."

The two men had only gotten to know each other in the weeks since Tarrago—having been assigned to the same team by Goth Sullus himself—and had taken a liking to one another. They'd both experienced similar travails in the Legion. As for the rest of their six-man team... that was more complicated. They were good fighters—a little vindictive, but capable—but when talk came to Legion days, they never had much to say.

"This is not our ship," Bombassa observed. "Whose is it?"

Exo gave an apologetic smile. "Wraith's."

"The fool who shot at us with blaster cannons?" Bombassa sat up again, this time successfully resisting Exo's attempts to push him back down. "We are prisoners? We must take the ship. We—"

"We're not prisoners," Exo said, gesturing to his blaster rifle. "See? What we *are* is lucky to be alive. A bump on the head for you is pretty good, considering how jacked up things could have gotten. He could have killed us, bro."

"Hmm," Bombassa growled, sounding not at all convinced. "*You* feel good about this. I do not."

"Trust me," Exo said. He leaned against a counter containing a tumbler bot encasement. Wraith had some serious tech on board from what Exo had seen so far—like he'd raided a Republic supply closet. "Wraith told me he left the Legion after they used him up, same as you and me. Only he's been making his living on the smuggler and merc circuit. We have a shared goal, and trust me when I say, he can help. He's legit the best leej I ever served with."

Bombassa poked a forefinger into Exo's armor. "You, I trust. But this man..."

"Is probably listening in," Exo said, eyes shooting upward at the ceiling. "Aren't you, Wraith?"

"No," came Wraith's voice over the comm. "Look, Exo says you're willing to work with me. You want some ships, I want my crew. And you have the hand—which I'm not willing to kill a member of Victory Company over—but you don't know where to use it. I do."

Bombassa shot Exo a look. "Why did you tell him we didn't cypher the location of the fleet?"

"Because we didn't," Exo said. "Stop acting like a point. This gets the job done a lot faster than sending thousands of probe bots into space and hoping one gets lucky."

Bombassa folded his arms. "I'm not acting like a point. I don't trust your friend."

"I don't trust you either, pal," Wraith replied. "But if I wanted to kill you..."

Bombassa growled again. "What of the rest of our team?"

"Contact 'em and tell 'em to meet us at the Cresweil Bazaar on Porcha in two days. And tell them not to show up looking like commandos. We gotta shake any potential tails before we get to our destination."

"Sound good?" Exo asked, pleading with his eyes.

"Very well," said Bombassa.

Exo clapped. "Yes! See, Wraith, I told you he'd listen. We really are working for the same thing."

"I'm working for *me*, Exo. If the Legion gets saved in the process, I won't try and stop it. But I'm not getting dragged into your little revolution."

***

Keel switched off the comm and leaned back in his seat. He turned to Ravi, who was calculating navigational jump points for after they left Wayste's atmosphere. "Still listening in?"

"Yes," Ravi said with a nod. "They are discussing what to do if you were to double-cross them. They do not seem to trust you."

"I wouldn't trust me, either." Keel rubbed his chin. "Think they'll try something?"

Ravi shook his head. "They seem to be leaning toward working with you."

"Good."

"That is probably the last mistake either of them will ever make."

"Or, if they're like me, they'll get to relive their mistake over and over again. Like when I left that planet with you on board my ship."

Keel flipped a switch that locked and unlocked a predetermined series of doors, letting the two shock troopers move about. Allowing them some freedom of movement ought to gain Keel some goodwill, but he wasn't going to let them go wherever they pleased.

"You seemed happy to have me along, as I recall it," Ravi said.

"I was acting. Just like with Exo." Keel flipped on his autopilot and swiveled his chair to face his navigator. "Ravi, I can't *believe* he joined up with Sullus. What's he thinking?"

Not looking up from his console, Ravi said, "You should ask him."

"Trust me, I will."

Ravi's fingers danced across his display, then stopped. He placed his hands in his lap. "I have the jump coordinates determined, per your instructions. The shock troopers on board transmitted the location of the rendezvous to the rest of their team."

Keel nodded. He flipped the comm back on. "Exo, I wanna leave atmo and make the jump. Time's wasting. Did you tell your team yet?"

It was Bombassa who replied. "Yes. Are we free to move about the ship?"

"It's all yours except my quarters and the cockpit. I'll come back and show you around once we reach hyperspace. Wraith out."

Keel angled the *Six* upward, feeling the force of its thrust as the ship climbed through Wayste's stratosphere.

02

Phasia, on the Planet Demetrion

The zhee armada came out of hyperspace and hit the beautiful garden world of Demetrion first. Ten heavily armed, fully loaded former Republic next-gen battle cruisers smashed through the local system defensive fleet first, leaving a diplomatic frigate burning into atmo. The spreading debris field of the local corvette-heavy defense group assigned to guard the world expanded away, forming dozens of new navigational hazards for the pleasure traffic that had Demetrion as its destination.

Phasia, the capital city of this high-end luxury world, reacted quickly. Klaxons erupted across the sculpted city as bots and automated warning systems instructed the citizens to seek shelter immediately. Routes to the underground hyperloop system Demetrion boasted to the rest of the galaxy about revealed themselves on devices and every form of advertising. Gone were the promises of endless delights, culinary adventures, and once-in-a-lifetime experiences. Now adventure-vacationers were advised to flee into the tunnel system that had also been designed as a doomsday bunker of sorts, seeing as it was eight stories deep.

The zhee battle cruisers were utilitarian, with a workmanlike weapon system courtesy of the House of Reason. They had barely been secured from orbital descent before they were dumping assault transports out into the blue skies above palatial Phasia.

The eight-minute approach to the marked LZs the MCR technical advisors had set up for the zhee attack force seemed like some momentous pause before an approaching storm. In that brief time the citizenry raced for the automated escalators and lifts that would lead them down to the main platforms and then into the hyperloop rail tubes. At every level, heavy blast doors with alabaster facades were marked with ghostly bluish laser light holograms indicating countdowns before the bunker system would seal itself off from the outside world.

The first orbital strikes hit west and east of the city, destroying the underground escape arteries buried beneath eight tons of rock. Orbital strikes fell under the "weapons of mass destruction" category and were considered a war crime by the House of Reason—which meant only the House of Reason could authorize the Repub Navy to employ such dire measures. But to the zhee there was no such thing as a war crime... as the citizens of Demetrion were about to find out.

With zhee dropships landing across the city, a Legion scout detachment, Bravo Company, Seventy-Eighth Recon, rotating in on leave from some hot zone out along the edge, reported to the *Zephyr*, an assault carrier in cradle at the liner docks. It was the same ship that had brought them in only a week before. And as the first wave of zhee assault shuttles touched down all along the outskirts of the sprawling gardenscape that was Phasia, many of the two hundred and fifty odd legionnaires were buckets up and ready to give battle despite the odds and circumstances.

The Seventy-Eighth Recon was facing a military force of upward of ten thousand radicalized zhee deploying the new N-20 battle rifle system and sporting an advanced armor protection harness similar in effectiveness—without bucket, due to zhee religious concerns—to legionnaire armor.

The navy commander of the *Zephyr* was still busy trying to recall all navy and marine personnel when the Legion rode out from the carrier's assault cargo decks in convoy on scout-cycles and heavier all-terrain tactical engagement carriers (ATTECs), along with motorized utility light equipment (MULEs) armed with mounted N-50s and automatic rocket pods. The first engagements between the light mobile Desert Rats of the Seventy-Eighth Legion Recon and the zhee—now organized into a kind of loose military force—were brutal and fiercely desperate. In normal circumstances the zhee were a pretty tough stand-up fight against the Legion, especially when the zhee had the weight of numbers and access to working military equipment hodge-podged out of whatever weapons bazaar they'd been hovering over as of late. But now the zhee had state-of-the-art weaponry and armor, air support, ship-based artillery support, mechanized transportation, and limited jump capability as provided by their armor.

And... there were a lot of them.

Within minutes, it wasn't so much a battle as a brawl.

It was quickly made clear to the Legion captain commanding the Seventy-Eighth that a "win" for the Legion meant simply buying time for more civilians to get down into the bunkers and seal the main doors behind them. So for the next two hours, the Legion scout teams made the zhee troops pay dearly for every street, alley, and block. Still, the zhee noose slowly closed about the city—and looting and mindless destruction had half the city in flames.

At one point the Legion managed to hold five blocks near the center of the city, where they'd set up effective vehicle-based kill zones at major intersections. The zhee tried to take the rooftops but were held at bay by Bravo Company's highly decorated sniper teams. With casualties mounting on both sides, and the zhee war leader growing more and more frustrated by the minute, the zhee pulled back and called in an orbital strike on the five Legion-held blocks.

For the next twenty minutes, ship-based energy weapons, tuned to high intensity by the direct power feed from the battle cruisers' technologically advanced weapons and reactors, eviscerated the Legion-held redoubts inside the fortified city center. Buildings exploded outward, sending collapsing facades and shattered glass in every direction. Massive structures toppled over onto the dug-in ATTECs, burying the defending legionnaires alive. Massive beams carved street-wide gashes through the surviving buildings, and through the mules that had been operating from the alleys. Temperatures in the area rose to upwards of three hundred degrees. Streets turned to muck as impervisteel transformed into its molten state.

And at the end of it all, the Seventy-Eighth Legion Recon, to a man, was wiped out.

Fighting at the *Zephyr*'s docking cradle continued for a while longer. The ship's PDCs held the zhee at bay for much of the day. But in time, the zhee took the main engine compartments and forced the ship's captain to surrender.

So it was that by the arrival of the evanescent purple evening, Phasia was under complete zhee control.

At around midnight, the entire crew of the *Zephyr* was beheaded in a mass execution in the Gardens of Reason beneath the Capital Tower, which was then set on fire from the inside. It glowed like the apocalyptic torch of some end-of-the-world giant for most of the night, while the city was pillaged and looted, its remaining citizens savaged. The city's salvageable art, artifacts, physical credit reserves, and goods were loaded aboard transport and cargo shuttles to be carried off into orbit.

The only good news for the victims of what would come to be known as The Sack of Phasia was that their subterranean bunker held. The zhee tried, during the entire time of the raid, to violate the entrance to the hyperloop system, but it had been well designed, and they were unable to get at the hidden survivors below.

Barely twenty-four hours after it all began, the zhee departed, taking the *Zephyr* with them. As a parting farewell shot, they fired a crustbuster—yet another banned weapon of mass destruction—at the center of the city, right at the main access door guarding the subterranean high-speed rail system. There were an estimated twenty-four thousand citizens of the Republic seeking shelter down there at the moment the planet around them suddenly split open and turned to molten lava. The crustbuster left a smoking crater fifty stories deep, not only killing every last refugee, but destabilizing Demetrion's crust, preventing it from being safely inhabited for the foreseeable future.

The zhee did not stop there. They also hit the nearby worlds of Hexa, Muranto, and Callista. None of the cities of those planets suffered as dire a fate as Phasia, but all were looted, ruined, and burned. And all the while the zhee chanted their blasphemies and fired their blasters into the smoke-filled skies above the gutted ruins.

At last, their bloodlust temporarily sated, the zhee returned to their deadly battle cruisers and leapt back to Fortress Gibraltaar, their new base at Ankalor.

Unity House
Utopion

The schedule of a Legion commander, the highest post held by any Legion general officer, was hectic, to put it mildly, on any average day. Today… was not an average day.

Legion Commander Keller had just extricated himself from another useless question-and-answer session with a House of Reason select committee tasked with integrating special protected alien minority species into the Legion. The committee had all kinds of studies that supported their aim of diversifying the ranks, and they were demagoguing hard to get their latest pet project of the moment done. Several sector capitals had seen "spontaneous" ral-

JASON ANSPACH & NICK COLE

lies and marches break out in support of letting non-human species join the Legion. All of the protestors held pre-coded digital holo-signs that were supposed to look homemade. This was, after all, the cause of the moment.

But Keller suspected this Q&A was really nothing more than a probe to figure out what the Legion was actually up to in lieu of the... *problem* at Tarrago. Keller had gone into the meeting with his usual poker face, and he'd given them all the same-as-he-always-had common-sense reasons why the Legion needed to remain human-only. At least the House wasn't once more asking for special exceptions for non-males—not after what had happened the last time.

Still, both of these issues, as far as the House of Reason was concerned, were always up for negotiation. After all, pounding these particular drums got the House of Reason backbenchers a lot of votes among the aliens. "Alien diversification" was always a talking point in which to tear down the Legion, while conveniently ignoring how equally human-dominated the House of Reason was—and the rest of the Republic, for that matter. Only the Senate had any sense of true representation, due to the Constitutional requirement that their membership include representation from every sentient species and every planet in the Republic.

For the Legion generals and the NCO core, the backbone of the Legion, this issue was never up for negotiation. They saw it as a play to once more lower fitness and training standards in yet another attempt to weaken the Legion.

Because that was really the goal. To the House of Reason, the Legion was the real threat. And for good reason.

The distinguished delegate from Obregon had even wanted to allocate funds to develop a new non drill sergeant–based boot camp, replacing the fundamental training overseer since time immemorial with a new kind of instructor called a "military lifestyle and career coach."

Keller, who never laughed in public, had suddenly guffawed, and then quickly covered the involuntary eruption as a dry cough. The colonel who served as his adjutant might have actually sworn audibly within the Council chambers.

After that things got real quiet, and the House of Reason focus group was soon gaveled to an end.

Keller left the hearing room located within Unity House, a massive and very ornate tower complex that hovered over Utopion Prime, and made it to a nearby government landing pad ten minutes later, relieved not to have been waylaid by yet another delegate or senator seeking to sound out the Legion's loyalty to the Republic with yet another series of questions about everything but the thing they really wanted to know and couldn't talk about.

They were nervous.

They had reason to be.

Because the Legion had the Constitutional right to end the rule of the House of Reason and the Senate if it chose to.

In an emergency, the Legion could invoke the nineteenth article—known as the Champion Clause, or simply "Article Nineteen"—contained within the Galactic Republic's Constitution. This allowed them to assume control of the government for up to six months. Most of the generals had advocated for years that such a maneuver was nearing execution.

But six months didn't buy a lot of time to do what needed to be done. Every House of Reason member had to be arrested and tried legally, and then new elections needed to be held so that the House of Reason could be restored and free of corrupt influence. The Senate was a bit easier, though nearly as time-consuming—it could simply be dissolved, and then it was left to the home worlds to elect new senators according to local custom.

But all of this was politics. Not something the Legion wanted to participate in. Not something it was designed to participate in. The Legion did war, and Keller had no clue why the early legionnaires had thought the Champion Clause was a good idea.

The shuttle sent to transport Keller to his next meeting landed on Government Pad Thirty-Three, and the adjutant, Colonel Speich, signaled Keller that it was time to board. They were standing inside an expansive and beautifully appointed boarding lounge. Of course, everything about the House of Reason's governmental offices and facilities was beautiful. Off mic, any member would've joked: "If you can't have the best, why get into politics in the first place?"

It was an old joke they only told each other.

As Keller shut down his briefing notes and locked the file with a code, an older man entered the boarding lounge. He was a tall, stoop-shouldered academic type in tweed, his scrawny neck wrapped in a scarf. Long, broken nose. Wispy white hair.

He made straight for the general of the Legion in long active strides that made clear his intentions were pur- poseful and that those intentions were to engage in con- versation. He had come seeking an audience regardless of hell or high water. Whatever that meant.

Keller sighed and put on his dress uniform jacket. He'd been going over some reports that didn't mean anything. Of course the House of Reason had every camera in the facility pointed right at him and his tablet.

"Excuse me, Legion Commander Keller," began the old academic.

But the adjutant colonel, a short, iron-gray-haired bulldog of a man, cut the academic off five steps out. Keller knew that Colonel Speich could kill the man in about two point four seconds with his bare hands alone. He was even a little bit faster than Keller, who did PT with any Legion unit he could find. Every day. He took pride in running young leejes into the ground as he dragged them through sixteen miles of the most grueling terrain he could find, in formation, at the double.

It pleased him to see them throwing up.

It was displeasing that, at his age, he could make them do that. There was a time, not long ago, when that would have been an impossibility. The young leejes were too strong for that. But not now. The effects of the constant meddling by the House and Senate had taken a toll.

Keller especially liked runs that landed on payday. Because the NCOs and the battalion commanders prac- tically begged him to ruin their troops for the weekend before they ruined themselves in the bars. It was not uncommon to have legionnaires pass out in their racks for upwards of twenty-four hours after Legion Commander Keller had finished one of his little runs. Those same legionnaires found that their muscles had turned to iron chains and cramped into immobility as they lay down for just a moment after the grueling morning run, waiting for final payday inspection. For the rest of the weekend they moved like ruined old men.

"The Legion Commander has another appointment to keep, and we're already late," said Colonel Speich in his usual all-business, don't-make-me kill-you staccato bark.

"I understand," began the old academic a bit fustily. "I was just wondering if he had a moment for an old leej from Psydon."

Keller heard that, and so did Speich. Psydon was a bad conflict. It had been a little bit before Keller's time, but the old veterans who'd been his first NCOs had been there, and they'd told him some pretty crazy stories about that brutal conflict. If you were at Psydon, you deserved a measure of respect. It didn't buy you everything. But it did buy you something.

"You were at Psydon?" asked Keller, as though he were challenging the old man to tell another lie.

The old man nodded and seemed to stand a little straighter, though his bony shoulders remained bent.

"I was. Sergeant, Tenth Recon. Pathfinder. Call sign Creeper. I got hit at the Aachon Reservoir."

Everybody knew about the Aachon Reservoir. It was the kind of battle where legends and heroes were made. And where they died too.

Speicher clasped his hands and stepped back, and Keller stepped forward and shook the old vet's hand, murmuring, "Sergeant."

The Legion might have been slowly changing from what it once was, but it hadn't changed so much that it had forgotten the leejes who'd gone before.

"What can I do for you?" Keller asked.

The old man cast his gaze about. He knew they were watching. Knew they knew what this meant. He, too, was casting the dice. Letting them fly. He was siding with the Legion once more. For now.

"After Psydon," said the old man, leaning in close, "I joined the intelligence services."

Keller nodded. He knew Dark Ops well. Relied on them more and more. But he didn't know this man. Some... other intelligence group, perhaps? Those made him feel uneasy. Nether Ops? They were the devil.

"Nether Ops... to be specific," said X, the old academic, calmly. "And I have some very important information I think you're going to need to hear. May I accompany you? I feel that my life is in danger, Commander."

***

The shuttle lifted away from the high landing pad alongside the government tower and joined the outbound traffic racing through Utopion's skies. Keller sat facing opposite X. Colonel Speich was seated in a flight chair across the shuttle's narrow aisle. Keller assumed a distant observer's poker face that he'd found worked best in just about every situation.

X settled himself in his seat and cast his melancholic gaze out the porthole at the beautiful land below. "The mass of men lead lives of quiet desperation," he said, as though he were speaking only to himself and only observing the heavy ship traffic over Utopion. Out near the Grand Council Hall, the immense bulk of a super-destroyer waited, hovering just over the ornately sculpted monument to social justice government at its pinnacle.

Keller said nothing, content to wait and see how the hand of the other man sitting across from him was played out.

"Thoreau," X murmured.

Keller had no idea what that meant. He wasn't interested in poetry, or some history lecture. In ten minutes they would reach Legion HQ and the interview would be over. The man before him would either say what he came to say... or he wouldn't. In a few minutes the opportunity would be lost.

"The 'mass of men'—that's the important point in that little bit of phrasing I just repeated. Or rather, it's my point, Commander."

Keller, who'd decided to see this through without saying a word, suddenly lost his patience and sighed. "What is your point?"

X turned to face the commander. Studied him intently for a long moment. As though he were trying to see if the younger man before him was the man required for this moment, this time, this hour come too suddenly.

X nodded to himself as if having reached some conclusion. "But not them," he said X, tilting his head toward the porthole and the grand majesty of a super-destroyer riding just over the top of the Grand Chamber of the House of Reason. "They are not the mass of men. Not when you can ensure that the Constitution is used as your own heavily armed lifeboat. That makes them a little different than the rest of us, doesn't it, Commander?"

Keller had been clenching his fists. Becoming aware of this, he flexed his fingers and wished for a little range time. Heck, he wished for a company and a mission. He'd always been a leej in that way.

After composing himself and running a quick hand across his dress uniform, he said, "No. It does not."

And then nothing more. No commentary of bitter indictment against the takers who only ever took. Just a loyal soldier who knew he was on the losing end of things and still did the right thing anyway. Still kept his shield locked with his brother legionnaires. Still held the line despite the odds. It was the only way when one was surrounded. Hold on to the known. Stay true.

"They," said X, nodding again toward the House of Reason beyond the porthole, "have just turned over Fortress Gibraltaar to the zhee. On Ankalor."

Keller's face, a face of a cool, calm, controlled card player, dropped. Shock and disbelief were replaced by rage. Not a loose word or gesture escaped him, but the effect of X's revelation was like some airstrike that had hit the bunkers far below, ravaging his unseen subsurface. The ground merely shook, but everything underneath had become chaos and destruction. Death and darkness.

"And ten of those new battle cruisers the navy didn't tell anyone they were developing... they gave the zhee those too. Specifically to their new war leader... Karshak Bum Kali."

Now Keller clamped his lips tight. His eyes smoldered like smoking hot coals.

"The House of Reason is hedging their bets, Commander," said X finally. "And they're betting against the Legion."

After a long pause during which Keller bored holes into the face of the unconcerned old man across from him, he finally muttered through clenched teeth, "Proof?" Even though he knew that everything this man was saying was true. Knew that they, the perpetual high and mighty scumbag lizards of the House of Reason, would do something like this. Something *exactly* like this.

X reached into his tweed jacket and produced a memory device. He handed it to Keller, who passed it to Colonel Speich. Speich began the process of unlocking the file on his personal device.

Keller returned to staring at X like he wanted nothing more than to murder the old man. But his gray eyes were somewhere else. Murdering someone else.

Murdering many someone elses, most likely, thought X. *Possibly even the entire body of the House of Reason.*

"It's time," said X softly. "Legion Commander."

Keller came back as if from far away. Suddenly seeing X again.

They shoot the messenger, thought X briefly. *They always shoot the messenger, don't they?*

And then he dismissed that thought because it wasn't true. It just felt that way all the time.

"Time for what?" Keller asked.

"Article Nineteen."

Keller didn't move. Didn't flinch. Didn't show the slightest bit of surprise. Because the old man sitting in front of him was right.

"You have six months. It's not impossible. But it can be done," X continued.

"In the middle of a hot war?" Keller seethed.

"Actually," said X brightly with a brio that seemed almost whimsically insane. "That's the perfect time. You'll be the saviors on the other side of this."

"According to the Nineteenth," Keller said, "we would have only six months to arrest, try, and adjudicate the House of Reason. If we reach a guilty vote based on a judgment of Failure to Lead, then we have to hold elections immediately. We do not have the full weight of the Republic Navy, we have no support from the civilian or governmental leaders, and we're scattered across the galaxy—mainly across the Tarrago sector—fighting a war against a new enemy that's put up the stiffest fight we've faced since the Savage Wars. What you're suggesting may not be impossible, but it might as well be."

"It's not impossible," murmured X once more. "You just need to make an opening move that scares the living daylights out of your enemies. Let's them know you mean business, Commander. Serious business. They'll scatter, which works best, or they'll fight. Which allows you to destroy them en masse. But to do that you'll have to go—and this is an old myth from the Earth stuff if you believe all that—but they used to have a saying back then: You will have to go Roman."

Commander Keller knew exactly what that phrase meant. Better than X did.

Colonel Speich handed his personal device across the aisle to the commander. Keller took it and studied it grimly for a moment. The look on Speich's face was pure doom. And a sickly one at that.

After a moment Keller lowered the device to his lap, as though it were forgotten, unimportant now that its terrible secrets had been witnessed. He looked at the old man known as X and knew at last with whom he was actually dealing.

"What do you propose?" he asked.

And that stunned X for a bit—though the old spy didn't show it. He hadn't expected the Legion commander to reach the conclusion/realization the man had just reached— at least, not for a few more days. Which showed, in that moment, that Keller *was* the right man for the moment. *This* moment. The right man to lead the Legion through its Constitutional duty to take control of the Republic and restore the democracy.

To start a Constitutional crisis. And finish it.

X gathered himself as though some cold wind had passed by and chilled him to the bone. Then he said what needed to be said and what needed to be done. What *would* be done, regardless of the consequences.

"It's time go Roman on the zhee, Commander."

03

The trim and fit young Legion captain who was to give the briefing on the tactical overlay of Fortress Gibraltaar on Ankalor, a zhee home world, stood in the shadows, waiting for the general officers to take their seats at the front of the briefing room. There was only one holographic projection; Keller wanted to look these men in the eyes. Only Major Owens, who was still involved with the situation at Herbeer, was represented by hologram. Keller would inform Owens of his promotion as the top leej in Dark Ops once he saw the man in person.

Aides gathered in the back with tablets and comm. A moment later Legion Commander Keller, in fatigues, stepped forward and addressed them.

"Gentlemen," he began. "What we have long suspected might happen has finally happened."

He said this in a matter that was blunt and terse and underwhelming. There were no dramatics, no histrionics, no hyperbole or gravitas. None of those things were ever present when legionnaires spoke to one another at any level. It had been trained out of them in favor of truth in communication. It was truth over all else, in general.

And every commanding officer present today was a true legionnaire—not some point who'd been foisted on them by the ever-wheedling, ever-boundary-pushing House of Reason and all their endless functionaries.

So this secretive little briefing room deep in hyperspace was a place of truth. There wasn't room for anything else. There wasn't time left for anything else. Words meant what they meant. Which was a phrase they'd learned all the way back in basic training, and learned again in Legion Command and Staff. The galaxy and the House of Reason might play their endless word games, changing meanings to fit the current agenda, or political want, but not the Legion. Here... words meant what they meant. And truth reigned supreme.

"The Grand Council of the House of Reason," continued Keller, "has armed the zhee with a base and ten warships. This came to us three days ago via a confirmed friendly Nether Ops source. It was verified by operators on the ground within twenty-four hours. Obviously the House of Reason is anticipating that we will either be destroyed fighting the rebels calling themselves 'the Empire,' or they intend to betray us once and for all by using the zhee at a crucial moment to free themselves of the Legion and the threat of Article Nineteen."

Keller paused and stared at all of them. Giving each a moment to digest the information he'd just delivered. "Given what we know about their clandestine treatment of legionnaires in the synth mines of Herbeer, I believe it to be the latter.

"Now, if you will all check your devices, you will see that you are receiving a blue book file that was part of your curriculum at Legion Command and Staff. But this is not a training exercise. I repeat that as per SOP. This is *not* a training exercise. It is a formal request by the current Legion commander, myself, to the required amount of serving general officers, to implement an Article Nineteen vote. The relevant information fields have been filled in within the blue book, and you may now review the charges brought against the House of Reason."

Keller folded his hands and stepped back.

If even one of them voted against him, he would be arrested by the rest and turned over to the Republic for trial, facing charges of sedition and seeking to overthrow the government. That was the safety check. Any general officer included in the vote could stop the process. And the perpetrator.

It was also part of the reason why the House of Reason pushed so many points to the rank of general.

On screen behind Keller a pending quorum vote tally appeared in ghostly holographic numbers that swam across the briefing room wall. Both options—"assent" and "do not assent"—were now at zero.

For the next ten minutes a quiet tension filled the room and only the sound of the devices being tapped at could be heard as the generals reviewed the charges on the tablets below their stern faces. Halfway through the ten minutes, X, who was lurking in the back behind the aides, lit his pipe and puffed it to life.

Then the votes came in.

Assent.

Unanimous.

Keller felt a wave of relief, though he'd never truly believed these men would deny him. For a long quiet moment the weight of what had been decided fell over the room. There was no turning back. The die had been cast.

Keller stepped forward once more to the briefing podium.

"I will arrange the arrests with Major Owens and begin a formal impeachment process of the Council. I'll take the Fourth and Twelfth Legions to take Utopion. I intend to implement martial law without much fuss. The House will be too busy running to stir up much trouble. And after Tarrago, their polling is at an all-time low. So, Urco and Moss, you're with me. Signal your legions to prepare for rapid deployment once naval units loyal to us have formed the new Legion fleet."

The two generals nodded at their commander.

"Moving on," Keller said, as he stepped back to allow the generals to watch the presentation he'd prepared to accompany the next bit. "At present many of our allied naval commanders are scattered across the edge. We'll recall them to Cononga to begin loading the bulk of the Legion for sustained operations once we've secured the capital, and then to deal with this new threat at Tarrago. We can't hit the latest rebel of the month until we clean up our own back yard. Once the delegates are arrested, the rest of the navy will have to be vetted, and that done quickly.

"Of course, we expect the House of Reason to form a government-in-exile and attempt to declare invalid our

Constitutional right to take control of the Republic for six months. So we'll have two forces working against us at once. The Black Fleet will be seeking advantage during the chaos of regime change, and the House of Reason will be seeking to arm unreliable factions—such as the zhee and the MCR—to use against us.

"Therefore we must send two clear messages, at the same moment we take control and arrest the House of Reason. First, that the Legion is in control of the Republic—and second, that a new level of harshness is in effect."

The strategic display of the galactic political situation was replaced with the simple title of the operation: *Turning Point.* The letters hovered in an ephemeral ghostly white, belying the permanency they implied.

"This will be our message to the citizens, and enemies, of the Republic, gentlemen. *The Legion is in control.* And we will restore the Republic to good governance, whatever the cost. And to convey that message... we are going to make a very dire example of a threat to every law-abiding species in the galaxy."

***

The briefing ended, and the five generals whom Keller had appointed as the Legion's governing council in lieu of the House of Reason moved on to the next meeting in Keller's personal quarters, adjacent to his office.

The mood was somber as the other generals returned to their divisions and commands, bearing the unseen burden of what had been agreed upon. And of what would be required. They had either committed treason, or they were saving the Galactic Republic. The history that would be written in the years to come would judge them. That was the only thing that was truly known.

Inside the private conference room, Colonel Speich assured the generals they had total EM security. Then this second meeting began.

"Our next step is to divvy up the work that needs to be done regarding arrests, trials, and a new election," began Keller. "But before we get to that, and the security plan to deal with this new menace known as the Black Fleet—I know what they're calling themselves, but they damn sure didn't earn the title of 'empire'—we need to agree on the opening move. I've decided to send a message to both of our foes, and to the galaxy in general. It will be extremely harsh, but in the end it will save more lives than it costs. Of that, I'm sure. This will be total war.

"We're hitting our new base on Ankalor. The Republic finished construction of Fortress Gibraltaar ahead of schedule, and instead of allowing the Legion to take possession of it as planned, they turned it over to the donks—I mean, the zhee." He stopped. Article Nineteen freed him from a lot of the House of Reason's word games, including the slippery game of political correctness. Donks. He began again. "Most of our companies are involved in current combat operations in various minor conflicts. But we have three legions destined for other hot spots that can be reassigned and ready to move within the week. We're forming a new corps and folding all three legions, along with some other stolen, borrowed, and begged assets, into a combined arms assault force transported by three assault carriers. What we need to determine is who will command the corps and lead the operation against Fortress Gibraltaar. I'll take suggestions from you now."

The generals shifted and reviewed their choices. It was General Rohm who threw out the first names like he was showing two pairs and jack.

"Top of the list is Hannubal. Then Samax. And of course... me."

"Need you for Utopion, Rohm," said Keller without the slightest trace of apology.

"Hannubal is daring, but he wouldn't be my first choice at all," said General Daeros. "But... he also might just be the right leej for the job. He's damn sure bloodthirsty enough. No question there."

Keller nodded.

And on it went. There were other suggestions from other generals. But in the end the consensus was General Marcaius Hannubal.

The Bloody Wolf.

"Then it's agreed," said Keller. His voice somehow filled the quiet room with a sense of understated gravity that made the reality of what they were doing come home to all of them. "I'll appoint Hannubal to the rank of Praetorian general and give him command of the task force I've assembled. He'll lead the assault with the order to wipe out Fortress Gibraltaar. He is to make an example of the zhee taking up arms against us, and to serve notice to the galaxy that the Legion does not play House of Reason games. When we go to war... it is total war. It is actual war. There are no boundaries, no conditions. No lines we will not cross in order to achieve not just victory... but conquest."

He made eye contact with every general. They assented with bare but sure nods.

"Moving on..."

***

When the planning for the implementation of Article Nineteen was complete, Keller left for his private office. Marcaius Hannubal was already waiting in a chair, staring out the window at the passing light show that was hyperspace.

Out there, thought Keller as he moved to his desk, the entire universe was speeding by. And it was a different universe than the one he had awoken to this morning. The members of the House of Reason had no idea that their entire galaxy had just changed in the space of a few hours. Even now they were still playing their games. Thinking they were comfortably secure.

General Hannubal stood as Keller entered, then sat when the Legion commander took his seat at his desk and bade him do likewise. Colonel Speich hovered invisibly nearby.

"I trust Speich has briefed you so far, Marcaius?"

Hannubal nodded. He was a young man. Or rather on the older side of young. Thirty-nine. He'd come up through the Legion officer corps fast as an infantry platoon leader—on Ankalor, incidentally. Then as a heavy infantry company commander. A special warfare team leader as a major, and then off to Command and Staff up through to general. He was daring. He had five misconduct charges, all dismissed, all filed by point officers at various episodes in his career. But of course every real legionnaire had some of those.

He had been lucky. Avoiding the quagmire of missed promotions by the point system.

He was bloodthirsty. Or at least that was the al-ways-whispered rumor about him ever since the blood-bath at Haclydion.

Haclydion had been a bad conflict no one wanted any part of. A planet that couldn't govern itself due to bad trib-al alpha politics, constantly appealing to its patrons in the House of Reason to put down any rebel uprising its mis-management had caused.

Some years ago, the Legion was sent in to put down a particularly nasty MCR-driven insurgency that was trying to put in power a rebel leader worse even than the corrupt President for Life currently running the planetary econo-my into the ground and looting its treasuries and natural resources to boot. The legionnaires were getting needless-ly killed on long pacification patrols out in the bush, and they were constantly prevented from hitting the MCR base because it lay within the boundary lines of a sympathetic tribal district. Tired of this, Brigadier General Hannubal—though this was never proven—assembled an ad hoc strike force of legionnaires not in armor or kit, marched them three days through disease-infested jungle, climbed a mountain, came down the other side, and wiped out the MCR base on the sly, leaving no survivors and making sure that every body was decapitated. The base turned out, in retrospect, to have been supplying IEDs and weapons to the rebels. The ad hoc strike force then returned back over the mountain, back through the disease-infested jungle, and reached the Legion base within the week. All of this was accomplished while the whole strike force was supposedly on leave after a rotation in from the field. An IG review showed that no armor or leej weaponry had been used in the strike.

Video footage acquired by the rebels the day after showed the remains of a bloody massacre at the MCR base. Within days, the rebellion died off, and MCR recruitment dropped sharply once most everyone realized they did not want to be as badly massacred as those who had been well behind enemy lines, in a secure and fortified position, had been.

In the dead of night.

Without a shot fired.

It was then that the natives began to call the general the equivalent of the Bloody Wolf. Though their "wolf" was actually a fast-moving saurian raptor that hunted at noon.

Hannubal had never admitted to the raid, and though it had almost cost him his career, as far as the navy and the House of Reason were concerned, within the Legion it made his reputation as a general who got things done no matter what.

Now, sitting in front of Legion Commander Keller, the man known as the Bloody Wolf seemed the opposite of all the infamy that had almost crucified him in the media at the time.

The Legion had been accused by all the major news networks of "making monsters."

"This is a simple operation," Keller began. "It's an attack on a fixed position. There are two shield generators in play. One mushroom cap over Gibraltaar and one planetary defense shield tied into the core tap grid. We're sending in a kill team to take out the shield generator array located in the Sarum Harassa neighborhood in Ankalor City. Like I said, it's an attack on a fixed position, and you'll have full orbital support from our ships. Nothing more than a simple operation to take an entrenched position, just grand scale. The zhee are foaming at the mouth for a chance to die for one of their gods in battle... and we'd like you to help them."

Keller thumbed through a menu and brought up a schematic of the base. Then he looked at the younger man soberly.

"How would you take this base, Marcaius?"

Keller knew full well that the young general had already spent twenty-four hours developing a plan, and the Legion commander had a pretty good idea, or at least so he thought, of what General Hannubal was going to ask for to complete the op.

The assets had been stacked and arranged. Ready to be committed at the drop of a hat from all across the nearby sectors. A drop fleet. Air cover. Heavy armor. The works. And all of it in support of what would be, at the end of the day, a bunch of leejes going in there to wipe out everyone. Because that's what it had to be. It had to be total. And it was... what it always was. What it always came down to.

Sending men in to do what needed to be done.

Hannubal didn't lean forward to check the map one last time. He knew what he was going to do. Instead with a brief nod he committed once more to the plan he'd walked through the door with. With one arm over the back of the chair and one boot kicked out in front of the other like some Caesar from ancient days he spoke with an ease that belied the awesome destruction he was about to rain down on the zhee. Calmly and with total confidence, he told his superior how he was going to murder them all for daring to even think insolently about who was in charge of the Republic. The zhee had it coming. They'd brought this on themselves with their mass uprisings, their suicide bombs against civilian targets. Their terror. Their unwillingness to live and let live.

Keller had expected the worst from the Wolf. He had half-guessed how he would do it. But what Marcaius Hannubal said stunned Legion Commander Keller.

"This can be done without the casualties the tac assessment AI tells us we're supposed to take, sir. I don't need the entire fleet in orbit, initially, and I'd like to take the assault carriers in at the same time the KT does the insert on the planetary shield array. I don't need navy interceptor cover either, and we'll use our own armor. We'll hit the target with all three legions and the assault carriers, and pin their commander so he can slip away."

Keller hadn't expected a commander to want to go in without fleet cover... but it made a kind of sense. Pin Karshak Bum Kali before he could slip away into any one of a million bolt holes inside the zhee slum networks. Going in to that nightmare hellhole would cost good legionnaires their lives for no reason. And with no guarantee of the high-value target's capture.

Hannubal continued.

"The longer we wait, the more the zhee mullahs will begin their call to arms. Pinning down their war leader quickly allows us to dictate terms. If they see a fleet in orbit, those dress-wearing donkeys will pull everyone they can out of the slums in Ankalor and surround the place with their own females and children. Plus they have control of the planetary shield array. They'll throw that thing up once they get their first sniff of trouble. Tac assessment puts our casualties much higher if that happens, because we all know the women and children are just as vicious as the donk male. And the mullahs don't mind strapping explosives on the females and their kids. It has to be now, and it has to be quick. This is a knife fight in a blind alley, sir. First one to cut deep wins and gets to walk away."

Keller caught Colonel Speich staring at him, and the look was not good. Speich was a cautious, conservative officer who did everything with business-like efficiency.

"Okay," said Keller slowly, leaning back in his chair. "Then tell me how you take the base and get Karshak Bum Kali alive? Because I need him for the next move. Everyone else, not so much."

"There are three defenses we need to overcome to take the fortress," said General Hannubal. "The air defense turrets beyond the defensive shield. The outer ring trench system. And the central fortress itself, built inside the rock. I just need those three assault carriers, the three currently picking up the legions and armor. Re-route them to the arsenal at Duram Hatam, because we want the old-issue gear that actually works—the tactical armor from the Kublar days. And they've still got racks and racks of N-42s; those platoons will want those babies, sir. Twenty-four hours to load out, and then we jump. Low-altitude capital ship jump insertion right into the atmosphere southwest of the fortress. Assault carriers descend to below five hundred, and they can't be hit until they're within visual of the air defense turrets. I have a recon company and a few other assets en route to HOLO into the area of operation and play a few dirty tricks before we ring the bell."

Hannubal reached forward and expanded the terrain map surrounding the fortress complex. He drew the map down toward the southwest coordinates until they were over an area the map labeled "Alpha Zulu Zero Three."

"These," continued General Hannubal, "are the facility's blaster, heavy weapons, and explosive ordnance ranges intended for training use. The zhee won't be here because they don't train, and it's outside the defensive shield that prevents us from firing from orbit. A long berm protects our LZ from direct fire from the base. We'll offload HK-PP armor and strike teams here. They have to cross a quarter mile of open field to hit the trenches, but we'll be using SMAFF to cover the assault. Our drop ships will run ops out of the assault carriers, which will lock forward deflectors and form the IDS system. At that point they'll be invincible against anything the base can throw at their forward deflectors.

"We start the ground operations immediately at first light. Surprise, speed, and overwhelming force will take us inside the trenches quickly. Once we assault through the three rings of the trench network, we can take the main complex with explosives and flamethrowers. Counter-sniper and anti-armor teams will keep the base's rock-side turrets, anti-armor, and sniper teams busy so we can get at the front door. But there's no two ways about it, Commander: we can't get much more surprise out of this than that. It's a big rock sticking up out of the desert floor. And the fighting in the trenches will be brutal. But if we move quickly and violently to exploit our gains, we can do this with as little loss of life as possible."

Keller said nothing.

Colonel Speich moved forward.

"As you've noted, General," he said to Hannubal, "the air defense turrets that surround the facility will be able to hit the incoming assault carriers before they put down on the LZ. Those carriers can't integrate deflectors and form the IDS until they're down and centrally slaved to one another's power plant systems. To avoid the fire from the towers, you'll have to put down outside their range. But then the indirect fire you'll take from the fortress will tear your armor and men to pieces as you cross open ground to get into the trenches."

Hannubal nodded; the man's point was salient. But he countered.

"That's why we need to come in fast and get inside their indirect fire radius. Using the training ranges for an LZ accomplishes this. The energy gun batteries on levels forty-six and seven aren't ranged for targets that close to the base. As for the air defense turrets, I've already HOLO-dropped a long-range company in the Ankalor wastes. They're masquerading as Guzim Haxadi, a local tribe of nomadic zhee who live deep out in the desert. The installation's ground radar will track them as just nomads coming in to do trade. They'll reach the southwestern air defense turret at dusk the night before. My plan calls for them to free climb the rock it's built on and take the battery by stealth. Once inside, they'll have access to the air defense network grid. Disabling that will allow us to bring the assault carriers in. That's assuming the zhee haven't suddenly become competent coders who can rewrite targeting and acquisition code destroyed by an algo-worm."

Keller leaned back and checked his watch. "Agreed, Marcaius. Now I've got to meet with the rest for phase two of the operation. Once they activate the planetary shield you'll be trapped down there. So we're going to knock that down so the fleet can come in and support operations against any kind of counter-response."

04

Captain Chhun hunched over the conference table in Victory Squad's team room. This was the squad's fourth stint aboard the *Intrepid*, which now felt more like home to Chhun than any other place he knew, apart from his family's place on Teema. Already Victory's squad flag—featuring a koob skull with thunderbolts crossed behind it—hung prominently behind the tactical planning table. The rest of their memorabilia—from countless ops dating back to the Battle of Kublar—would be shuttled in later. Interior decorating wasn't really a priority right now.

But filling team vacancies was. Sticks was recovering well, but getting used to a cybernetic leg took some time. Lots of physical therapy. Chhun had figured that Wraith would take Sticks's spot, so he hadn't really conducted a search prior to the Herbeer mission.

And then they lost Pike.

Victory Squad could get by with only five Dark Ops leejes most of the time. But four... that wasn't going to fly.

Chhun scanned the list of names Major Owens had sent him; it was lit up on the surface of the tactical table before him. At this point, Chhun had been in Dark Ops for so long, he didn't really know too many men serving in the Legion proper. He was relying on Owens's recommendations, and had asked for help from Bear, the newest member of the team, thinking he would have better knowledge of who could make the jump from Legion to Dark Ops.

He tapped on a sub-section of the list, causing the grouping to enlarge and show head shots and mini-bios.

"How 'bout someone from Synth Squad?" Bear asked. "They're all on the ship for now, and you saw them in action first-hand. I know that's important to you, Cap."

Chhun nodded slowly. "It is, but the only one I'd go for is Rowdy. And it sounds like he'll be on Herbeer for a while yet."

"Let's sort by commendation and service levels," Bear said, tapping the table a few more times to make the holographic overlay dance with new data.

Chhun looked over the info and shook his head. "Yeah, see... this is disappointing. I mean, look at some of these PT scores. I know every leej feels like his class was the best, but honestly, you think these guys would have made the cut back when we first joined the Legion?"

Bear let out a snort. "Hell no. Thank the points, brother. High standards mean hurt feelings, right?"

"Just find somebody who can shoot!" Masters called out from the sofa lounger, not taking his eyes away from the holo game that flashed before him. "They can—ah dammit, stupid campers—they can stay in the back with an N-18. That way they won't have to run until we get them in shape."

"Maybe you should go into full VR and haptic, so you won't die so much," suggested Fish, who was watching Masters play. "Lose the controller."

"That's called easy mode," Masters said, selecting a new loadout and a new kit. He was playing as a Savage marine against the Legion in an FPS that hearkened back several centuries. "Besides, I run around shooting stuff all the time as it is. When I play a game, I wanna be able to kill people while sitting on my ass."

"Shoulda been a pilot then."

"No kidding," Masters said, his attention fixed on the screen as he spawned aboard a Savage lighthugger. "So what do you think of my plan, Cap?"

Chhun was still studying Owens's list. "That might be the best option we—"

A soft chime came from one of the legionnaires' helmets, which were resting in a gear cubby built into the far wall. Someone was attempting to reach one of them through a private L-comm channel linked directly to a bucket. That was unusual—that would normally be done only while on combat operations.

Masters put his controller down, wincing as he saw his assault-class character die from a grenade blast. He moved to the shelf, then looked over to Chhun. "It's coming from yours, boss."

Chhun grabbed the bucket and saw that someone had placed a sticker of a pink cartoon cat on the side. "Thanks for that," he said dryly, shooting a look at Masters.

He placed the helmet over his head, drowning out his squad's chuckles as the bucket's operating system booted up.

Incoming secure transmission. Accept? Y/N

"Accept," Chhun said, not wanting to flick out his tongue to hit the proper toggle. Not until he cleaned the thing out. Who knew what kind of grubby handling this thing had been subjected to during the little sticker prank.

"Hey, glad you're all right," came the voice from the other end.

Chhun smiled. He hadn't known how he would feel about hearing from Wraith after the way they'd parted. But it had been Wraith, after all, who had sent Lao Pak to Herbeer with Victory Squad, and Chhun felt that Major Owens's life had been saved due to their early arrival. So yes, Chhun felt okay hearing from Wraith. Happy, even.

"Thanks. Good to hear from you, Ford. Keel, I mean."

"Actually, Wraith is fine for the time being. Kind of keeping Keel on the down-low because of some company I've got. You get Owens?"

"He's fine. In fact—"

"Look, not to cut you off, but I found Exo."

Chhun's eyebrows went up. Exo was exactly the type of leej he needed back on the team. Wraith, too. Perhaps if the two of them could join...

But that wasn't going to happen. At least not until Wraith recovered his crew.

"Really? Good. Hey, before you go any further, I know I said that the team would help you get your crew back after the Herbeer op, but, uh... we're gonna be busy. Real busy. It was crazy, Wraith. Leejes—real leejes, not those easy-pass guys the points brought in—were all imprisoned on Herbeer, just like the major. Keller has a plan."

There was a pause, then Wraith said, "So Exo works for Goth Sullus now."

"What?"

"Yeah. I was surprised too. He's going after the same Nether Ops team as me. The reason Broxin wanted my crew was because one of them is a biological passkey to control some unmanned fleet. A big one. Can't get near it without the key. We're headed there now."

"An unmanned fleet? Like, just sitting there?" Chhun asked. This was... amazing. "Is it in good shape? Whose was it? Aliens? Savage marines? A whole fleet, really?"

Wraith didn't seem to share Chhun's enthusiasm. "How should I know?"

"Wraith, this is big. An additional fleet at this stage could swing the balance of power. The Legion needs those ships."

"Sure, because there's no chance that they aren't made up or inoperative." Wraith's voice dripped with sarcasm. "But yeah, that's sort of why I'm calling you."

Masters tapped Chhun on the shoulder. "Who is it? What're they saying? Is it your sister? Your mom? How did they get L-comms?"

Chhun waved off the interruption. "Wraith, if one of your crew is a *key* to… what, access this fleet? … and you're missing your crew, then how do you… I don't know, get in?"

Wraith cleared his throat. "I, uh, found a *skeleton* key. Don't worry about it. Look, I gotta go. Get the approval from Owens or whoever to remain on standby. I'll contact you again."

"Right," Chhun said, still thinking about the fleet. "But what does that even mean, this bit about a key? Is everything on a master-slave control system?"

"Sure," Wraith said, sounding somewhat flummoxed.

Chhun nodded. This was huge. Ford leaving, Exo leaving, it now seemed like that had happened for a reason. "Yeah, okay. And hey, Wraith."

"Yeah?"

"Be careful."

"Eh, we'll see. KTF, Chhun."

The *Indelible VI*
Porcha System

Ravi shook his head at his captain. "Skeleton key?"

Keel gave a wide grin. "Pretty good for off the top of my head, right?" He stood up and adjusted the blaster holstered to his thigh. He moved around the back of his chair, squeezed the upholstery as he arched his back, and heard a series of small pops.

Ravi looked up. "You are going to speak with the shock troopers now?"

"Yeah. It's about time."

"And should I come with you?"

"In case there's trouble?" Keel shrugged. "I can handle it. They're both former Legion, so I think they'll be more talkative without you there. No offense."

Ravi nodded, indicating that none was taken. "There is a thirty-eight percent chance they are laying a trap for you."

"See?" Keel said, moving to the cockpit's door. "Good odds. Besides, I already know you and the *Six* will be playing guardian angel. Just don't activate the stun bursts if I'm standing next to a bulkhead. Last time the bump I got on my forehead was there for almost a month."

"Considering that the lyconlore was strangling you, I feel the tradeoff was acceptable."

Keel grinned. "And out the airlock he went. I want you to work on something for me."

"What?"

"I want you to contact Gannon on Porcha."

Ravi furrowed his brow. "I thought the two of you hated each other."

"Yeah," Keel said, raising his eyebrows. "We do. Call him and set up a time for us to talk."

Before Ravi could inquire further, Keel opened the door and left the cockpit. He felt his for blaster one more time, making sure that it rested just so in its holster. Most likely, Exo and Bombassa would be in the main lounge. It was the most comfortable and spacious section of the ship. And that was a good thing, because if they were there, Keel would see them before he entered the room. They wouldn't be able to jump him there. And if they weren't there... well, then Keel would have his guard up.

The two shock troopers were in fact in the lounge, sitting on a padded bench, helmets off and rifles between their knees. Keel stopped at the end of the corridor, leaning against the bulkhead rather than entering the room.

"There's a 'fresher down that way," Keel said, nodding in the general direction. "In case you want to get cleaned up. I've got some extra sets of clothing, too." He paused to look at Bombassa. "Might be a little small for you, big guy."

"We're good," Exo replied, looking around. "This the ship they gave you after you volunteered to go deep?"

Keel shrugged. "More or less. I made a few modifications since then."

"Looks nice, man."

"Yet to see a better one out there. You want the tour?"

Bombassa shook his head firmly. "No. Another time. I want to know why you almost killed me."

Keel gave a half grin. "You said it yourself: *almost*. If you had a better way of everybody getting out of that little standoff alive, you fooled me."

Bombassa frowned as Exo said, "Look, it was a tough situation for everyone. You're good, Bombassa. No harm. But I'm sayin' this is gonna be good for us all. We have the key, Wraith has the location… I'm telling you, it's all good."

Keel sauntered over to a round table. "Why don't we all sit here? You want something for your head? I don't entertain much on the *Six*, but the bar's pretty stocked."

The two shock troopers made their way to the table while Keel opened a cupboard and pulled out a bottle. He placed it in front of Exo. "I know you're a beer guy, but you liked this stuff too, right?"

Exo held the stout green bottle in his hands and smiled. "Tabrizzi rye. Yeah, this'll do." He nudged Bombassa. "You want some?"

"No."

"How 'bout some caff?" Keel asked.

"Water is fine."

Keel retrieved a tumbler and two mugs and set them on the table. He filled a carafe with water and poured himself and Bombassa a mug while Exo measured out a modest portion of rye. Keel tossed a caff tab into his mug and watched as the water heated and darkened into the stimulating drink.

"First cup this morning," he said, making conversation like it was the most natural thing in the galaxy. Like the three of them hadn't all had weapons aimed at one another only an hour earlier. Like Keel hadn't shot at the two shock troopers with the ship they were now inside.

"So, you talk to any of the old guys?" Exo asked Keel.

"Nah." Keel blew on his drink and took a sip. It was hot and bitter, with just a hint of nuttiness. "I've thought about it. But... I'm basically AWOL. Don't want to put anyone in a bad situation. You?"

Exo stared at his drink and exhaled through an open-mouthed smile. "No. I think... when I let my enlistment expire, it kinda shocked the guys. Maybe hard feelings. I don't know. And then, you get out into the civilian world and things are so different... Everything just sort of slipped away."

Keel smiled. "I'll be honest. I can't really picture you as a civilian."

Exo laughed. "Wasn't for me. But... the Legion. That wasn't for me either. However bad it was when you left, Wraith, it got worse. Anyway, it wasn't long before I took some private contracting jobs. There's always a demand for former Legion. Pay is better. Bosses can be just as bad, though."

Bombassa remained silent, rubbing away water condensation on his glass like rain-wipers on a speeder. He had a story, Keel knew. Former Legion, disgruntled or idealistic enough to join in open insurrection against the Republic. The man didn't have to like Keel, but things would go a lot smoother if he did.

"So, uh," Keel said, "you guys catch much of the news?"

Exo shook his head. "Not really. Been sort of busy."

"Devers is dead."

Exo gave a wolfish smile. "I know. I saw it happen." He drained his glass. "It was on Tarrago."

Keel arched an eyebrow. "The holofeeds said he died when his destroyer blew up while assuming a blocking position between Tarrago and your little fleet there."

"Don't believe the news," Exo said.

Bombassa growled. "We shouldn't be talking about this."

"What?" Keel prodded. "Don't speak ill of the dead? Because me and Exo both knew Devers, and the only bad thing about him getting dusted is that it didn't happen years ago."

"That's not what I mean," Bombassa said. "This information isn't supposed to leave the Black Fleet."

Keel smiled. "Look, if there's anything that might convince me that your little insurrection isn't all bad, it's that you're taking out points like Devers."

"That's what I'm saying, Bombassa," Exo said, slapping the table for emphasis. "A lot of the leejes out there, if they knew that Sullus wasn't playing when it came to the points... I bet the whole Legion would join up."

Bombassa sighed and took a drink.

Keel followed suit, sipping his caff. "I can't imagine the three of us are the only ones disillusioned with the Legion. You're probably not far off, Exo."

"Nah, I'm right on target." Exo leaned back in his seat. "So, what about you, Wraith? Why didn't you rejoin Victory Squad? What're you doing dressed up like a spacer, digging up the bones of old Republic spies?"

Keel shrugged. "First year or so, that was all I could think about. Complete the mission and rejoin. It was killing me that you guys were in the fight—doing raids, snatches, kills—and I was just floating around mixing up with pirates and other criminals looking for who-knows-what.

"I'd call in my reports, which weren't much beyond exposing places where the Republic governors weren't doing their jobs and the MCR or some local warlord was working with impunity. The open secret is that if you find the right administrator, the law doesn't apply out on the edge. I've seen a governor tie up a garrison of leejes with rules of engagement so complex that they have to get four separate legal opinions before they can switch off their safeties, let alone open fire. All the while, the bad guys run free.

"So anyway, I included it all in my reports. Names, locations, even holographic evidence. And... *nada*. Nothing ever changed. So I asked myself, 'Why am I putting my neck on the line here?'"

Exo leaned forward. "And the answer was...?"

Keel frowned. "There was no good answer. And every request to get back on the team was denied. So I left the Legion and went to work for myself. I do all right for myself, and KTF still means something in my line of work."

Exo drained his glass of rye and motioned for a refill. When Keel obliged, he looked to Bombassa. "So, that's two I'd categorize as disillusioned, and one that was simply screwed out of his career."

"That so?" Keel asked, eyeing Bombassa.

The imposing trooper gave a half nod, raising his eyebrows in an expression that seemed to say, "That's about the whole of it."

"See, Sergeant Indigo here," Exo began, pointing his thumb at his partner, "was a model leej NCO. Saw a lot of combat out on the edge. Even had a stint in the One Thirty-First. Anyway, MCR had been playing revolution on some planet, and the leej had 'em pushed all the way into the mountains. Last-stand stuff, but they were dug in. Bombassa and his company got the call to go up there and finish the job."

"Hard work," Keel said, draining his caff and getting up to place the mug in the auto-clean. "Slow and methodical. I remember when Victory Company had to clean out those Brongi rebels from the Maltinian peaks. Took forever, but we got it done for Pappy."

"Time wasn't a luxury we had," Bombassa said, his deep voice reverberating through the *Six*'s very frame. "A point named Castick was looking to make the jump from captain to major, but he was years away, even if he did everything right. Word was, his House of Reason sponsor swung a deal to get him a battlefield promotion if we could finish off the MCR by Unity Day."

Bombassa seemed to be slipping back to a different time, dredging up painful memories. "There was no waiting for MOABs. No requisitioning an inferno unit to burn them out of the cave. Just charge and kill. Charge and kill." He stopped, considering something. "I suppose, in its own way, it was like the Savage Wars. We just pushed, knowing that as many of us that ate it... more of them would die. By the end, the last cave and tunnel system, there were maybe ten of us left. It was enough."

"What happened?" Keel asked.

Bombassa sighed, as though the weight of that battle still hung heavy around his neck. "It was no Kublar, but it *was* another example of how the enemies of the Republic were standing up to even the Legion."

"Someone's gotta take the fall, right?" Keel surmised.

"Sergeant Bombassa," the dark legionnaire said, sounding like a historian reading an old document. "In your rush to secure for yourself personal glory on the field of battle, even at the expense of the lives of your fellow legionnaires, you knowingly and willingly disobeyed orders that, if followed, would have prevented the needless deaths of your fellow soldiers. You violated not only the code and traditions of the Legion, but you disgraced the uniform and the very brotherhood you have sworn to serve. You are hereby and forever banished from the Legion, dishonorably discharged and forever carrying with you the shame of your actions."

Bombassa paused, the slightest hint of tears welling in his eyes, not of sorrow or self-pity, but of rage. "The shame of my actions!" he shouted. "I saved as many of my men as I could from that worthless point. And in the end..."

"Guess who got the promotion?" Exo said to Keel.

Keel shook his head. "I'm sorry. I knew it was bad."

"It's cancerous," Exo said. "There's nothing left for the Republic but to burn it down and let a new order rise from the ashes. Maybe better, maybe not. But... can it get any worse?"

A silence fell over the three men.

Bombassa's face was fixed in a faraway stare. "That was the fiercest fighting I'd ever witnessed... until Tarrago."

"What happened on Tarrago?"

"He got a medal," Exo said, clapping Bombassa on the shoulder. "For fighting hard while his men died—same as on Bronga—to complete the mission. But this time for a reason. And the point dies at the end of the day. Bombassa took a capitol building, captured a governor, and commandeered a corvette. Fighting got so bad he had to finish the job without his blaster rifle."

"So what'd he use?" Keel asked.

Bombassa's eyes switched into the present again, cold and deadly. "A cutting torch."

05

"These guys seem legit," Keel said to Ravi as he dropped back into his seat in the cockpit of the *Indelible VI*. "Well, I mean, Exo was already legit. But the other guy, Bombassa, he knows his way around a blaster."

"He seems professional, yes." Ravi paused for a moment, placing his hands in his lap. "This is a volatile situation, Captain. There is a chance—forty-six percent—that you and the shock troopers engage in violent activities."

"Kind of counting on that."

"I mean violence against one another," Ravi clarified.

Keel checked his chronometer and hyperspace positioning, tapping pensively at a flashing light. "Well, there's always a way out. Anyhow, if all goes well, all that violence can be leveraged against whoever is holding my crew captive. The..." Keel snapped his fingers. "What were they called? Cybils?"

"*Cybar.*"

"Yeah, them." Keel flushed a drive core that read a little hotter than he liked. Getting Leenah back would be nice. The ship was already showing signs of her absence. And the truth of it was, so was Keel. He missed her. He wanted to pick up where they'd left off. Wanted to see if this might be something worth turning his life upside down over.

Ravi looked up from his console readings. "The two shock troopers are attempting to communicate with their team over the S-comm, but the holo-communication system does not seem to be capable of working through hyperspace."

"Glad Garret was able to crack into those comms. Should go a long way to help avoid a double-cross."

"Unless *you* are the one who commits it," said Ravi.

Keel rolled his eyes. "It's not a double-cross if *I* do it. I'm a scoundrel. They should know better."

"Speaking of which, Gannon is still on standby."

Keel looked at the flashing comm light on his dash. "Oh, right. I forgot why I even came up here. Did he seem scared?"

"Incredulous is the word I would use," said Ravi, twirling the tip of his black mustache. "But he agreed all the same. I think he is curious."

"He oughta be ready to wet himself. Here goes nothing."

Keel activated the comm, and Gannon, a perpetually scowling spacer who wore several days of black stubble, but not quite a beard, winked onto the holoscreen.

Gannon stared at Keel and guffawed. "By the six fates of Barseev, it really *is* you."

"What?" Keel held out his arms. "Lotta people out there tryin' to pass themselves off as me?"

"One Aeson Keel is more than enough," Gannon said, reaching toward his holocam as if to activate a switch. "I just wanted to see if it was really you, or if Ravi was pulling my leg. Didn't think you had the nerve. Well, bye."

Keel gave an exasperated eye roll. "Just when I think I've met all the stupid the galaxy has to offer, I see you and I'm reminded that it's all relative. Don't cut the comm."

Gannon paused, straightening himself out on what seemed to be a stool. The area around him was dark, maybe a garage. The solitary light in the room shone down directly on top of him, casting elongated shadows down his face and covering his eyes.

He leaned back, his features disappearing into the darkness completely, and gave a dry, humorless laugh. Reappearing in the light, he said, "Y'know, Keel, you wouldn't have had Ravi call me if you didn't need me. And for a guy who needs *my* help, you're not doing a bang-up job of buttering my bread."

"You're talkin' about the insults?" Keel asked.

Ravi gave him an apprehensive, warning look.

Gannon nodded. "I'm talkin' about the insults, yeah."

"Oh," Keel said, bobbing his head up and down like he'd just seen the light. "See, that's because I haven't forgotten what happened at Crickar."

"I was *made*," Gannon said, as ready as ever to wade into this long-standing feud. "You oughta understand it and move on like all the others."

"All the others are dead."

"And they don't complain. So whaddaya need?"

Keel folded his arms. "I should shoot you. Not hire you."

Gannon laughed. A greasy, unpleasant sound. "You've been threatening to kill me for going on three years, and I ain't dead yet."

Ravi shot Keel a look as if to say, *He's got you there.*

"I've been busy," Keel said to Ravi, his look imploring. He refocused on Gannon, growing stern. "You remember that job on Brissy Six? The one with the royal crown?"

Gannon rubbed his hand under his chin, emitting a sound like sandpaper working over a rough board. "Yeah, I remember. Most money I ever took in on a job—even after paying the Wraith his cut."

"You remember how we distracted the royal guard?"

Gannon's lips curved into a wicked smile. "Oh yeah."

"Well, I want you to do the same thing on a mark coming into Cresweil."

The smile didn't depart from Gannon's face. "Or what? You'll kill me? No thanks, Keel. I'll take my chances."

"Well," Keel said, leaning back in his chair and fiddling with the cockpit's sensor array just above him, "I *will* kill you. But that's not why you're gonna do it."

Gannon let out a snort. "What, you got my mommy all tied up somewhere?"

"He has fifteen thousand credits," Ravi interjected. "Half now, half when the job is satisfactorily completed."

"No kidding." Gannon's tone changed. He was interested, letting his words out like a curious viper. "That *does* catch my interest. What and when?"

"Ravi," Keel said with an inclination of his head.

The navigator superimposed a basic Republic shuttle over the holoscreen. Its wingtips and nose were all painted black, like the fins of some reef-dwelling shark.

"This is the shuttle you'll be looking for," Keel said. "No information on where it will dock, but to reach the bazaar, a registered station will be required. Estimated arrival time is tomorrow at fifteen hundred hours, local time."

"And when do you get here? 'Cause I'll need at least two days to get it taken care of."

"Then we'll show up two days from now," Keel said. "The marks will wait for us."

"Okay, yeah," Gannon said with a slow nod. "Send me the money and I'll get you all set up."

"You'd better." Keel looked to his navigator. "Ravi, send him the money."

"'I'd better?'" Gannon scowled. "Space off, Keel. I don't need your money."

Keel stared coldly at the man on the holoscreen. "Maybe not, but you're gonna take it. And you're gonna do the job. Because if you don't... I've got the credits to pay Wraith to make good on all those threats I've let slide over the years."

"Wraith ain't gonna..." began Gannon, but his words trailed off at the sight of Keel's unyielding stare. "You're bluffing."

Ravi leaned over, placing himself in the holo's view. "I don't believe he is. This is very serious. Wraith owes Keel a favor, and you will certainly be it."

Gannon swallowed. "Look, Keel—"

"Get it done."

With a slow nod, Gannon said, "Yeah. Okay." He leaned forward and cut the holofeed.

Keel didn't so much as blink until the screen went to standby.

Ravi gave a quick "Hmm" as commentary on the interchange. "I am wondering how long you will continue this Wraith-Keel duality charade. Surely the word will get out before long that you are one and the same. I calculate an eighty-three-point-six percent chance that a member of your old kill team shared this information with Lao Pak."

"Keep your cards hidden until someone calls."

"And I suspect you are planning on killing Gannon no matter how good a job he does for you?"

Keel gave a fractional shake of his head and a half-smile. "Ask me no secrets and I'll tell you no lies."

Ravi twitched his mustache. "I will ignore your sudden enthusiasm for platitudes and instead ask, why have you not killed Gannon already? He certainly deserves it."

Keel reached for the hyperspace controls. "Same reason I didn't kill Lao Pak back on Pellek. Because he might be useful."

He pushed abruptly on the controls, causing the *Six* to dump out of hyperspace with a lurch, as though he had ignited counter-repulsors to brake in mid-flight. "That felt convincing enough."

Ravi eyed the captain. "We are now feigning a mechanical failure to provide Gannon the needed time."

Keel rose from his seat. "That's right. Make sure the *Six* reads a plausible failure in case either of our passengers has the wherewithal to check the logs. And give me something showy to fix back by the drive reactor."

Ravi's fingers danced over his console. An audible pop and groan sounded from the port side of the ship. A siren sounded immediately.

"Yo!" Exo shouted over the ship-wide comm. "There's a bunch of smoke filling the ship!"

Keel gave his navigator a confused look.

Ravi shrugged. "You said to be showy."

Legion Destroyer *Intrepid*
Cononga System

Chhun hadn't expected Major Owens to take a shuttle from the super-destroyer *Mercutio* over to see him on *Intrepid* when he passed on Wraith's report. But here the major was, standing inside the doorway, shades on, working over a wad of gum.

"Get dressed," Owens ordered after looking over Chhun's down-time uniform of mesh shorts and a Legion T-shirt. "I'm bringing you to a meeting with Commander Keller."

Chhun smiled. "This is pretty much how I was dressed the first time I met the Legion commander."

Owens popped a bubble between his teeth with a loud snap. "Not this time. This is the big one."

"We get to find out why all these destroyers are staging out here?"

"Yep." Owens nodded toward the kill team's dormitory. "So let's go, because I need to talk with you about Wraith before the briefing."

Chhun left for his footlocker. "I'm not shy—we can talk while I get jocked up. I'm guessing the Legion commander wants me in full battle rattle instead of dress blues?"

"Good guess," Owens said, following Chhun past the rest of the kill team, who pretended not to eavesdrop.

In his room, Chhun pulled off his shirt, revealing abs of impervisteel.

"You young guys," complained Owens. "Doesn't matter how many sit-ups I do," he slapped his stomach through his Legion fatigues, "I still got the padding."

"That's because you eat too many carbs," said Chhun, pulling on his synthprene under-suit and moving to his locker to armor up.

"Drink too many is more like it," Owens said with a chuckle. "But Mrs. Owens doesn't seem to mind it. When I actually get to see her, of course."

Chhun stepped into his boots and felt them seal around his knees. "You gonna try and see 'em?"

"Talked to 'em on holo," Owens answered, sniffing and looking to the side. "That'll have to do for now. My girl, Neese, is growing like crazy."

Chhun nodded. He knew the feeling. Comms and holos were all that he'd seen of his family in what seemed like eons. Only for him, there were no children, no wife. Just parents who seemed to age a decade between each op. The last time Chhun saw them, his father looked as though he'd lost fifteen pounds, and his hand constantly trembled. Chhun's mother told him it was probably just stress. Nerves. Nothing to worry about. Chhun worried anyway.

"You wanted to talk about Wraith?" Chhun said.

Owens grunted an acknowledgment. "Keller wants an after-action report about the mission planning. And I've got it written up, ready to transmit. My understanding is that Captain Ford went AWOL, abandoning the Legion and Victory Squad. And our previous discussions gave no indication of anything else. So you'll understand my surprise to hear from you that Wraith is in the field, calling in intelligence reports outside the chain."

Chhun sighed. "It's... complex. Yes, Wraith left the team instead of joining the mission, but I didn't exactly try to stop him. I think he came in from the cold and then back into action too quickly to adjust. Couple that with Nether Ops kidnapping his crew... I think we got what we could out of Captain Ford. At least for a while."

"He helped you accelerate your mission's timetable through the pirate."

"Yeah. And I'm not saying you didn't have it handled, but we came at the right time. And now he's dug in with a Black Fleet strike team."

Owens's furious gum-chewing ceased, and his mouth hung slightly open. "He's *what*?"

Chhun lowered his voice, holding his armored sleeve in his hand. "Yeah. They're after some kind of fleet. Unmanned. That's why Nether Ops took his crew. One of them had insider knowledge. And... Exo is with them."

"With Ford?"

Shaking his head, Chhun said, "With the shock troopers."

A silence fell between the two men before Chhun quickly added, "Don't know why. Ford's working on it. He says for Victory Squad to stand by, though. And I think we should."

"No can do. Keller wants me to put you guys on something big. We've been planning a major operation. This is going to be it, Chhun."

"Did he ask for us specifically?" Chhun felt his final piece of armor snap around his left arm.

"He asked for the best." Owens snapped his gum. "That means Victory."

"So then you don't *have* to send us?" Chhun leaned inside Owens's bubble and spoke quietly. He looked around the room to see if he was being eavesdropped on. "Listen. This is bigger than what Keller has in mind, whatever it is. I just... have a feeling."

Owens gave a slow, repeated nod, as if listening to music. "Okay. I can get you out of this one. But we won't be making this a regular thing. Command isn't going to be happy if my best assets are out doing whatever it is Wraith has in mind. You'll soon find out that Victory Squad is going to be kept busy. Real busy."

***

The *Intrepid*'s bridge war room was as crowded as Chhun had ever seen it. All five of the pentagonal room's walls were lined with staff and command officers from the Republic Navy, Marines, Army, and Legion. Captain Deynolds stood beside a round holocomm table, with Major Owens at her side, along with the head marine and army brass stationed on the ship.

If every other destroyer, frigate, and corvette amassed at Cononga had their command rooms packed like

Intrepid's, there was no way the holoprojectors could render them all. But the holoprojectors didn't try. Only Legion Commander Keller was being projected, alone in the center of the holotable, and that was surely true in every other ship in the fleet. This show was his to run.

"I want to thank you all for being here," Keller said, and the buzz of conversation died down. "I promise to keep you no longer than absolutely necessary. While I have every confidence that our location won't be divulged to the House of Reason—as you know, Cononga is one of the friendliest planets in the galaxy to the Legion—the House will no doubt notice your absence from your battlenet positions. So I'll make this quick."

Keller seemed to eye everyone in the room through his holographic projection. "We are on the verge of beginning a campaign, under the authority provided to us by Article Nineteen, to depose the House of Reason."

Chhun shifted from one foot to the other. This was it. This was really it. The Legion was going to shut it all down—to finally curb the malignant hand of the House of Reason and the Senate. He was witness to history.

"You have all received the dossier that outlines, in detail, our reasons for taking this step. It is not a decision we make idly, or rashly. It is a decision that brings me no joy. For many years now we have made every effort to avoid this very outcome—and have been stymied at every turn. But now the time has come. The time to fulfill our duty to protect the Republic—even from those threats that come from within."

"As I am sure all of you here assembled will agree, this is a course of action that has been a long time coming. It is not a response to any single event, to any single failure of the House and Senate. Having said that, the revelations about the clandestine punishments taking place in the synth mines at Herbeer were certainly... salient. The illegal imprisonment of legionnaires and political exiles. The implicit cooperation with Gomarii slavers. All contrary to Republic law. Our slicers are working to recover further incriminating evidence from Herbeer's systems, but we already have more than enough to make a compelling case to the galaxy that the House of Reason has long been operating unlawfully and must be held accountable.

"I remind you all that the Constitution of the Republic names the Legion the rightful protectorate of the galaxy's liberties. Thus we stand prepared to invoke Article Nineteen and remove the current House and Senate so that a new government, one willing to represent its citizens, can be built."

Keller paused, letting the weight of this settle. The room was dead silent. They had all known what Keller would announce, but it was another thing entirely to hear him actually say the words.

"You have also received the dossier revealing General Hannubal's battle plan for the attack on Ankalor, and your specific roles therein. I know this strategy probably comes as a surprise—that a quick strike on Utopion, designed to remove the House of Reason from power and disband the Senate, is what you believed would happen. I know it is that goal that led you to risk all and stand with the

Legion here and now. However, after considering the aid and counsel of a former legionnaire serving in Nether Ops, I am confident that Ankalor must be our initial target. It is not enough for the Legion to invoke Article Nineteen; we must bring the people of the Republic on our side. This strategy will allow us to achieve that goal. It is our best chance for Article Nineteen to fully succeed."

Keller rocked back on his heels. "It is also our moral duty. I remain surprised that the House of Reason made a deal with these demons. I can only surmise that it is the repeated failures of Admiral Landoo and her forces that caused a desperate House of Reason to arm the zhee. Ostensibly as 'protection.' But the result... was predictable. The zhee have already used their new ships to attack both Legion forces and Republic worlds, as you all know. We won't let that stand. We *can't* let that stand."

The Legion commander's voice remained calm and cool, but it was infused with passion. With steel. "The zhee on Ankalor cannot be allowed to remain an unchecked fighting force. Nobody in the galaxy wins when zhee have battle cruisers. We have a moral obligation to protect the Republic even as we remove the House of Reason's poison from its veins. We will show the citizens of the Republic that the Legion, when unfettered from the demands and control of the House of Reason, stands for peace, order, and justice."

A murmur shot through the room like an electric current through water. Keller stood still until the noise died down.

"Questions?"

Keller's eyes caught the upraised hand of Captain Deynolds.

"Captain Deynolds?"

"Sir. With Admiral Landoo essentially in hiding from the Black Fleet while at the Bantaar Reef, aren't you concerned that this action will provide the Black Fleet an opportunity to consolidate gains with their… dreadnoughts?"

"I am," said Keller, the creased lines of his face reinforcing the words. "However, it is my opinion that the Black Fleet at this time is not our primary threat."

When it was clear that there were no further questions, Keller gestured to someone unseen, and a holograph of Major Owens appeared beside Keller's on the holotable. "Major Owens is the sector commander of Dark Ops at galaxy's edge," the Legion commander said. "As his immediate superior was a House of Reason appointee now relieved of command, I've given him command of our infiltration on Ankalor. Major, is your team prepared?"

Owens cleared his throat. He and Keller had planned out Dark Ops's role in the assault for hours on end, scrutinizing every detail. And now it was time to let the rest of the force in on what he had prepared. "I have Zenith Squad set to infiltrate and take down Ankalor's planetary shield in advance of the fleet. That will prevent the zhee, or those sympathetic to the zhee under the sway of the House of Reason, from putting it up and preventing our attacks."

Chhun felt a pang. This was the mission Owens had spoken of earlier. Chhun knew Victory Squad would have been first choice. But he had begged off as a result of Keel's tip, and now Zenith had gotten the honors. He was already second-guessing his decision.

"That leaves the shield protecting Fortress Gibraltaar," Owens continued. "It's built to Legion specs, enough to protect it from orbital and artillery strikes. And a kill team isn't going to get past that security. It will have to be taken down the hard way—through a direct assault."

"Thank you, Major." Keller's hologram faced the rooms. "I needn't tell you that Major Owens's and Dark Ops's role is critical to our success. With the planetary shield down, we will initiate a planetary bombardment eliminating all zhee military facilities. The Legion, Marines, and Army will then drop onto the planet and take its cities."

Chhun found himself nodding his head in agreement with the rest of the leejes, operators, hull busters, and featherheads. This had been a long time coming. The zhee had been given every chance to live peacefully in the galaxy and yet had never failed bite the hand holding the olive branch. And now that they were armed and equipped by the Republic, the Legion couldn't let them sit unchecked. They couldn't leave their rear or flanks exposed to such an enemy.

When the briefing ended, Chhun filed out with the rest on board *Intrepid*. He hoped that whatever action was still before him, he would play a role in restoring freedom to the galaxy.

06

The *Indelible VI*
Dead Space

"You sure there's nothin' I can help you with?"

Keel lifted up his black welding goggles for a moment so he could look around the corner at Exo. "Nah, afraid not. I think I've got it, though." He went back to his work, sending brilliant white-blue flashes dancing across the hull of his freighter. Luminous balls of ghost-white sparks sprinkled onto the deck like fairy dust.

It was all for show, of course. After putting a stop to the smoke—a simple venting duct Ravi had overloaded and re-routed into the life support air streams—Keel had spent the last two days breaking and repairing non-critical sections of the *Six*, always "on the verge" of finding the elusive problem that kept them from jumping into hyperspace to join the rest of the shock trooper strike team.

But the time wasn't wasted. Through it all, Keel had worked hard to play the role of potential recruit. He'd asked about Goth Sullus, the Black Fleet, tactics, objectives—anything he could think of to make himself sound interested, but not *too* interested. It was a skill he'd picked up in the first year he'd gone out into the cold, and something he now did better than anyone he knew.

He examined his torch work with an artist's eye. "I bet that does it. Ravi'll have to run a full systems check before we make the jump, but I think I got it."

"Cool," Exo said, but his voice betrayed a certain reticence. Perhaps... sadness?

"Don't sound so busted up about, huh, pal?" Keel said, removing his gloves and stowing his torch in its case.

Exo gave a half-hearted laugh. "The thing about the Black Fleet—the Empire, officially—is that it's like the Legion, but it ain't. You know?"

"Not sure."

"So, militarily, it's KTF, even if we're not allowed to use those words. I mean, Black Fleet is full-on kill them first. Like, almost scary."

"Coming from you," Keel said with a lopsided grin, "that *is* scary. When I was an officer, no one in VC ever accused Exo of being timid. Pappy used to call you one of his pit-maulers. You and Chhun."

Exo nodded, a whimsical, melancholy expression on his face. "That's probably the biggest thing. There's no one like Pappy in Black Fleet. Or Chhun. Or you, for that matter. The officer class doesn't have any points, sure, but it's full of guys who play the attrition game, you know?"

"We have twenty and you have ten, and we'll spend fifteen to win," Keel said with a knowing nod.

"Exactly like that. When we took Tarrago's moon, I mean, it was well thought out. It was tactically sound. But dude, we lost so many men that I ended up being the ranking leader until Sullus showed up. Casualties were that bad, bro."

Keel looked down at his scuffed black boots. "War's gonna be a bloodbath if it keeps ramping up."

"I know it. That's why this is important, though." Exo clapped his hands as he spoke, as though he were rallying a team of athletes. "We get this fleet, strike a blow at Utopion, purge all the garbage... war's over. I know the Legion will see the sense of it. I know it. Keller should have busted up the House a long time ago."

"Probably," Keel agreed. "So that battle on Tarrago, when Sullus showed up. That's when he did his little space wizard schtick?"

Exo laughed and shook his head. "Yeah, but it wasn't a trick, man. I saw it myself. Dude was legit tossing people around like... telekinesis. I dunno. Like a superhero. I've never seen anything like it."

"Who has?"

"If I'm being honest... it freaked me out a bit. I thought about just dusting him while his back was turned to me. Another leej almost dropped him, so I know he ain't invincible."

"So why didn't you?"

"So, for this split second, the barrel of my blaster is swinging across his back. Dude was all over the place. No regard for clear firing lines. And I get this urge, like, dust this monster right now. And then—and I swear I'm not making this up—it's like I hear Sullus inside my head saying, 'Don't.'. Crazy, right?"

Keel stared compassionately at Exo, then nodded an affirmative. "You sound like an insane person."

Exo laughed and balled up a fist, playfully threatening to punch Keel, who held up his hands in surrender.

"I've seen a lot of stuff across the galaxy," Keel said, rubbing his chin with the palm of his hand. "But space wizard is a first—legends on technologically undeveloped worlds aside. Doesn't sound like you can lose with a space wizard on your team."

Exo shrugged. "Maybe. Maybe not. Numbers aren't great, and the boys blowing up the shipyards caused some serious harm. They all say it doesn't matter, but that's propaganda. It hurt."

"What makes you think it was Chhun?" Keel asked, motioning for Exo to follow him back to the ship's main lounge.

"Because no one else could have done it. Dude is untouchable, doesn't even know how good he is."

Keel nodded. "He was something else. I'm sure he wasn't alone, though."

"He's the type of guy the Black Fleet needs in command."

Keel opened a cupboard in the lounge and pulled out a unit of ale. "Get you something?"

Exo nodded enthusiastically. They clinked the necks of their units of ale before both taking a long pull.

"That's the second time you've mentioned needing new leadership," Keel observed. "Your brass doesn't have what it takes?"

"I dunno," Exo said, examining the label on his drink. "Almost everybody is a washout or has a grudge—like Bombassa. Don't tell him I said that about him, though. But that goes all the way to the very top. Rumor is that Admiral Rommal is only there because he got burned by the Republic—something about his wife—and wants payback. And then there's General Nero..."

"General *Nero*?" Keel asked.

Exo laughed into his bottle as he took another swig. "I know, right? Pretty sure they're all using aliases. But Nero's the closest thing to a point I've seen since joining up. He's not incompetent—not by a long shot—but he's definitely in it for himself."

"I get it. 'If the Legion won't make me commander... maybe these guys will,'" Keel said.

"Exactly."

"Why not reach out to Chhun?" Keel suggested with an upturned palm. "Recruit him onto your side."

"One," Exo said, enumerating his coming point by tapping on his forefinger, "I'm not a golden boy like Bombassa. I saved Sullus on Tarrago's moon and led the charge to take the gun, but when the awards came, they went to the people who got shot down, not to the leejes who shot shit up."

"Sounds familiar."

"Too familiar," Exo said.

For a moment, Keel felt a spike of adrenaline—maybe hope. He didn't *want* Exo to be mixed up with the other side, so hearing his friend sound disillusioned was a promising development. Whatever faults might be found in the galaxy, Keel didn't think this Sullus was the answer. He thought back to how concerned Tyrus Rechs had been about the man. That old bounty hunter had known a thing or two; if he was worried about Sullus, that was good enough for Keel.

In fact, the more Keel had heard about how the Black Fleet operated, the less he saw it as a viable government. Better than what was in place now, perhaps, but worse than the Legion. And Exo hadn't exactly painted a sterling picture of its leaders. "At least they're not points" wasn't the highest bar to clear.

"So, this Nero guy," Keel said, looking casually to see if Bombassa was anywhere around. The big shock trooper wouldn't take kindly to this sort of exchange of classified information. The only times Keel got anything of use were when the man wasn't around. "You think he'd sell you out?"

Exo shrugged his shoulders. "Who knows? Price is right…? I wouldn't be surprised."

Keel nodded and let it sit there, not wanting to sound too interested. "So what's the second thing?" he asked after gulping down another mouthful of ale.

"Hmm?" asked Exo absently.

"You said 'one,'" Keel said. "That usually means there's a second reason. Why else wouldn't Chhun be a good fit for your 'little cause'?" He winked as he finished the sentence. Exo believed in what he was doing, but needling him about it was fun.

"Ain't nothin' little about conquering a Republic planet, bro."

"Fair enough," Keel said. He drained the last of his beverage. "Want another?"

"Yeah."

As Keel attended to the refreshments, Exo said, "Two is because Chhun is a true believer. He's the most Legion leej out there. And he wasn't like that before Kublar. I thought for sure he was done during that last tour on *Chiasm*. And then all hell breaks loose, and now he's a Dark Ops lifer."

"Has to matter," Keel mumbled.

"What's that?"

"It's because it all has to matter," Keel said, sliding a fresh drink to Exo. "Chhun isn't willing to let it all be for nothing. All the boys in Victory, all the missions in Dark Ops... Worst thing that can happen to a guy like Chhun is to hear that none of it mattered. That all that death was for nothing." Keel saw Exo watching him intently. "You either break free, like I did... or you keep doubling down."

But even as he said it, he wondered if that was true— whether he had really broken free. Wasn't he still helping the Legion, helping his friends? Wasn't that the point of conversations like this one with his old buddy—to get an edge on the Sullus threat? Was it? Or was he just feeding himself enough line to go rogue for good... or, hell, even take Exo up on his offer to join the Black Fleet.

He wanted room to maneuver. To do what felt best at the time.

"Ooah," Exo answered. "I know that's right." He took a big drink, set the bottle down, then picked it back up to chug away what was left. The empty bottle was set back down with a resounding bang and a hard-edged sigh of satisfaction.

"Another one?" Keel asked, wondering if Exo would think he was trying to get him drunk. Which was a good trick, when you wanted someone to talk. But if that had been Keel's plan, it wasn't a conscious decision.

"Nah," Exo said with a wave of his hand. "I'm good. I'd take Chhun in a heartbeat, though. There's a lot of guys I'd take if I could. That's why I'm doing this, bro. I'm doing this to save them."

"I believe you," said Keel. And he did.

"On second thought, one more won't kill me," Exo said, stone-faced. "More of the rye if you've got it."

Keel got up and poured Exo a generous shot.

Exo knocked it back, hissing like a snake as the fire burned down his gullet. "One more," he said. He drank again. "Okay, last one."

"You sure?" Keel asked, his concern genuine. He didn't know if it had always been this way with Exo. Certainly it hadn't been in the Legion. But the Dark Ops team *had* found him in a slum bar on Utopion.

Keel's mind cycled through all the reasons why Exo might be drinking so heavily. The fighting on Tarrago's moon? Exo would have killed a lot of leejes. Yeah, that was probably it. The guilt of that... Keel knew something about that. You had to kill that guilt, remind yourself that it was them or you, because it's *always* them or you. And maybe Exo couldn't do that. He was the sort of guy who ran on emotion, who was fueled by his passions. Cognitive dissonance wasn't something a guy like him could do, even if he believed it was for all the right reasons. This war against his brothers had to be tearing him apart.

Exo finished his last drink. Slower, but not slow.

Exo stared at his empty shot glass. "Nero's supposed to rejoin the shock troopers at Tusca soon. Been recovering from an injury at Tarrago during the raid. I wouldn't be sad if his shuttle never arrived. Wouldn't have been sad if he'd died at the shipyard with the rest of his boys."

Tusca. That was where Tyrus Rechs had been killed when his ship went nuclear. It was where Keel had *almost* dusted Devers. A place he'd barely escaped from—and left in bad shape. But the point is, he'd called it in—which meant Dark Ops surely would have checked it out. So how could Nero and his shock troopers still be staging there?

Keel pondered all this in the few seconds between Exo's words and his own innocuously performed question: "What's on Tusca?"

"Training grounds," Exo began, and for the first time, he might have slurred his words—slightly. Tabrizzi rye was potent. "Nero has the rank and file training something big, bro. Not like the fleet we're after kinds of big, but part of the plan."

"A plan your friend has no part in." The voice belonged to Bombassa, who walked into the room shirtless and with a white absorption towel ringing the back of his neck.

"How was your shower?" Keel asked.

Bombassa gave a hard stare in reply, then looked down to Exo. "You are drunk?"

"I'm fine," Exo said, cradling his empty shot glass in one hand. "And don't worry about Wraith. He's out of the Legion. Points did him wrong same as you and me."

"You should not be speaking so freely. You know this." Bombassa reached down and grabbed Exo by his elbow. "Come on, get up."

Exo jerked his arm free. "Get off me, man! I'll stand on my own."

To his credit, Exo stood without wobbling. So much so that Keel wondered just how much the drink had actually affected him. He'd met some prolific drinkers who could put away copious amounts of booze without showing any of the adverse side effects, and Exo seemed to be in that category.

Keel watched as his two shock trooper guests stared at one another. His comm chimed, breaking the tension.

Ravi's voice came over the comm. "Captain Keel, the hypotheticals for our jump are coming out clear. I think you have repaired the problem, but I'd like for you to run through a final reboot with me in the cockpit."

"Be right there," Keel said into his comm. He looked at Exo and Bombassa. "You two are welcome to join me if you want."

"No," Bombassa said, before adding as an afterthought, "thank you."

"Nah," Exo said, shaking his head. "My turn for the shower." He made his way down the hall.

With Exo out of earshot, Keel caught Bombassa's eye and nodded toward the galley. "There's caff in there." As he moved past the hulking shock trooper, he patted him on the shoulder. "Take care of Exo, huh?"

***

Ravi was reading a book on his holoscreen when Keel reached the bridge. It was in some language Keel couldn't identify, and featured a painting of a man on a horse by a hedge of roses. It looked old.

"Tell me that's not what you're using to plot our hyperspace routes," Keel said, dropping into his seat.

"Hoo, hoo," laughed Ravi, turning off the book. "This was long before hyperspace."

"Any luck finding it?"

Ravi shook his head. "The hand is not aboard the *Indelible VI*. Your friend Exo likely slipped it to one of his other team members before we left Wayste."

"Why would he do that?"

Ravi tilted his head to the side. "Probably so we would not steal it. And given the circumstances, this was a wise move."

Keel sighed. "Okay, contact Gannon and see if—"

"I have done this already."

With a half frown, unsure whether this was welcomed or annoying, Keel said, "In that case, I need you to contact Harvel Keene. He runs the spice route along Tusca. I need him to look for someone named—"

"Nero, yes, I called it in the moment I heard your discussion."

"Ravi, don't do that. Don't be so… nosy."

The hologram arched an eyebrow. "A Republic-model frigate with black-tipped markings has been seen jumping into various systems along that hyperspace route. Nero is not showing up on any of my searches, so I cannot give a reliable probability, but the ship markings do match what we have seen from vessels converted for use in the Black Fleet. A shuttle from that frigate has dropped planetside at each stop, carrying a man who is buying up antiquities and art. The last sighting of him was at Womaf."

"So, what, he's on a shopping trip?" Keel asked.

"Works of art declared by the government as distinct and protected cultural identifiers, and thus not to leave indigenous worlds, are always easiest to find in the edge's night markets."

Keel thought about this. "If he's jumping from system to system on his way to Tusca, after Womaf he'd hit Olik and then Tusca itself. Ravi, how long—"

"Based on the timing of the last sighting at Womaf and the average time spent on-planet, I estimate Captain Chhun's kill team has nine hours to catch up with Nero on Olik. If not, they will have to find him on Tusca itself."

"Okay, let's get Chhun on comm."

Ravi gave a curt nod and worked his console. The comm light flashed to show it was attempting to make a connection.

"Ravi," Keel said, cautiously, "did Harvel tell you all this?"

"Harvel did not see anything," Ravi said, his eyes fixed on a scrolling array of text strings moving much too fast for Keel to decipher. "I went through Moma."

"Moma!" Keel exclaimed. "He's an info broker, Ravi. How much did you have to spend?"

"Forty thousand."

"*Forty thousand*? Are you out of you mind? Ravi, how could you spend forty thou—"

"Here's Chhun," Ravi said.

Keel clamped his jaw shut and stared hotly at his navigator. Forty thousand credits blown in the time it had taken him to pour a couple of drinks.

"Wraith, what's going on?" Chhun asked, his comm connection on voice only.

Keel mouthed, "I hate you," to Ravi, then said to Chhun: "So, you got your team on standby, right?"

07

Chhun paced outside Captain Deynolds's office. Wraith had just delivered up to him the possibility of capturing of one of Goth Sullus's top men, the general alleged to be in command of the shock troopers. Something like this could be huge—it was the equivalent of the House of Reason removing Legion Commander Keller from the picture.

So Chhun had taken this information to Owens and Keller—had proposed that Victory Squad take the *Intrepid* to the Olik system in an attempt to capture this "General Nero." Wraith had said the general just might be willing to sell his warlord out if the offer was right.

But Legion Commander Keller had dismissed Chhun, wanting to speak with Owens and Deynolds privately about the operation. That didn't sit well with Chhun. Not because Keller didn't have every right to do so, but because it seemed to Chhun that it meant the Legion commander was leaning *against* authorizing the mission. And this wasn't the sort of opportunity that came around more than once.

It would be up to Owens to convince Keller now. At least Chhun had sold *him* on it. He had an ally in the room.

Now it was just a waiting game, while his team sat jocked up and ready to move, shorthanded as they were.

He stared at Captain Deynolds's door, willing it to open with his every thought.

And then it did.

Owens strode out first, with Deynolds behind him. Chhun wanted to run up and ask what happened, like an excited child hoping his grandparents had brought presents with them on a visit, but he restrained himself.

Owens said nothing for several seconds before casually acting as though he'd just noticed Chhun standing nearby. "Oh! Chhun! I almost forgot you were out here." The major broke into a wide grin before Chhun had the chance to say something he might regret. "Ops approved," Owens continued. "Deynolds ordered the ship to jump, and we are now cruising through hyperspace to nab us a five-star bad guy."

"We should arrive in roughly seven hours," Deynolds said. "Before then, I'll want a coordinated plan of attack drawn up *with* contingencies."

She was right about that: there would definitely need to be contingencies. If Nero behaved like Wraith suggested, they might have to take him on the ground, or in the shuttle in atmosphere. Or possibly on board the freighter itself. *If* the freighter was even there. There were numerous variations, and each required a well-cultivated plan that could be enacted at a moment's notice.

Chhun nodded at the captain. "I'm ready to discuss the operation immediately. I can have my team assembled anywhere on the ship inside of ten minutes, as long as a speedlift is open."

Deynolds gave a fractional nod. "Command room in ten minutes then." She turned to go.

Chhun held up a finger. "Captain, there's one thing I'm sure we'll need."

"Yes?"

"A high-speed squadron of raptor featherheads— er, pilots."

Deynolds gave a slight smile. "I know just the ones." She headed off down the corridor, leaving Chhun and Owens together.

"How bad was it?" Chhun asked his commanding officer.

"Not as bad as you think," Owens said, pushing his shades up onto the bridge of his nose. "If we weren't planning a major kelhorned invasion of an entire planet, I don't think he would've blinked. Plus, he expected you on Operation Turning Point to take down the shield generator, and when he learned that R&R wasn't the reason you begged off… well, that didn't sit well with him. But I'll take the heat on that. Point is, he agreed. So this is your free pass to do something other than kill donks. Because when you get back… you and Victory Squad are gonna be in the thick of it on Ankalor."

***

Masters adjusted the plasteen strips tied around his wrists. "I hate this. Cap, are you *sure* we gotta kit out like this?"

Chhun pulled himself away from the manic hustle of the surrounding docking bay on board the *Intrepid*. Outside the shielded bay door, the swirling, haunting folds of hyperspace blurred past. Not much longer until the ship arrived at Olik.

The strips Masters was complaining about were designed to make the Legion armor capable of surviving limited exposure to the vacuum of space. Masters knew that. But Chhun played along.

"No telling what kind of nut we're going to have to crack to get at Nero," Chhun said. "So it's just like it was back in Liberty Scouts: Stay Prepared."

Masters dropped his head and sulkily replied, "My mom didn't let me join Liberty Scouts."

"You didn't miss much," said Fish, who was standing just inside an assault pod attached to the bottom of an armored transport shuttle.

"What're you talking about?" said Bear. Like Chhun, he was staying outside of the cramped pod for as long as possible. "Liberty Scouts was awesome. That's how I first learned to shoot a blaster rifle."

A lull in the conversation followed as the kill team checked and re-checked their equipment, waiting for the order to load up into the assault pod. Smaller than assault shuttles, assault pods were launched like missiles from larger craft. They were less powerful than the piloted assault shuttles Chhun and his team had used to breach

JASON ANSPACH & NICK COLE

capital ships through the years, but that was precisely the point. A standard assault shuttle would rocket straight through a transport shuttle, and everyone wanted this "General Nero" captured alive.

Chhun looked over to the standby assault team made up of Republic marines—the guys who'd be sent out if his kill team found itself on the wrong end of a blaster cannon. Walking through the crowd was Major Owens in full kit, a navy pilot at his side. The pair made their way straight to Victory Squad.

"Captain Chhun," Owens said on reaching them. "I want you to meet Lieutenant Dax Danns. He's the squad leader for Raptor Strike Squadron 101—Star Reapers. He's assigned to make sure you don't get shot down once you launch."

Dax had a dark complexion and a charismatic, mega-watt smile. He moved his flight helmet from one hand to the other to shake with Chhun. "Nice to meet you, sir."

"You too, Lieutenant." Chhun looked around the docking bay, searching for the taxied Raptor starfighters.

Dax seemed to sense what he was looking for, as he pointed Chhun in the right direction. "That's us over there, and we'll be nearby the whole time. No way we'll let a kill team get vaped while the Reapers are in flight."

Chhun studied the ships. The fixed-wing Raptors had the usual white hull with gray streaks, all except for one, which was metallic gray with bright green streaks. That must belong to the flight leader. "How'd you get the okay on a paint job like that?" he asked. "Not exactly reg."

Dax chuckled. "By not having a CO with a stick up her ass. Captain Deynolds okayed orders to let us customize our birds after we got our tenth confirmed. And," Dax tilted his head, clearly impressed with himself and filing his fingernails against his dark green flight suit, "only took me a week clearing out pirates outside of Honnifer to pitch out my ride. Rest of the squad's only a few kills behind. Probably get it done today if Black Fleet launches fighters."

"They're the best," Owens said, raising his voice to be heard over the all-comm updates, mechanical noises, and general chaos that was a docking bay at general quarters—battle stations.

"Glad to have you out there," Chhun said.

The shipboard comm interjected itself into the conversation, calling for all pilots and appropriate personnel to prepare for launch.

Dax smiled. "You get a chance to do a favor for a kill team, you take it, right? Get-out-of-dead free card in case the House of Reason ever jumps down my neck." Laughing at his own joke, Dax pulled his flight helmet over his head and started running toward his Raptor squadron.

"Okay, Victory," Chhun shouted, turning to face his team. "You heard the magic voice. Time to climb inside and get cramped."

Owens knocked on Chhun's shoulder armor. "Save room for me in there."

This wasn't a surprise; Owens had his rifle and was jocked up for combat. "You sure, Major?"

"Not letting a team down two men get after it solo. We aren't that desperate yet."

Chhun nodded. Owens had proven on Herbeer that his time in command hadn't atrophied his fighting ability. "Masters is our spear tip. Why don't you take jump master?"

Owens looked like he wanted to object to being placed at the end of the line, last one out of the pod. But he only nodded, removed his shades, and pulled his bucket over his head. "Rock and roll."

Command Bridge of the Black Fleet Frigate *Monstrous*
Olik System

Pehl Turek walked slowly across the bridge of the Black Fleet frigate tasked with bringing General Nero to Tusca from his recuperations on Tarrago. Not the most important mission in the galaxy, but infinitely better than his time as first mate aboard the long-haul transports traveling from one end of the galaxy to the other.

His hands were clasped behind his back as he observed his modest crew. Only five were needed on the *Monstrous*, unlike the two dozen needed to man a destroyer. He wondered, for a moment, the crew size needed for one of Emperor Sullus's dreadnoughts. Some day he would find out. But for now... he was in command. Finally.

From a family steeped in Republic Navy tradition, Captain Turek found himself an oddity. Four generations of sons had all served in the navy, to a man. Turek's three older brothers had done their part as well. But Turek didn't test well enough to serve as an officer—that's what they said. He could perform the necessary duties expected of an officer. He was quick on his feet, made good practical decisions, was suited for a life in space, but when it came to the necessary entrance examinations... he always bombed. Enlistment was his only option. The first Turek son unsuited to serve as an officer in the Republic Navy.

So his father told him to skip the navy altogether. Told him there'd be more money and fewer headaches just taking a commission with a mercantile spacer. And no shame.

But shame was all Captain Turek ever felt. Because he knew he'd failed. He knew his father had told him not to enlist because he didn't want to introduce to his retired navy brass buddies his three officer sons and the swab who couldn't cut it. His father never said that out loud, but Turek knew it was true.

And that was why Turek experienced a soul-stripping inward flush of warmth every time he entered a spaceport, sat through a Republic customs inspection, or gathered with his siblings. That was the worst of all. At every wedding or funeral, they would appear resplendent in their white dress uniforms. And there he was in an ordinary suit, explaining for the hundredth time to a distant relation why he, Pehl, wasn't in the navy like everyone else. Or even in command of the cargo hauler he served upon.

But I'm in command now, Turek reminded himself, his brief tour of the bridge complete.

That was all it had taken for him to join the Back Fleet. Just the acknowledgment that he had been overlooked— that there was a place for him in the coming new order.

"We want men of merit," the former Naval Academy instructor, now recruiting for the new emperor, had told him. "And we know you were born for the stars, clipped and grounded by the Republic. And I think," the man said during that clandestine comm discussion in the stark loneliness of deep space, "that it's time you take command of your future, and a ship in our fleet."

A simple frigate, while a step up from a deep-space hauler, was still the sort of starship people were given command of when their career was all but over. But for Captain Turek, *Monstrous*—with its modest command crew, its meager detachment of shock troopers, and its single squadron of tri-fighters—was *everything*. He would do his duty well and please his superiors. He would be noticed. He was ready for greatness. Ready for his destiny.

And so, when the Republic destroyer burst into subspace, already within firing range, Turek did not hesitate.

"Shields!" he screamed, in time to prevent all but the first deadly turbolaser from impacting his thin hull. "The general?"

A comm and sensor officer studied the dash. "Sir, the general just exited Olik's atmosphere and is on a trajectory toward *Monstrous* docking."

"Republic Raptors!" screamed the security officer, giving words to the visuals they all saw through the forward viewport. Starfighters, practically miniature compared to the hulking destroyer from which they came, poured out of a shielded docking bay.

"Scramble all tri-fighters," Turek ordered. "We need to buy the general time to reach us."

Turek's helmsman swiveled in his chair and got his captain's attention. "Sir, oughtn't the general return to the planet?"

Captain Turek shook his head. "The planet will be swarming with legionnaires before long, if the general is their target. His best chance is to reach *Monstrous* and escape with us. Have jump coordinates at the ready."

"Yes, sir!"

The ship lurched and rocked from the concussive force of turbolaser fire impacting in brilliant explosive flashes on the shield array. *Monstrous* couldn't take much of this. Not for long.

"Captain Turek," the weapons officer called out. "Requesting permission to engage the Republic destroyer."

"Don't bother," Turek said, dismissing the idea with a wave. "We'd be lucky to get their shields to even flicker. Power down all batteries except for starfighter defense, and channel it to increase shield strength. We don't need to out-punch them, we only need to last until the bell rings."

Raptor Strike Squadron 101, "Star Reapers"
Olik System

Dax Danns roared out of the *Intrepid*'s docking bay and into open space. This was always a surreal sensation. Inside the bay, the noise from his Raptor's thrusters was deafening—and then it all went deathly quiet once he was out in open space.

Massive turbolaser blasts shot from *Intrepid*'s batteries over his head. Carnage in energy form advanced to wreak havoc on the much smaller frigate, hammering its shields so ruthlessly that Dax could actually see the protective energy screens rippling.

"All right," Dax called into his squad comm. "Form up on me, Reapers. We in, we out, and we fast on this hop."

"Scope's picking up a Republic-model transport shuttle exiting orbit," called Reaper Four, his report coming just as Dax saw the same on his screen.

Dax tapped in a preconfigured request to his Raptor's AI, asking it to plot an optimal intercept route. "Thirty seconds," he mumbled to himself.

And probably four minutes before the shuttle reached the frigate. Not much time, especially if the Black Fleet had any halfway competent starfighter pilots scrambling to intercept.

With an easy push of his flight control stick, Dax aimed his ship straight for the frigate itself. His plotting computer beeped at his wide variation from its highlighted course.

"Where you headed, Reaper One?" the *Intrepid*'s CSG—Commander, Starfighter Group—inquired over comm. He was a year into the position, and Dax knew that the guy wanted little more than to be back behind the stick.

"Gonna swing us around the frigate's docking bay," Dax said, knowing that his squadron would follow him without his giving the command. "If they launch fighters, I want to have the drop on them."

"Priority is the shuttle," reminded the CSG, his voice stern.

"Roger," Dax said, increasing his speed as the fixed-wing craft scanned for incoming fighters. "We got time for the detour, boss."

The Raptors swooped alongside the frigate, flying parallel to the craft. These frigates always reminded Dax of boxy, oversized speeders with two massive drive engines protruding from the back. The Reapers raced past the engines, lining themselves up to fly directly toward the distant shuttle, the frigate's docking bay still ahead.

Flashes of turbolaser fire from *Intrepid* cast their green glow inside Dax's cockpit like flashes of lightning on a night drive. Soon, magenta flashes erupted from the frigate in response.

"Whoa!" called out Reaper Four.

"What is it?" asked the CSG from *Intrepid*. "What's the SA?"

"Frigate's guns are trying to tap us," reported Reaper Two.

Dax throttled forward as the *Monstrous*'s blaster bolts streaked behind him. "Just kick up the speed, Reapers. Those guns can't track small and fast."

The squadron increased its acceleration, quickly burning through the distance between them and the frigate's hangar bay. And just as they came near, the larger ship began spewing forth slick and agile tri-fighters, painted matte black, just as in the reports from Tarrago.

"That's what we're looking for," Dax called out. "Paint your targets and punch right through, Reapers!"

Tri-fighters jinked in hopeless attempts to escape the unanticipated barrage of starfighter fire tearing into them mere seconds after they emerged from the shielded docking bay. At least a half dozen tri-fighters were immediately vaporized as the Raptors' blaster cannons ripped through their wings and cockpits. Even so, more continued exiting the frigate until it seemed there were two tri-fighters for each Raptor.

"Mother, this is Reaper One," Dax called in to his destroyer. "Vaped six tris, count a couple dozen more. Must have 'em packed in tight in that frigate."

"Copy, Reaper One," the CSG replied. "Launching Black Hawk Squadron to engage fighters. Don't let the shuttle get away."

"Not plannin' on it," Dax said to himself.

He executed a spiraling corkscrew that locked a tri-fighter in his sights, then sent linked blaster bolts burning into the tri-fighter. One more hash mark to be painted beneath his fighter's canopy.

"Reapers Two and Three, form up on me. Let's keep that shuttle from getting back home. The rest of you keep those fighters busy."

"On it, boss!"

"Right behind you!"

The three Raptors pushed through the thick screen of Black Fleet fighters, picking off targets of opportunity as they fell into their sights. Soon Dax was through the swarm, and the distant shuttle was in view from his canopy, growing larger as he streaked toward it.

"Reaper One, one of you picked up a tail," called Reaper Nine from the maelstrom. The three Raptors had formed the three points of a triangle, moving in formation toward the shuttle. "Coming up behind the port-side Raptor. Is that you, Three?"

"Yeah," replied the pilot. "I can tell something back there is shooting at me, but I got no joy—I can't see 'em!"

Dax frowned. "Two, Three, break off and keep an eye on each other. But if the tri puke follows me... do me a favor and vape 'em."

"Acknowledged, Reaper One."

The two Raptors rolled away, peeling in large, inverted arcs that afforded each pilot the opportunity to look up and see more clearly their wingman's situation. Peals of blaster fire chased Reaper Three's maneuvering Raptor, glancing across its wing and bringing down its shields.

"Shields down!" Reaper Three reported. "Tri-fighter is still on my six... can't shake him loose."

"Hang tight," said Reaper Two. "I'm coming around. Damn it... this guy won't stay still. I can't get him locked."

Blaster fire shaved away paint stripes and sizzled impervisteel as it seared past Reaper Three. The pilot sounded concerned, a man sensing his demise. "Get this guy, dammit!"

"I'm trying!"

Dax looked over his shoulder at the knife fight behind him and swore to himself. He pulled his Raptor up hard and looped around, orienting himself with a barrel roll and assuming a collision course with Reaper Two. "Nose down, Three!" he ordered.

The pilot pushed in stick-forward and performed an abrupt dive, giving Dax an opening at the pursuing tri-fighter. Reaper One didn't hesitate. Two alternating blaster cannons sent four energy bolts into the center of the tri-fighter's cockpit, igniting its flammable gases in a quick burst, and Dax flew through the exploding wreckage.

"Thanks, Dax," called out a relieved-sounding Reaper Three.

"You can thank me at the club," Dax replied, already falling back into formation. He looked with a furrowed brow at the intercept readings. "Sket! We gotta disable this shuttle yesterday!"

"Be advised," the CSG announced over the comm, "hostile frigate has lost shields. Expect power to be routed to laser batteries. Eyes open out there, Reapers."

The shields were down? Dax had an idea. "Mother, this is Reaper One."

"I hear you, Reaper One."

"Blow that frigate apart!"

"I... what?"

"That shuttle's got a chance to dock hot... and the moment it gets inside... hyperspace. We gotta deny its ride out of here. By the time the shuttle starts calculating its own jump, I'll have the engines disabled." Dax could see the auto-turrets under each shuttle wing attempting to track his approach. He would attempt to knock those out before swinging around and hitting the engines. "Hope I don't blow the whole thing up," he mumbled to himself.

"All craft," the CSG called, urgency in his voice. "Concentrate all firepower on the hostile frigate. The captain and I want it left a junk field."

Responses of confirmation poured in.

Over his shoulder, Dax saw the *Intrepid* pummel the small freighter with its overwhelming batteries. Raptors unloaded their full complement of missiles before doing striking the hull with their cannons.

The shuttle pilot must have realized what the Republic was playing at. The transport vehicle began turning away. But its movement was like that of a geriatric mule—these suckers didn't come close to handling like a Raptor.

Dax smiled as the shuttle pilot made a fatal error, exposing its starboard engine unit to him. He locked on with a concussion missile, but rather than firing, he primed it for a mirror position. He would go in with cannons first, loop, then fire at the opposite engine as quickly as possible, trusting the missile to home in on its pre-arranged target. "Thank you very much!"

Blaster bolts tore into the shuttle's starboard engine unit, causing the ethereal blue glow to fade out into a lifeless, scorched black even as the shuttle's wings adjusted for hyperspace travel.

Dax began his loop.

"They're about to jump away!" warned Reaper Two.

"C'mon..." Dax pulled his Raptor hard, pushing it to the very peak of its ability. He fired nanoseconds after seeing the green lock flash, then watched two spectacular things from the view out of the top of his canopy window. The first was the frigate *Monstrous* erupting into scores of miniature explosions, which blossomed and bloomed until a flowering eruption seemed to issue forth from the center of the starship, causing it to break apart as if pulled by a thousand dragons in a thousand different directions. The second thing Dax saw was his missile arcing to the last operative engine on the shuttle. It drew nearer, nearer... and then exploded in a white concussive wave of energy...

... just as the shuttle made the jump to hyperspace.

Wide-eyed and with a small voice, Dax cried, "No."

It was gone. The shuttle was gone.

"Reaper One," called in the CSG. "What's going on, what happened? We've lost visual on the shuttle. Advise—did it reach hyperspace?"

"Yeah, it did," Dax sighed. "Be advised, they—" A new ping from the sensitive scanners in the nose cone of his Raptor arrested the words as he uttered them. "Hold up. I see them, Mother! They jumped, but it was a nanosecond too late. Sensors show the disabled shuttle not a hundred kilometers away. That's as far as she got."

"Roger that, Reaper One. Protect the target until we can recover with tractor beam. Nice work, Reapers."

08

Legion Destroyer *Intrepid*
Hangar Bay
Olik System

Masters's leg jittered up and down like he'd just consumed fourteen cups of caff before entering the tight confines of the assault pod. Chhun tried to pass the seemingly endless time by counting each time Masters's knee went up and down, but he couldn't keep up.

Finally, Bear gripped the volatile limb at the lower thigh and held it down. "Dude. Relax."

Shaking his head as though he were trying to remove water from his ears, Masters said, "Sorry. Can't." His opposite knee began its own nervous ride. "These things are death traps. I'm not going to be able to relax until the doors open and I'm shooting bad guys."

Fish leaned forward from his jump seat and looked past Bear to Masters. "You do realize that we haven't even left the ship yet, right? Shuttle's still on the deck."

"No kidding it's still on the deck," Masters bit back. "That makes it even worse. Because that means there's probably a huge dogfight out there and they're holding us back so we don't get blown up. Only they'll still send us out into the blaster fire if it looks like Nero might get away, and then everybody will know why we're there and it'll be like a game of smear the stier."

"That's not gonna happen," Chhun said. He didn't want his men to dwell on the unpleasant idea of being vaped inside their cramped tube, never knowing what hit them until they were consumed by a gaseous fireball. "Focus on your job, KTF, and we'll all be fine."

"I dunno, man," insisted Masters. "We've been in here, what, fifteen minutes? And no one has said nothing to us about it. If the shuttle was out there, we'd have gone for it. If it was on the surface, we'd have dropped. If it was on board a ship, then we just sit tight until the fighters clear a path and then it's us plus a bunch of hullbusters against whatever. But what if it's one of those three gigantic ships they have? That's gonna be a lot of work, man."

Owens shook his head. "Calling it a frigate over the battlenet. If it were a destroyer, we'd feel it rockin' the shields."

Masters seemed not to hear it. "It's gonna be one of those huge ships and then we're gonna punch in and have to fight through three miles of phonies. That's what it's gonna be, man. I know it."

Over a private comm channel, Owens asked Chhun, "What's up with this kid?"

"It's how he deals with waiting," Chhun said, not at all concerned. "He's got a neurotic side. We've learned to live with it; it's best to just let him go."

"Huh," answered Owens. "I don't remember him being like this when I was still active with the squad."

"Lots of things have changed since then. No offense."

"All good. You hearing anything on your comm that I'm not?"

Chhun smiled inwardly. "Don't figure they'd tell me something they aren't telling you. I was about to ask you the same thing. All I'm getting is 'kill team stand by.'"

Owens made a clicking noise with his tongue and said, "Let me contact the hullbusters, see what they know."

"It'll pass the time if nothing else."

"Marines," Owens barked into his comm on their open channel. "This is Major Owens embedded with Legion Kill Team Victory. One of you hullbusters have any hints about what's going on? We're sitting in the dark here—literally."

"Just waitin' on you, Major," answered a voice from the Marine comm channel.

"Say what?" Owens switched to a private comm with Chhun. "They say they're waiting on us."

"What?"

"Yes, sir," the marine answered. "Orders are to follow your team to assault the shuttle. We're all waiting here outside the containment dock."

"The shuttle is *on board*?"

"Yes, sir. Tractored in and isolated in the CD."

The CD, containment dock, was a specially armored and shielded bay used to contain hostile or suspect starships brought on board with tractor beams. Vessels were kept there until a team could scan, clear, or otherwise sweep the ship to make sure it wasn't rigged or outfitted to explode or attack. An unfriendly starship could do a lot of damage if it was allowed to go hot inside the general docking bay; it could wipe out entire fighter wings, not to mention the scores of crew nearby. But in the containment dock, the damage an explosion could do was minimal. A ship turned into a bomb would be free to detonate, but it wouldn't matter—the force of the blast would be channeled and vented through shielded release ports, causing no significant damage to the ship itself. And if they started firing blaster cannons, the offending ship would barely make a dent in the quadruple-thick, shielded walls.

"Looks like the shuttle is there, waiting on us," Owens informed the rest of the kill team.

"For how long?" asked Fish.

"How long?" Owens relayed the question over the marine comm.

"Been waiting about five minutes. I was about to send a couple boys to wake you leejes up."

"Cute," Owens said.

"Nice if someone would've told us," Bear said, adjusting his helmet between a pair of mammoth hands.

Chhun hit the button to open the assault pod. "We know about it now, so let's get going."

Outside the assault pod, Fish pointed toward a couple dozen marines on the far side of the hangar bay. "I see the hullbusters. Containment Door A."

"Hustle up," ordered Chhun, setting the pace for his men to follow as they moved toward their objective. He looked from left to right, counting Raptor starfighters as he went. There were fewer of them here than there had been when his team first entered the assault pod, but Dax's black-and-green starfighter stood out among the ships that had returned. The pilot had done his job, and now it was up to the kill team and marines to finish it.

As the team moved, a naval petty officer approached. "Are you the kill team?"

"No," Masters shouted, "we're the basics parade. Next show is at fourteen thirty."

"I have orders for you to report to Containment Dock A."

"A little late, spacer," Bear said, shouldering his way past the messenger.

"Orders received," Chhun said. "We're on it."

Victory Squad reached the gathered marines. Chhun, with Owens, approached a marine captain making himself conspicuous by the way he walked up and down his line of kneeling hullbusters, slapping them on the tops of their green helmets and giving final reminders and instructions.

"I'm Captain Chhun, Dark Ops," Chhun said, both hands gripping his N-4 at the ready, allowing a curt nod to do what a handshake otherwise would.

"Captain Kenny Johnson," the marine replied. "My fire teams are ready to seal off the containment bay and watch for any space rat holes they might try to use to get around you. I also have some men with experience doing CQC from Rawl Kima, in case you want an additional team assaulting the shuttle."

Chhun nodded. The captain was fresh-faced, young enough that had this been before Keller's dismissal of the points serving among those loyal to the Legion, Chhun would have figured him to be an officer appointed to the marines because his government sponsor didn't have the clout needed to get him command of a starship or in the Legion.

"How long you been in?" Chhun asked, slinging his blaster rifle and opening his breaching kit, looking for the best tool to crack open the shuttle's ramp. Since it was a Republic model acquired by the Black Fleet, a slice patch would probably be enough go get her to open up... though Chhun preferred the boom.

"Eight years, sir."

"Good." Chhun found the slice patch and paired it with the proper class and model of the shuttle he could see through the transparent blast door window leading into the containment bay. "Not a point?"

"No, sir," the captain answered, all business.

"Good," Owens said, speaking up for the first time. "Legion don't like points."

"Sir, the Legion saved my father's life on Psydon. I don't like points, either."

"Ooah," said Fish from nearby.

Chhun caught the attention of his team. "Okay, I'm set to breach. I want a twin column formation with Masters taking lead. Captain Johnson, position your men to keep our backs and have your CQC boys and a corpsman standing by. We'll use them as a Quick Reaction Force if things get ugly."

Chhun took a deep breath. He hoped that wouldn't be the way this all went down, but with the general apparently in command of the entirety of the shock trooper force on board, and with the knowledge that men like Exo were serving as shock troopers... yeah. This could really suck.

JASON ANSPACH & NICK COLE

A warning siren sounded in the docking bay as the heavy containment doors pulled apart, revealing a damaged transport shuttle sitting inside. The ship had a pair of fixed swept wings at its rear and a sleek rounded cockpit at its fore. It had two forward-facing light blaster cannons, one built into the frame beside each wing. These looked to have been scorched and made inoperable, if that was the work of Dax and his Space Reapers, Chhun would have to buy them all a round.

Chhun held up his arm, fist balled, indicating to his team that they'd gone as far as he wanted them to go. Of course, the L-comm provided him the means of simply *telling* his men to halt, so the visible symbol was more for the marines, who likewise halted. He then motioned the fire teams where he wanted them and waited as they ran around the perimeter of the hangar to set up crew-served N-50 blaster cannons.

When he was satisfied that everyone was where they needed to be, Chhun and his team began moving toward the target. They moved smoothly, because being smooth meant being fast. And being fast was what kept them alive.

The shuttle gave off a hiss, and its yellow underbelly lights flashed to indicate that the ramp was coming down. The kill team halted and took up fire positions. So much for having to blow it open. It looked like the general had ordered his troopers to go down with a fight. Chhun only hoped that Nero himself could still be taken alive.

"Think they're coming out to surrender?" Masters asked over L-comm.

Bear pumped his shotgun for a maximum energy charge. "Would you?"

"If I saw myself standing outside?" Masters asked. "Oh, hell yeah. Gotta be cray-cray to want a piece of this."

"You're crazy all right."

"Maintain comm discipline," said Chhun.

The ramp lowered, a white cloud of vapors escaping and obscuring whatever lurked in the darkness inside the shuttle. In his mind's eye, Chhun could see the brilliant intensity of blaster bolts zipping through like thunderbolts from a cloud. But none came. Instead the haze dissipated even as the ramp lowered. Then, as if they had been waiting against the ramp itself, the bodies of two shock troopers came tumbling out. The glossy, black-armored soldiers slid and rolled down the ramp, clattering onto the deck and then remaining still.

"Should we shoot them just to be safe?" Fish asked.

"Hang on," said Chhun. His bucket's IR could see a figure approaching the top of the ramp from inside the shuttle itself. He wore a black uniform and a long overcoat that went down to his mirror-shined boots. In his hand was a simple blaster pistol, held so the grip faced outward.

"This is General Nero," called the man from inside the shuttle. "No doubt there are legionnaires, perhaps even a kill team, waiting for me outside. I'm surrendering the pistol I used to kill these men you see before you."

Chhun's bucket showed Nero slowly squatting, the weapon held out and visible the entire time. He placed the blaster on the floor, stood just as slowly, and kicked the weapon. It banged and spun down the ramp like a child's toy dropped on a staircase.

"I'm coming out now."

General Nero walked down the ramp, a look of supreme confidence on his face, even though both of his hands were resting on the top of his head. Chhun's bucket tech scanned the man's face, looking for a match in the Legion database. This guy was leading his own little Legion, using the same tactics and command structure. The presumption was that he was former Legion himself. But the processors came back empty—no record on file.

The kill team moved in, weapons ready.

"I surrender," Nero said, a slight grin on his face. "I trust Legion Commander Keller wishes to have a word with me? We're old friends, he and I. I was once a shining star in the Legion."

At once the kill team moved with a frighteningly unified speed and purpose that served to wipe the smug smile from Nero's face and replace it with what Chhun knew to be a deep-seated concern for his own well-being. It was a look the kill team had seen many times before.

Bear grabbed him by the collar bone and send him down hard on two knees while Masters ener-chained his arms. As Fish placed an isolation hood over his head, he held it open just long enough for Chhun to say, "He does. But my team wanted a word first: Go to hell, traitor."

09

Cresweil Bazaar
Porcha

Technically, the Cresweil Bazaar was not a city, though if it were, it would be the most populous on the entire planet. The bazaar started as a sort of planetary initiative just after the Savage Wars. It was the brainchild of then–Cabinet General Muuvi the Belligerent: sell at the bazaar and pay the government a flat three percent. No customs, no tariffs… no questions asked.

Porcha managed to keep the Republic looking the other way by hemming and hawing over what they declared to be culturally exclusionary policies that prevented the planet from formally joining the intergalactic government following an alliance during the Savage Wars themselves. That line of negotiation—coercion through guilt—proved to be so effective that even when Muuvi the Belligerent was killed and dragged through the streets in a revolutionary uprising, the Republic stayed away.

Or maybe they just liked to use the bazaar for their own purposes.

For Captain Keel, it didn't matter all that much. Porcha wasn't unique to the galaxy, but it did mark a vital port where one could buy and sell just about anything. It had therefore become a regular haunt for Keel when he was first cutting his smuggler's teeth after leaving his brothers in Victory Squad.

Keel wore black trousers with yellow stripes running down the side and a generous, white open-collar shirt beneath a brown lurr-hide jacket. He had insisted that Exo and Bombassa dress the part of spacers as well. Exo wore some of Keel's clothes—a blue vest above an orange shirt with brown pants and dusty black boots. The ensemble was both baggy and snug, as Keel was taller but less powerfully built than the broad-shouldered, barrel-chested former legionnaire. Bombassa was altogether too large to wear anything of Keel's and had to settle on a pair of sandy coveralls. Keel didn't remember where he'd picked them up.

"I feel stupid," Bombassa complained. The whine of one of the many observation bots and courier drones that thickened the sky sounded overhead.

"You look fine," Keel assured him. He looked up at a drone, which seemed to have taken an extra second to hover ten meters above their table. Most cities had ordinances restricting bot and drone traffic to make it less intrusive for the organics. But Cresweil Bazaar wasn't a city.

"He looks like he killed a mechanic and put on his skin," chuckled Exo.

Bombassa flitted his eyes from Exo to Keel. "See?"

"Can't be helped," Keel said, trying not to roll his eyes. The last thing any of them should want was to get identified as military. Cresweil reacted violently to anyone they believed might be there to enforce that now-forgotten three-percent tax... or to shut things down on behalf of some Republic world tired of not having their exorbitant tariffs paid out.

Keel watched as a vendor at their corner gestured demonstratively at an N-4 rifle he held in one hand, seeking to convince a prospective buyer that what he held was the weapon the shopper was looking for. The vendor, who wore a flak jacket bulging with charge packs and fraggers, jammed a fresh pack into the N-4 and fired several rounds into the air, as if to demonstrate the reliability of his inventory.

Exo and Bombassa instinctively jumped, while Keel sat on impassively. "Relax, guys."

Scowling, Exo said, "Yeah, well, shock trooper training kind of requires that sort of response, bro."

"So does Legion training," added Bombassa, giving Keel a hard look. "Or at least... it once did."

Keel gave a sardonic half smile. "Well, around *here*... jumping at the sound of blaster rifles shot into the air reveals you as a fresh-off-the-ship sucker. Or a soldier. And neither of those do well on Porcha."

Exo looked around. At first, Keel thought he was scanning the crowd for the rest of his team of shock troopers to arrive. But instead he said, "When's our drinks getting here?"

A server—some species that looked like a hybrid of snake, octopus, and human—emerged from the interior of the cafe. The three men had taken advantage of the sunny weather and sat outside. As the server slithered toward them, its torso upright like a gorgon, its tentacles delivered drinks to the various patrons sitting among the maze of tables.

"Here you go," a fairly attractive human-like face said, delivering three drinks.

Keel nodded a silent thanks, while Exo practically dove for his drink.

"I said bring me two!" Exo called out after the server. He fished out a pulpy citrus rind that floated with the ice on the surface of the red liquor. "She better not take her time," he mumbled to himself.

Bombassa took a sip of his own drink, made a face of displeasure, and set it back on the table. He looked to the steaming cup of caff Keel had in front of him. "Why are you the only one not drinking?"

Keel held out an open palm plaintively. "Because *one* of us has to stay sober." He leaned back in his seat and scanned the bustling streets. "When is your team supposed to arrive? You'd think they'd be waiting for *us*."

Exo bottomed out his glass and breathed a ragged sigh. "They said on the comm that they hadn't left the ship before now. Probably got lost on the way."

"Swell." Keel thumped the side of his drink. If the shock troopers had spent all their time holed up in their ship, then there was no way that Gannon could have had the opportunity to perform the task he'd been hired to do. Which wasn't the worst thing in the galaxy, but it certainly took some options off the table.

Through the teeming crowds of the bazaar, three men pushed through the throngs of people like drops of water in a pan of hot oil. They each had the high and tight quarter-inch haircut popular among Republic marines and other combat personnel. They wore black T-shirts, parade-polished black boots, and black fatigue pants. The bulge of their concealed blasters was obvious.

"Oh, brother," Keel said upon catching sight of the coming shock troopers. They were moving at a slow jog and looked as though they were part of a city garrison out for some friendly PT in the streets. More than a few bots and drones seemed to be monitoring their movement from overhead, and every shopper, vendor, or gang member they jostled past responded with the most telling of glares. It was obvious the guys had never been in Dark Ops with the way they were drawing attention to themselves. Keel wondered if they were ever even Legion. Their entire manner seemed somehow… off.

He glanced over at Bombassa and Exo. They didn't convey any sense of warm-heartedness over the pending reunion. Their faces were all business.

"Your friends are making quite a scene," Keel observed dryly. "They all former Legion like you?"

Exo exchanged a look with Bombassa before focusing his attention on Keel. "They're shooters, and they *say* they're Legion."

"But…" prompted Keel.

"They don't know the Legion," Exo continued before looking around for the absent server. He eyed Bombassa's drink and smiled as the shock trooper slid it in his direction. "Thanks," Exo said. "Hot out today." He took a large gulp. "Anyhow, yeah. They get how the Legion works, but in that way that makes you feel like they weren't actually *in* the Legion. 'Bassa thinks they were RA or marines embedded with leejes."

Keel looked to Bombassa to see if the big man was willing to provide any elaboration.

Bombassa shrugged. "They are quiet whenever talk of former units, commanders, shared acquaintances—things like that—come up."

"I guess as long as they know how to fire a blaster in the right direction," Keel offered, blowing away a column of steam rising from his caff, a hot drink for a hot day, but that never bothered him. "I mean, look at the MCR. You can start out as paramilitary, be as sleek and professional as you want, but at the end of the day, it takes a hell of a lot of blasters to go up against the Republic. Eventually you just need bodies."

Bombassa grunted in agreement while Exo finished off his second drink. He snapped his fingers in an attempt to gain the server's attention—to no avail. "What's a guy gotta do to get his second drink, threaten the waitress with a blaster?"

"You *had* your second drink," said Bombassa.

Exo winked. "I had *your* first drink. Still waiting on my second."

Keel laughed, and Exo smiled. "So you're right about the numbers thing," Exo said, clinking two round chunks of ice at the bottom of his glass. "I've always said the whole point of throwing in with Sullus is to get the Legion to open their eyes and add their strength to the fight. That's how the House of Reason comes down. Sheer force."

"If they go for it," Keel countered.

"Yeah. But how about you? Why don't you add yourself to our numbers, Ford?"

Keel gave his most patronizing smile and slowly shook his head. "Because there's a lot more money to be had as a free agent."

"Some things," Bombassa said, his voice earnest, "are more important than money."

"Not from what I've seen."

Keel's comm chimed, and he looked down at the signature pattern lighting up from the comm unit attached to his shirt. "That's Ravi. I'm gonna take this inside. Too many ears for hire out here to talk about anything *real* important, fathom?"

"The Black Fleet is important," Exo insisted.

Keel winked. "Sure. Don't let your buddies make the mistake of unpacking those blasters they're trying to hide when they show up. I wouldn't like it, and neither would any of the dozen or so others watching them come your way."

The shock troopers arrived at the table just after Keel disappeared into the quiet darkness of the main building.

***

"Okay, Ravi, go ahead." Keel was sitting alone in the darkest corner booth he could find. The niceness of the day, combined with it being hours before the rush of sellers and buyers done with a day's trade and demanding drinks to celebrate or mourn business deals, left the place empty enough for Keel to keep close watch on anyone who might be observing him, but there was still enough interior buzzing to provide a din of conversation to drown out his voice.

"I am watching the shock troopers' craft via TT-9 observation bot. Gannon is only now making his move, though one soldier remains on board."

"Yeah," Keel frowned, "Exo said they packed themselves inside like pilgrims on a lighthugger, waiting for us to arrive. This is the first chance Gannon has had."

"I know this too," Ravi said. "I have been monitoring their S-comm transmissions."

A pair of Hools walked by, their venomous spines shining wet at the tips with their lethal poison. They approached the bar, the rest of the patrons giving them a wide berth. Keel loosened his blaster pistol as one of the two aliens looked menacingly toward him. Keel gave a fractional nod, his face unreadable. The Hool turned away and made demands of the bartender, a beat-up looking servitor bot.

"Anything else of interest going back and forth on the comms?" Keel asked.

"Nothing of note. They are expected to report in to whomever their handler is, but this is Bombassa's job, so it has not yet been done." There was a pause, then Ravi provided his interpretation of their flexibility. "It seems this team has a great level of freedom afforded it. They talk as ones authorized to do whatever is necessary to complete their mission, free of interference."

"Good to know in case we want to take them on a detour or two before getting Leenah and Garret."

"And Prisma and Skrizz," Ravi added.

"Sure."

"Gannon and his men are forcing their way onto the ship. They are moving very well. I am impressed, actually."

"I guess we'll find out if the guy inside has time to raise an alarm."

Ravi didn't answer.

"What're you seeing? Can you risk sending the feed to my datacard?" Keel removed the small rectangle from his pocket and flicked its corner to wake it up.

"I would not recommend that," Ravi said, somewhat absently. "There are enough slicers looking for data that a tri-streamed transmission might be observable. Perhaps if Garrett were here..."

"Okay, so you give me the play-by-play."

"There's not much to be said. Two of Gannon's men are outside, blasters in hand. They are dressed... it looks paramilitary. I am going to magnify the bot's cams and see if I can identify anything peculiar. They are doing... very well so far."

"Gannon knows his way around a blaster."

Again, Ravi gave no reply.

"Ravi?"

"Captain Keel, Gannon is employing the use of MCR soldiers. I can see the relevant insignia on their uniforms."

Keel groaned inwardly. It didn't surprise him that the mids would take a job for hire—they needed the money to stay relevant. And it wouldn't surprise him if Gannon had made pals with a local MCR general. Gannon was the type who always looked to firm up his own self-important beliefs. He lived in a world where he was, in spite of all evidence to the contrary, the most skillful smuggler and merc the galaxy had ever seen. Any time he didn't live up to that infamous and prestigious title... well, that was other people's fault. Never his own.

"As long as they do the job and don't blab about it, that's not the worst thing in the world."

"I am not so sure the job they've done is the one you have hired them for."

"What?" Keel practically shouted, shifting abruptly in his seat. A nearby green-skinned arine looked quizzically at him. "Sorry," Keel mumbled, holding up a menu card at his elbow. "These prices... try the tyrannasquid."

With the alien disregarding Keel with a shake of his head, Ravi painted a picture of what Gannon was up to. "They are exiting the ship now. I see Gannon is holding something... it looks to be a forge-vault case with a handle."

"Probably thinks there's something valuable in it," Keel said.

"Yes, nigh-indestructible cases typically are used to house valuable items. This is a most helpful observation."

"Shut up, Ravi. What else?"

"The MCR are running back and forth with armloads of weaponry. Blaster rifles... I see det-crates... charge packs... Oh, an aero-precision launcher."

Keel frowned. That was to be expected. Fighting a war was expensive, and the mids no longer got the funding they once did when they seemed like they might be a credible threat to the Republic. "No sign of the shock trooper on guard?"

"Of a sort. They are carrying out his armor. And the armor belonging to the others."

Keel was about to say something about how they wouldn't have anyone capable of putting it to good use when Exo burst into the cafe.

"Yo! We gotta go right now. Our boy on the ship is in trouble!"

"Ravi, I gotta go," said Keel, rising from his booth and flipping a credit chit onto the bar counter, between the two Hools.

"Understood. I will cycle the *Six* on preflight standby."

***

The sunlight was painfully glaring compared with the subdued darkness of the cantina's interior. Keel squinted through the searing radiance and saw Bombossa and his three shock troopers with weapons out, clearly agitated.

They weren't the only ones. The denizens of the bazaar seemed to have had their suspicions confirmed that the three jar-headed men in black shirts and fatigues were some sort of foreign military power. A multitude of fingers, fins, flippers, tentacles, and claws pointed at the shock troopers, with just as many guttural shouts and angry whispers into comms.

"We need to get out of here," Keel said.

Bombassa looked around and soaked in the hostility. "Yes. Someone forced—"

"Tell me on the way," Keel said. "Where's your ship?"

"Two kilometers east," answered one of the conspicuous shock troopers. "Pezzola Docking Bays, E-13."

"Couldn't find a closer spot?" Keel quipped, and then he was running into the crowds of the bazaar, blaster in hand, leaving the shock troopers to stand and look at one another.

As Keel raced down the crowded streets, people took notice of his blaster pistol—and the five armed men moving in his wake. They gave him a wide berth, occasionally arming themselves, but not causing any trouble. The resulting open lane allowed Keel to kick into full speed. Glancing over his shoulder, he saw that only Exo was able to stay within a few meters of him. Bombassa, while imposing and fit, lagged behind, his large frame unable to move lightly and quickly enough. The shock troopers, for their part, had the fitness level of your standard marine: they were in shape, but they weren't Legion-conditioned.

"Ravi," Keel called between exhalations, breathing cyclically through his nose as he ran, "whatcha got on Gannon?"

"They've loaded into a caravan of three speeders and are heading in the opposite direction of you on a parallel avenue. If you cut into the alleyway on your right, there is an eighty percent chance that you will have an opportunity to intercept."

"You could've just said 'turn right,'" Keel huffed.

"Apologies, Captain. Turn right."

Keel peeled off and made toward the alley. An oblivious humanoid with a shriveled, tan face nearly walked right into him, narrowly escaping collision by jumping backward as Keel juked out of the way. The creature shook a nine-fingered fist and uttered curses in foreign and domestic tongues as Keel ran by.

The alley's sudden shade made it feel as though the temperature had dipped several degrees. After flat-out running in the sun's heat, the soothing cool was a welcome relief.

"Wraith!" Exo called from somewhere behind Keel. "Wrong way, man. Ship's down the other road."

"I saw someone with your armor moving down this way," Keel shouted back. "I think this'll give us a chance to ambush 'em!"

"Oh, hell yeah!" Exo exclaimed.

Keel jumped over an empty box stuffed with thick brown paper as he streaked down the alleyway. The intersecting street, some ten meters in front of him, was bathed in sunlight. Perfect. Anyone on the street would have a hard time seeing into the alley from the sun-drenched thoroughfare, but Keel could see them just fine.

And what he saw was the lead vehicle of the three-sled convey moving past. The speeder was cruising at a moderate pace, not drawing attention to itself. It was a getaway vehicle driven by those who thought they'd already gotten away.

Keel adjusted his pistol grip and went into a two-handed shooter's stance. He leaned forward slightly and walked slowly toward an optimal firing position. "C'mon..." he mumbled as the open-air sled rolled by.

The driver was an MCR insurgent wearing the usual MCR green fatigues. Apparently the mids weren't seen as a problem on Porcha the way the Republic or other planetary militias were. Gannon was seated next to the driver, with two more mids in the rear section.

"That them?" huffed Exo in a low whisper as he came to a stop next to Keel, blaster pistol ready. "We shootin'?"

"That's them," Keel confirmed, but waved his hand to let Exo know that despite this, he should hold his fire. "Here comes a second sled. On my mark... now!"

The two men began firing on the four mids traveling in the second sled. Keel sent a single heavy blaster shot from his Intec x6 into the driver's head, and two more shots into the chest of one of the stunned passengers sitting in the rear seats. The sled nosed down, scraping the road, before turning sharply toward Keel and Exo—and colliding with the corner of the building that the alley ran behind.

Panic erupted in the bazaar, and a flurry of humanoids and other alien species began running in all directions. A pack of kimbrin—though not MCR—surged into the alley, then hesitated in fear upon realizing that the blaster fire was actually coming from their chosen path of retreat.

"Move!" commanded Exo as he kept the two surviving mids pinned down in their sled. The vehicle wasn't armored per se, but the alloyed frame was designed to stand up to significant impacts. Indeed, the nose of the sled showed hardly a dent from crashing into the poured composite building, and it had stood up to Exo's blaster pistol fire. Keel knew his hand cannon could punch through... provided he could guess where to shoot.

"Changing packs!" Exo screamed. He pressed his pistol's quick release, caught the charge pack, and slammed in a fresh charge in a fluid, practiced motion.

"Exo!" The voice came from behind. Bombassa and the other shock troopers were swimming against the current of panicked and fleeing kimbrin.

"Here comes the next sled," Keel warned as an open-air speeder pulled around the crashed vehicle. This one, too, was occupied by four mids. But these men were ready, their blaster rifles sending automatic fire down the alley.

"Get down!" Keel yelled, his Legion training as a commander of men taking over. Perhaps it was something about having Exo at his side, but he felt like his old self in that moment. Whatever that might say about him.

Blaster bolts of a golden hue zinged down the alley, indiscriminately striking walls, street, debris, and fleeing civilians. The only thing they didn't seem to hit—thanks to the cover provided by the ambushed sled—was their intended targets.

As the third sled moved out of firing range, Keel popped up. At almost the same moment, the two surviving mids in the crashed sled did the same. Keel shot one man in the chest, sending him tumbling backward out onto the street and causing the repulsor sled to gently rock like a ship on the water. Exo took down the second man with three hits to center mass.

"After 'em!" Keel ordered. He ran up to the sled, pushed aside the body of its deceased wheelman, and leapt in. Exo made room for himself next to a dead mid in the back seat, almost losing his balance as Keel threw the vehicle in reverse and pulled the accelerator paddle on the half-wheeled steering column.

"Wait!" called Bombassa, still a good twenty meters behind them and picking himself up from the ground. He had thrown himself out of the way of the blaster bolts—and the feet of the panicking mob.

"Hold up for 'Bossa," Exo urged.

Keel shook his head. "No time. Next time he can hurry up." He surged the repulsor sled forward, pulling into the street in pursuit of the MCR. Keel would rather get dusted than allow Gannon to get away with another double cross. Not this time.

10

The speeder handled more like a pig than a pony. Every pedestrian, overturned food cart, or incoming blaster bolt Keel had to swerve to avoid cut down his speed noticeably. Most modern sleds were printed to be exceedingly light and agile—they could keep their speed while changing lanes or making hard-charging turns. Then again, those modern sleds wouldn't have stopped a blaster bolt from punching through to the interior. This sled, by contrast, was an old, safe, commuter speeder, meant to withstand a collision and travel in a straight line. Not exactly the sort of thing you'd pick for pursuit—and definitely not the sort of thing Keel would have picked for a getaway vehicle. But no one had consulted him. And in this case, that was a good thing. Because with the other two sleds as limited as his was, Keel felt confident that he could close the gap between them.

Golden blaster bolts raced toward him. Most of them were aimed too high and sizzled above his head, but a flurry of them were on target. Keel had to quickly reposition the repulsors to force a sharp rightward turn—or what passed for a sharp turn in this beast. The blaster bolts struck the side of the speeder with a rapid, triple-clang noise.

"They don't make 'em like this anymore," Keel grumbled, shaking his head at the close call.

Exo grunted in agreement before sending forth a charge pack's worth of return fire. The mids ducked low, suppressed for the moment. "Changing packs!" Exo shouted as he dropped his empty onto the floor and fished out a replacement from a pants pocket. "Really wish I had my AP launcher!"

Keel squinted at the sled they pursued. It was about twenty meters in front of them, with Gannon's sled further still. As the mids ducked down to avoid Exo's pistol fire, Keel spied a familiar black case with white, stenciled letters. "An AP might be an option. I see one in the sled now."

He pushed the speeder back into the center of the street, fighting the steering column as the vehicle struggled to adjust. He pulled the accelerator paddle on the steering wheel as hard as he could, as though by applying more pressure the sled would find some sort of hidden reserve and gain ground. But the gap remained fixed.

"Uh-oh," Keel said ominously.

"What?" Exo asked. He squinted through the bright sunlight and saw it. "Dude. Not good."

The mids were poking their heads up above the cover of the speeder, sending inaccurate blaster fire at Keel and Exo while simultaneously trying to open the aero-precision rocket's case.

"Dude, step on it!" Exo yelled.

"What do you think I'm doing?" Keel shouted back. "We need to dump some dead weight."

Exo looked around. "Like what?"

A blaster bolt flew by Keel's head so close that he could feel the heat just above his ear and smell his burnt hair.

He took one hand off the wheel and pointed to the wheel-man's corpse in the seat next to him. "Them!"

"Oh. Yeah. That's dead weight all right." Exo put down his blaster pistol and began to hoist up the body of one of the two dead rebels in the back seat. With a huff and a grunt, he tossed the body overboard, causing the sled to rock and the corpse to tumble behind them like a rolling rag doll.

The sled slightly, almost imperceptibly, increased its speed. Keel sensed it, a skill developed from years of flying the *Indelible VI* at and beyond its limits. "Now get the other two."

"Bro, I'm trying. This guy is wedged down beneath the seats. Not the easiest deadlift with blaster bolts flying at me."

Keel furrowed his brow and aimed his blaster pistol carefully above the windshield. He sent a single red bolt into the rear of the sled, just short of one of the mids, sending a shower of sparks flying like the crackling embers of a fire rising heavenward. Keel's blaster packed a considerably greater punch than most. The downside of his modifications was that a single charge pack could provide a maximum of six shots. Most blasters could expend ten times that before being spent.

The rebels dropped down low, not wanting to face a follow-up shot. Exo struggled to pull out the dead rebel in the back with him, whose arm was stuck on something beneath Keel's seat. No matter how much Exo tried to reposition it, he couldn't pull the man out. The arm worked like an anchor, keeping the corpse on the speeder's floor.

Keel fired his blaster pistol again. "Will you hurry up?"

"The kelhorned mid is stuck!"

"So get him unstuck! He's already dead. It's not like you can hurt him!"

Exo pulled mightily, and all at once, Keel heard a slick gashing noise. Exo fell back onto the seat as the mid's arm came free. A great, ghoulish gash tore through the rebel's uniform from bicep down to wrist.

"Good thing he couldn't feel that," mumbled Exo before dumping the body overboard. Another humanoid bread-crumb left on the trail, should Bombassa and the others want to follow.

"It's helping," Keel said. "We're gaining on them."

Ahead, the mids were opening the case and removing the AP launcher. Keel aimed his blaster pistol—last shot unless he changed packs while driving—and fired. The bolt struck the rebel in his clavicle, sending him spinning around and tumbling off the back of the speeding sled.

Surprisingly, the man didn't lose consciousness. He struggled to a sitting position, dazed, as Keel's sled raced toward him. Not wanting to swerve and lose speed, Keel pulled his lips back in a grimace—preemptively squea-mish about what was to occur next. The heavy, imperv-isteel bumper of the sled smacked directly into the rebel, and the sled roared over him, emitting several more thuds and bumps as the body was buffeted between repulsors and the speeder's undercarriage.

"Oh, hell no," shouted Exo, looking at the carnage be-hind the sled. "That's not how I wanna go out." He had climbed into the front seat and tossed the last man out of the sled.

"Hang on tight," Keel said as the sled continued to pick up speed. "If you get a shot…"

"Already on it. Just get us closer," Exo called out, unable to send accurate fire as the speeder skipped and hopped along the street. Keel suspected it had been a very long time, if ever, that this speeder had moved so fast.

The remaining rebel in the back of the speeder ahead of them brought the aero-precision launcher to his shoulder, while the rebel in the front passenger sheet sent two golden blaster bolts wide left of Keel and Exo. Keel ground his teeth. He was potentially down to seconds to live. Ravi could have told him exact numbers had he been along. If that launcher locked on to their sled, there would be no dodging it.

The rebel flipped up the targeting reticule. The two sleds were close enough that Exo and Keel could hear the tracking beeps of the launcher. Well, if they were going out, Keel wanted to be close enough to take out the mid who did it, too.

Keel squeezed the accelerator paddle harder still. "This might hurt a little…"

Keel's sled rammed into the back of the rebels' sled just as the solid locking tone sounded from the AP launcher. The rebel fell forward from the sudden lurch caused by the collision, and in an impressive feat of self-control—probably because he didn't want to blow himself up—he twisted his body as he fell and fired the missile straight into the air.

Keel followed the white smoke trail as the missile rocketed toward its zenith. But he had heard the lock. That thing would come back down soon. "Exo, jump on the other sled!"

Exo must have been thinking the same thing, for he had already placed a foot on the speeder's hood. He made the leap, crashing on top of the rebel.

Keel pushed his repulsors to their max, as if trying to drive *through* the sled in front of him, deftly swapped out a charge pack, and stood up in his seat. He adjusted the steering wheel to the right, causing his sled to veer away, then leapt with all his might to bridge the chasm opening between himself and Exo.

He slammed into the side of the other sled with a thud that nearly knocked the wind out of him, but his fingers found purchase, and his grip held. With his feet dangling, he scrambled to pull himself safely inside as the driver swerved and shifted in an attempt to shake off the would-be boarder.

Exo was busy burying his fists into the face of the rebel in the back seat. "You bitch!" Exo roared, scoring a glancing blow just behind the rebel's ear. "Try to kill me? Huh! Trying to kill *me*?"

The sled took a hard turn and jumped up onto a walkway, sending bazaar shoppers who'd thought they found a safe vantage point scattering like nebula roaches when the lights came on. The sled crashed right through a stand selling counterfeit datapad cases and accessories, and Keel was thrown back. His arms extended to their full length as his fingers gripped the side door, turning white as he just barely held on.

A body dressed in green fatigues darkened the sunlight, and Keel watched as a rebel fell out of the speeder and slammed into the walkway, rolling wildly with limbs that looked attached only by the threads of clothing that covered them. If the rebel was alive, he must've broken every bone in his body.

"Here!" Exo's face appeared over the edge of the sled, and his arm reached down. Keel grabbed it and allowed Exo to pull him up and in.

Keel stepped toward the front of the sled. The passenger, a kimbrin female, was unconscious—likely from the crash. A cut above her eye, just below her spiked brow, was bleeding heavily. The driver, a human, was reaching for his blaster. Keel leveled his own pistol at the man's face.

"Out," Keel ordered, gesturing with his head to indicate what he expected.

The rebel hesitated, and Keel primed his blaster pistol. "Out."

With a fearful swallow, the rebel stood up and hurled himself out of the speeding sled. He attempted to land on his feet, but the momentum caused his legs to go out from underneath him, and he tumbled into a nasty and awkward roll.

Keel dropped himself into the driver's seat.

"I would've dusted him," Exo said, taking hold of the aero-precision launcher.

Keel smiled. "We need to catch up with the lead sled or Gannon's going to get away. Dumped the weight faster my way."

Exo didn't reply. He rested the launcher on his shoulder and looked through the target reticule, seeking a lock on the last remaining sled. But the driver must have been aware of the danger she was in, as she slammed her speeder wildly along the streets, attempting to break the lock by blending in with every table, awning, tent, and stand on the way. She took a hairpin right turn and disappeared behind a corner.

Keel followed her relentlessly, slowly gaining ground through sheer skill of handling—and having two fewer persons on board.

"Almost got you…" Exo muttered. The sled took another turn, escaping around a corner. "Dude, Wraith. I need you to keep them in view."

"I didn't design the bazaar's grid," Keel shouted back. Indeed, the densely packed side streets were woven with innumerable alleyways and crossing roads.

Keel's comm beeped. "A little busy," he said in answer.

"Not as busy as you will be," Ravi replied. "The sled you are pursuing is heading toward what appears to be an MCR roadblock supported by truck-mounted N-50s and at least one heavy blaster cannon battery. If they see you, the odds of your sled being destroyed are well over seventy-five percent."

"So blow it up, Ravi." Keel assumed that his navigator already had the *Six* in flight.

"I am currently being pursued by three MCR Preyhunter starfighters." Ravi's voice was eminently calm. "There *were* six. I estimate only a four percent chance that I will reach and destroy the blockade before you, unless I open myself up to missile attack. Of course, if you still had some of those AI-enhanced missiles that Garret programmed..."

"I'd rather take my chances." Keel heard Exo swear behind him. The sled had darted around another corner before he could get a lock. "Do what you can, and we'll do what we can."

"Understood." The comm beeped an end transmission tone.

"Exo," Keel called over his shoulder. "If we're going to get these guys without being dusted ourselves, it's gonna have to be soon. Like, *now* soon."

Exo readjusted the launcher on his shoulder. "Okay. I got this. I got this. Just keep it steady as you can when we turn the bend."

As their speeder turned the corner sharply, skipping up over a sidewalk, Keel saw Gannon pointing frantically for his MCR driver to take the next right turn. If he had to bet, that would be where the blockade Ravi told him about lay in wait. "Gotta be now, Exo!"

Keel heard the launcher beeping in an attempt to lock on as the fleeing sled prepared to make the turn. They'd be clear before a lock happened.

The tone sounded out its progress. Closer. Closer.

The sled began to make a wide right turn.

Keel shook his head. They were getting away. It would be up to Ravi to take them out... if they didn't go underground before the *Six* dispatched its harassers.

Whoosh!

A concussive wave hit Keel in his back, almost making him steer the sled off the road. An aero-precision missile streaked toward Gannon's speeder. Keel hadn't heard a lock. Exo had blind fired.

And hit.

The missile led the escaping sled perfectly, slamming into its side at a perfectly timed intersection. A billowing fireball accompanied the boom, and the sled and everyone inside went flying in various degrees of wholeness.

"*That's* what I'm talkin' about!" Exo whooped. "Ain't nobody in the galaxy can do what I do with one of these!"

Keel shook his head in amazement. "You've got a talent, Exo."

"Damn right."

Pulling their speeder over short of the wreckage, Keel hopped out, blaster in hand. Exo followed suit. With the MCR sled's repulsors destroyed, the burnt-out shell of the vehicle lay on the ground in flames. The charred remains of one of the passengers lay half in and half out, its forearms and hands still whole, but everything else a blackened skeleton. Surrounding the scene were bits and pieces of seat fabric, twisted metal, scattered pieces of shock trooper armor, weapons, charge packs, body parts, and... the case, still clutched in death by Gannon, who, having been blown in two at the waist, was no longer quite himself.

"Salvage what you can," Keel ordered Exo before peering around the corner Gannon's sled had been attempting to turn. Up the street was the blockade, but a long ways up. Nearly half a kilometer. They might have still gotten a lock had they followed Gannon's sled around the bend, but there would have been no time to collect anything before the N-50s started firing. As it was now, several MCR soldiers were approaching on foot, and the sleds with the heavy weaponry seemed to wait impatiently as other rebels dismantled the barricade they'd built to provide them an opening.

"Better be quick about it," Keel reported.

"Yeah," said Exo, picking his way through a concentration of blaster rifles. He seemed to be looking for something specific. "These all look wasted. I think they nabbed our crate of fraggers and it went up when I hit the sled."

Keel nodded but didn't reply. He went back to Gannon and looked down at the man. "Tough break, huh?" He bent down and grabbed the case. The lock was broken, whether from blast damage or because Gannon had cracked it, he didn't know. Looking up to be sure Exo was still busy going through various bits of unsalvageable weaponry, Keel pried the case open. Inside was Kael Maydoon's severed hand.

Ravi's voice came over the comm, set low enough to be heard only by Keel. "I'm making my way to your location. Stay put."

Looking left to right, Keel pulled the hand out and flipped open his vibro knife. He made a quick sawing motion and came away with a finger, which he stuffed in his pocket. He tossed the rest of the hand into the flaming sled.

Then he approached the burnt corpse of another rebel—a human who was now little more than bone and ash. Keel dropped to his knee and cut the rebel's hand off. He placed the macabre souvenir into the case and sealed it.

"Any idea what's in here?" Keel asked, holding up the case for Exo to see.

Exo went stone serious. He held out his hand. "That's what I was looking for. Give it here."

"What is it?"

"Hand it over," Exo repeated, an edge to his voice.

"Relax, pal." Keel said, tossing the case to Exo, who caught it with both hands. "Maydoon's hand? Or is it some secret weapon of your space wizard boss?"

Exo sighed. "It's the hand."

Keel nodded glumly. "Thought I'd run off with it and leave you and your boys behind?"

Exo didn't say anything, but the look on his face said that that was exactly what he was worried about.

"I don't know about your little rebellion," Keel began before stopping himself. "Sorry. Your little empire. But as long as you're willing to do the right thing by me... we don't have a problem."

Exo kept his look hard, but then relented, nodding slowly. "Yeah. All right. KTF."

Keel blew out his breath in a laugh. "Sure. KTF. Legion-not-Legion. All that. Stick with me—*trust* me—and we'll all be fine."

Voices shouted orders and warnings from around the corner, and heavy footsteps echoed down the now-abandoned streets of the bazaar.

"Mids are coming," Exo said, setting the case on the ground and priming his blaster pistol, freshened with a new charge pack.

"Yup," said Keel, casually looking at the side of his blaster pistol.

"So don't you think we ought to get some cover or duck down an alley?"

The whining roar of a starship moving through low atmosphere began to fill the streets. Keel smiled as the *Indelible VI* raced along the avenue, strafing the advancing mids with a furious barrage of blaster cannon fire that utterly decimated the advancing soldiers. And when it reached the barricade itself, it sent the waiting vehicles to the scrap pile. Exo let out a long, awestruck whistle.

Keel looked around. The patrons in the bazaars crowded the darkened streets and alleys, as if afraid to come out into the sunlight. More likely, they were worried about what Keel and Exo might do to them.

The *Six* pulled around and slowed, rotating its ramp-side to face Keel. The ramp lowered, and pieces of paper and debris flew away with the ash from the wreck. The fires consuming the sled bucked and waved from the disturbance of the incoming repulsor engines.

"You coming?" Keel shouted to Exo. "Or do you wanna wait for your shock trooper pals to come get you?"

Exo hesitated, then shouted back, "I'll go up with you."

The two men boarded the ramp, and the ship lifted off. Keel and Exo held onto the mechanical struts that served to raise and lower the ramp they stood on and looked down at the swirling smoke and carnage-wracked streets below. As they gained altitude, the bazaar's patrons emerged from the shadowy streets, running toward the ruin in a mad dash to get their hands on the choicest pieces of salvage left behind.

11

The Carnivale
Utopion

X sat back in his seat, surrendering himself to gravity more than easing himself in. He let out a sigh, scanned the report on his datapad one last time, then tossed it onto his desk. The datapad made a particularly loud smack on impact.

X sighed. How could this have happened? How could he not have been aware of it until it was too late?

The datapad lay face down on the desk. X eyeballed it from beneath an arched eyebrow. It had made an awfully loud smack. He tilted the thin slice of technology up, just enough to see the screen. It wasn't cracked. He let it back down. Gently this time.

His hand went out, reaching for a cat that was not there. He needed it to be there. Needed for something soft and tactile to exist. To make itself available to him in times such as these. Impossibly hard times.

He will win who, prepared himself, waits to take the enemy unprepared.

These words, X knew, had proven their truth innumerable times since they had first been uttered in the ancient times. The proverb was one that X had lived and breathed. He was ever prepared, and ever patient.

There had been surprises, sure. Chaos and randomness could never be fully accounted for. But in this three-fronted war that was developing between Legion, Republic, and—X scoffed despite himself—*empire*, X had believed that the lines were drawn in such a way that he could view the game board and see the next move.

But now, the Legion had somehow—and the somehow was something he bloody well wanted to know—gotten word of the secret location of this Goth Sullus's chief general. A man named Nero. A man who, if Legion Commander Keller was to be believed, was someone else entirely. A player. Someone whom the higher-ups in the Legion would all know. Would have, at one point, called a friend.

And now the Legion had him. Sullus did not. And X, miserable fool, you just urged the Legion to strike at the zhee and topple the House of Reason. Though it certainly seemed like they had already made *that* decision prior to your speech. Yes. It very much felt like they were only giving you a polite listen.

It had also seemed, in his meeting with Legion Commander Keller, that the Legion's Dark Ops knew more about Goth Sullus than he did.

But then, he admitted to himself. *You don't know much of anything about Goth Sullus. Or his fleet. Or what he wants.*

X jotted down a note to himself, with real ink on thick vellum, to see about increasing the Carnivale's influence in Dark Ops. That had been a task left undone for too long.

So... now... it seemed that the Legion was poised for victory. The zhee would fall swiftly and hard. There was no doubting that. With Keller's carefully selected admirals and generals, with their sympathetic navies, armies, and marines, they would annihilate Ankalor the moment the zhees' Republic-supplied planetary shield was brought down.

And what then?

How would the galaxy react to a conquering Legion that had, only months previously, allowed themselves to be swollen with an officer corps of appointed lackeys? How would the galaxy react to a Legion using its substantial military might to clean up—with extreme violence of action—the mess that the Republic's government had caused?

The mid-core would probably be all right. Life might or might not change. If anything, they'd be pleased to see the core world elites being put in their place; after all, they'd long clamored for just such an outcome in their clandestine support of the bumbling Mid-Core Rebellion.

But the core would be a different story. Those worlds willing to fight—not that there were more than a handful of those—would do so. And those unwilling to touch a weapon themselves would nevertheless be sure to bring in every mercenary with a love of money and a blaster to spare. The Senate had already made steps in that direction by introducing the legislation to arm the zhee. The House of Reason had seen that as... reasonable.

And those poor blokes on the edge, X thought to himself. *What of them?*

Same war. Different name.

By X's estimation, it would mean a decades-long civil war. At a minimum. With two governments taking turns proclaiming themselves to be the true Republic. Of course, only one of them would have the Legion. But was that a good thing? There were too many variables. So much that could go awry. What if the Legion refused to relinquish power this time? What if, in defeating the Republic and this laughable toddler's empire of Goth Sullus, the Legion itself became the *real* empire?

X didn't like it. Maybe it would go well. But usually these things did not.

So how to prevent events from going where X believed they would go?

He flipped over his datapad and examined the screen. As if, perhaps, it might contain some new information. Some new way of doing what needed to be done. But it failed to provide even a distraction he might use to put off what came next.

X straightened himself and entered a very secure, very secret, and very off-limits comm key.

A holographic projection of Delegate Orrin Kaar of the House of Reason appeared before X in one-sixteenth scale. X thought he picked up on something like surprise, but the savvy politician quickly assumed an expression of delicate, careful concern. X knew that his own projection was sitting somewhere in Kaar's office. That it *had* sat there before the delegate chose to accept the call.

"This is Delegate Kaar. I'm sorry, who is this?" He spoke as though he were taking an unexpected call from a courtesy comm.

Kaar came across as a kindly man thriving in that gap between middle age and doddering senility. A man who expressed in his personage an understanding wrought from decades of experience, with eyes that promised tested wisdom to those willing to listen. The sort of man who had accomplished much but was not yet done. The sort of man who compelled those in his presence to join him for one last ideal.

X almost apologized for disturbing him. For reaching him at this supposedly secret key reserved for emergencies. Kaar was good. So very, very good. But X resisted, allowing a silence to fall between the two men.

"Well then," Kaar said, still congenial, but with a smile that hinted at annoyance. "This is a private key." He moved to turn off his comm.

"Delegate Kaar," X said, blinking first. "We do actually know one another. And as you no doubt see from my transmission credentials, I serve the Republic through Nether Ops."

Kaar gave a thoughtful look, as though trying to remember. "I'm sorry. I simply do not recall. What is it you need my assistance with?"

"It was at a Security Council briefing," X said, wishing to press the issue and not allow himself to assume a position of lesser import or authority. This would raise the delegate's hackles. That was the plan. "The zhee and MCR planned to destroy the House of Reason with a stolen Republic corvette. One of my agents here at the Carnivale was embedded with the rebels."

Kaar's face darkened. "Do not presume my acquaintance simply because you were required to explain how your reckless and sloppy work endangered the seat of this government."

X sat in silence. He had an answer, of course. But Kaar didn't care for answers or reasons. He was flexing his considerable political muscle. Showing X just how insignificant he was. And X, for his part, was happy to oblige.

"Perhaps you're calling to bring more dark tidings?" Kaar pressed on unbidden—and X knew he had him where he needed him. "What is it this time? Has the Carnivale *discovered* that the attack at Tarrago was done by a new group of rebels that they just *happened* to supply with the necessary ships and weaponry? Did you only have to stand by and watch them destroy the Seventh Fleet and take Tarrago and its moon in order to find this out? Is that not an accurate summation of the ridiculous actions of the Carnivale? Is that not the reason your department is the laughingstock of Nether Ops?"

X quelled a rising desire to protect his ego and pride. His goal here wasn't to be victorious in a pissing contest. And... winning a battle of egos was rarely without consequence. This call was for the long-term benefit of the Republic. And... the galaxy.

"Delegate Kaar," X said, doing his best to sound both confident and subservient, "the fog of war has made the best-laid plans into tragedy... *in hindsight.*"

Kaar grumbled as though he wasn't listening. "Set back relations with the zhee by years..."

"It is relevant that you mention the zhee," X said. "What men like you and I must ever and always do is to make the best decision with the information we have available.

I know that is what the House of Reason has done in its arming and equipping of the zhee. But... what if the zhee were taken off the game board before you were afforded the opportunity to use them?"

Kaar fixed his attention on X. Seeing him with an intent and purpose for the first time. "What do you mean?"

"Delegate Kaar, I have information you'll want to hear..."

Stealth Shuttle *Night Stalker*
Ankalor

Major Owens walked down the center aisle of the sleek stealth shuttle—or rather, his holographic projection did. The major himself was still safe aboard the *Mercutio*, four hours away from reaching Ankalor with the rest of the Legion fleet. The six men of Kill Team Zenith lined the walls of the shuttle, three on each side, strapped into their jump seats with buckets on and kitted out to do some damage. In the seventh seat, the commander's seat, was a Republic Army crewman, one loyal to the ideals and authority of the Legion. He wore a flight helmet with a black, opaque-looking visor going down to his nose.

A momentary sense of déjà vu struck Owens—a memory of a mission he'd once undergone using Republic combat sleds. It flashed through his mind like a passing current on a stream. It had been a long time since he'd driven in a sled, or a stealth shuttle. The interiors of the two vehicles were remarkably similar. Whether that was a testimony to some Republic engineer's ability to get as much out of

R&D as possible, or the result of a bureaucratic desire for one-size-fits all, Owens didn't know.

The chief difference was that this shuttle had been modified to place a rotating N-80 blaster at the rear door ramp. Owens loved when the N-80s, most commonly equipped on buzz ships, spat out their special brand of hellfire. An N-80 was essentially eight N-50 barrels taped together and spinning to unleash a near-constant stream of blaster fire. They ripped apart the air and the enemy alike. Its inclusion required that most of the bay that would typically be used for speeders was converted to supply the power needed to keep the beast running.

Far below the N-80, the shuttle, and Kill Team Zenith lay the city of Ankalor. The shuttle was maintaining a distant, undetectable, synchronous orbit, waiting for night to fall on the zhee city that protected the planetary shield generator. The planet was Ankalor, too. Ankalor was everything to the zhee who lived there. It was the planet, the city, and every village and hamlet in between. A traveler's nightmare even without the locals looking to gut you, fillet you, and grind your bones into an aphrodisiac powder.

"Legion base in the Ankalor Green Zone says that all is quiet," Owens said, his holographic image flickering as it moved through the outstretched leg of one of the legionnaires of Zenith Squad. "Quiet for the zhee, I mean. Bring that shield generator down and get back into orbit before daylight. The hammer'll be here to drop on them before the donks get the chance to order new parts."

"You heard the man," hollered Captain Drayus, the leader of Zenith Squad. "Donks ain't gonna get a pile of weapons and not try to use 'em on the rest of the galaxy. Ain't nobody that stupid, 'cept the House of Reason. Now I wanna see each one of you kelhorns ready to KTF once we get planetside."

"Ooah!" shouted the Dark Ops legionnaires with him.

Trident, a legionnaire Owens had grown to like while spending time on Deep Space Supply Station Nine, loosened his vibro-knife from its sheath. "Keep these handy if a zhee gets in close. Donks love knives."

Revo, newly promoted to sergeant and the junior man on the team, thumped his chest, patting his own knife. "Then the donks are gonna love it when I shank their shaggy asses with this one."

"Never pass up the opportunity to get a knife kill," said Drayus, looking at the holographic image of Owens. "Ain't that right, Major?"

"Ooah, Mal." Owens stood still a moment. "All right, Zenith. Just wanted to see you all face-to-face before the op began. I know you'll do the Legion proud down there."

"Or die tryin'," grunted Trident.

12

Chief Warrant Officer Della Cassius felt himself rocking in his pilot's seat as his shuttle skipped through the highest reaches of Ankalor's atmosphere. He quickly scanned all he could from the shuttle's cockpit window and then glanced down at his instrument panel. All was clear. No ships detected by passive sensors.

"How we hiding?" he asked his co-pilot, Warrant Officer Medgar "Hot Plate" Winnows.

Hot Plate tapped a dimmed screen of black with red letters, causing it to brighten. He scrolled through a series of readings—detected scanning devices, their strength, and point of origin.

"Scanners are showing separate readings from Republic UI-D33 and four different band waves of TQ early detectors. Probably aftermarket stuff used by the zhee. Legion's peer-scan showing strong but negligible chance of detection."

Cassius had never been spotted on a mission, and he'd flown hundreds of them for Dark Ops as a part of a special army wing known as the Gothic Serpents. The leejes might not have a high opinion of Republic Army in general, but they appreciated the Serpents' flying enough to know better than to call them basics. Of course, that didn't mean they didn't still get called featherheads. In the end it was about professionalism. If you proved to the Legion that you were capable and professional, the branch distinctions didn't matter much.

"How negligible?" Cassius asked his co-pilot.

Hot Plate sounded a wordless protest against having to answer.

"*How* negligible?" repeated Cassius. "You were the one who made the bet."

Hot Plate let a long beat sit between the two of them before reporting, "Point oh-oh-one-nine."

"I'm sorry," crowed Cassius, a smile showing in the half of his face not covered by his flight helmet. "I'm bad with numbers, Winnows. You know that. Is 'point oh-oh-one-nine' *more* than dot-oh-oh-three or is it less?"

Hot Plate hung his head. "Less."

"Okay, that's what I thought. But *you* said the Legion sensors on Ankalor would hit oh-three, easy. So when you said oh-oh-one-nine, I got confused..."

Looking over at Cassius, Hot Plate said, "Are you finished?"

"Not at all. This right here?" Cassius said, not taking his hands off the controls or his eyes from what he was doing, "This is a predictive indicator of the next four hours of your life until we get back to the station."

"Wonderful."

"And when we get back to the station..."

"Do I really have to wipe my entire section of the list?" Hot Plate asked. "I thought you said you like all music."

"All music except for *that*." Cassius smiled. The two men shared a playlist for use on long flights, a mix of their favorite music. Unfortunately—as far as Cassius was concerned—Hot Plate adored the crooning, nasal styles of twanging honk-tune musicians like Prettis Mahler, singing depressing songs about lost speeders, drunk and cheating wives, and living credit to credit. "Oh, yeah," Cassius said. "It's all gone."

The stealth shuttle banked, invisible to scanners, at risk only in the unlikely event that a watching eye, looking at the stars against the night sky, not only happened to sight it but also to track it. And even then, the technology that kept the bird invisible to sensors kept it from getting locked on by auto-turrets, launchers, and virtually every other piece of modern anti-starcraft weaponry.

Ahead, beyond the limits of Ankalor City and its Green Zone protected by Legion base Black Snake, was the massive fortress the Republic touted as the future of security, peace, and prosperity for the zhee species. Under Republic protection, naturally. The air around the fortress glimmered, an indicator that its powerful shield was operational.

Cassius flipped on the internal comm. "Two minutes out."

***

Viina Kop sat in the back of a flatbed repulsor truck, watching the night sky. His zhee partner, Guva, slept on the ground beneath his cloak, preferring to risk the venomous bite of a scowert rather than contort himself among the unforgiving ammunition crates and cold steel bed.

It was Guva who had received the orders through the chain of command. He was the senior, older than Viina by more than a decade. Guva guided Viina across berms and flat pans of ground, the old repulsor truck whining in protest when its tired engines were unable to lift it over the uneven terrain. And when at last the repulsor truck arrived at this wilderness location, well beyond the glow of Ankalor City, Guva pointed his hoof-like hand to the brilliant star, known as Kash the Unrepentant. "Here," Guva said, and then bid Viina's eyes to follow his hoof across the sky to another star, Herpio. "Here."

Viina nodded and swung the quad barrels of the anti-aircraft blaster cannon back and forth from Kash to Herpio as Guva settled down to sleep.

Hours had passed since then. Viina was tired but dared not tear his gaze from the skies. He could piece together his purpose based on the weapon entrusted to him and the heavens he monitored. What would it be? A Republic tri-bomber seeking to destroy his village? A warrior king flying a black dragon from one of the other zhee worlds, seeking to bring about the ascendancy of the zhee to the galaxy? Whatever it might be, it was happening on Ankalor. Blessed Ankalor, first home world of the zhee. Home of the rightful heirs and rulers of the zhee and the apostate galaxy, appointed by the gods at the foundation of all things.

Viina would not bring shame on Ankalor, should the gods choose him as a servant vessel.

A glimmer appeared in the sky, coming from just behind Kash the Unrepentant and moving toward the fortress. Viina had to strain his eyes just to see it. It was as if he were watching a spirit streak across the night sky, a ghost from the great lagoon of the dead.

"Guva!" Viina whispered, afraid that his voice might be heard, whether by spirits or by the Republic and their sensors. "Guva!"

Guva stirred beneath his cloak but remained quiet. He could sleep through the arrival of Varuud-Ma Kop, if such a thing were possible.

Viina still dared not take his eyes off the glimmering phantasm. It was moving fast, like a starship. *Act now, fool, or the chance is lost!*

Was the voice his, or was Viina being called by the gods themselves?

He let out a furious bray and sent white streaks of explosive blaster bolts toward the invading ghost.

***

The urgent warning tone sounded only seconds before the first volley of anti-aircraft blaster fire erupted around Chief Warrant Officer Cassius's forward window. Just long enough for him to look at the flashing red triangles indicating the position the shots were coming from.

"Incoming AA fire," reported Hot Plate, his voice calm, not giving way to the spike in adrenaline Cassius knew they both felt.

"Hang on," Cassius shouted into the ship-wide comm, almost in time with his nosing the flight control down to enter a dive.

They were less than two minutes out, and Cassius knew that the Dark Ops legionnaires in the back would be up and ready to disembark, and the crew chief would be ready to control the doors and get on the heavy N-80. Cassius hoped that the warning, slight though it was, would be enough for them to at least brace themselves and avoid serious injury.

Given the alternative—being hit square in the thin hull of the stealth shuttle—the evasive maneuver was the only option. The larger assault and armored shuttles could have taken the hit, but a stealth shuttle going up against the explosive bolts of anti-air blasters... that was not a fight this bird could win.

The next several seconds felt like an eternity. The shuttle dropped in altitude so abruptly that Cassius felt his stomach jump before the inertial dampeners caught up with him.

Hot Plate called in the contact to the air boss back on *Mercutio*. "We're taking AA fire from an unmarked position. Repeat, taking fire from an unmarked position over the Grodan Wastes."

There were anti-air towers strategically placed all around Ankalor, and although those towers were technically under the control of the Republic, this mission was definitely *not* Republic-approved—so the possibility of those towers being used against the stealth shuttle had been deemed a legit threat. Hence the route over the Wastes—far from Ankalor's anti-air defenses. Yet here was someone out here in the middle of nowhere, waiting for them with a mobile AA cannon. The question on

Cassius's mind was… who? And how did they know they were coming?

The stealth shuttle responded to Cassius's touch like he was married to it. He knew exactly how to make it move the way he needed it to and could *feel* the craft responding. More bursts flashed around the ship, causing it to shutter and vibrate, but caused no damage.

Boom!

Something rocked the rear of the shuttle. It wasn't like being struck with a missile or even peppered with heavy blaster fire; it was something Cassius *heard* more than felt. A new indicator light began to flash, adding its own warning tone to the cockpit's AI-conducted symphony of trouble.

Cassius felt his shuttle slipping; it was slow to respond to his stick and paddles. "She's feeling loose," he advised his co-pilot.

"Showing engine damage," Hot Plate responded.

"*Night Stalker*, this is Overlord." The comm relayed the message from *Mercutio*'s war room. "What's your situation?"

Cassius felt his shuttle tremor, and then control came back. He eased the shuttle out of the dive and into a new flight pattern, and scanned the holo relays. No trailing smoke, no visible damage. "We were hit by incoming AA fire. Engines are good. Hull integrity is good." The spray of anti-air fire continued to streak toward the position they once held. Whoever was shooting hadn't been able to follow the shuttle's descent. "We are eyes shut," Cassius reported, giving the update that told his air boss that they had reacquired operational invisibility.

"Affirmative," responded *Mercutio*. "We have a Legion Quick Reaction Force on standby in the Green Zone. Deliver your cargo and advise. We'd rather you get off planet, but the Legion base will do if needed."

"Copy," Cassius answered. He went to the ship-wide comm. "How's everybody doing back there?"

"Like a case of meal packs orbit-dropped into a mountain range," barked back one of the legionnaires.

That would do. If they could crack a joke, they were probably all right.

Cassius scanned his instruments. The dive had put them off course, and he'd have to loop back around to the insertion point. That meant another five minutes, unless he cut toward the city outskirts. With the likelihood of the zhee calling in an intelligence report, he decided that getting the team on the ground fast was priority one.

"Two minutes," he announced.

"Said that two minutes ago," said the Dark Ops team leader.

Cassius smiled and looped the ship around. "How're we reading?" he asked Hot Plate.

Hot Plate shook his head as though he couldn't quite believe what he was seeing on screen. "Everything looks good, Della. We dodged a close one."

Boom!

This one, Cassius could *feel*. The cockpit went ablaze with flashing lights and was washed over with shrill beeps and whines all competing to be the loudest, all saying the same thing: *This is bad.* Cassius had no paddle control, no thrust; he could feel the shuttle slipping away from him, beginning to wobble and pitch in the sky. Visuals showed a thick plume of smoke trailing behind.

He pulled on his stick, attempting to fight off the spin the shuttle was beginning to build up as gravity pulled the craft downward with no forward propulsion.

"We've lost primary and secondary repulsor engines," reported Hot Plate, his voice spiking with panic.

It was no use; Cassius couldn't maintain control. "We're going down," he called out, surprised by the calmness in his voice. It was so matter-of-fact. So clear and clinical.

The shuttle continued to spin, each revolution faster than the next. Cassius saw the darkened ground of the Ankalor City outskirts whirling past him in a blur and the star-speckled horizon twinkling in contrast. There was a part of Cassius's mind that held on to his training; he'd been flying shuttles for a decade. He knew that if he could coax the ship to land on its stomach, its landing repulsors might soften the impact.

The ground grew rapidly closer. The shuttle spun down between two tall buildings. It was a miracle they didn't simply crash into one. A wide dirt street seemed to pull them in...

Cassius heard himself scream just before impact.

His world turned black.

***

It was a burning sensation in his back that caused Cassius to first flit open in eyes in a pain-wracked consciousness. Everything was muted and blurred. He couldn't make out anything around him, though he knew on a cognitive level that he must still be in the shuttle's cockpit. An alarm, almost a whisper to him, kept a steady hum around him.

He tried to adjust himself, then cried out at a sharp pain in his leg. *That hurt. Don't do that again.*

The additional spike of pain helped focus his vision. He could see the instrument panel in front of him. The shuttle's canopy window was missing, revealing an empty street lit by fires inside steel drums, and a stucco wall painted with graffiti in zhee letters. Cassius looked down at his leg and saw that it was bent where it shouldn't be—in a place much too high, between his knee and hip. The realization that his femur was snapped brought on a new wave of pain and nausea.

"Hot Plate?" Cassius's voice was a croak, a whisper. "Buddy?"

He looked to his right and peered into the lifeless eyes of his co-pilot. The impact of the crash had sent Hot Plate's dash into his thighs like a meat cleaver. Pink muscle and tallow-colored fat lay exposed to the dusty cabin air. A dark pool of blood had already formed beneath him.

Cassius pulled off his flight helmet and felt the sweat on his hair bristle as each follicle was swept by the helmet's lining. He tossed the helmet on the seat next to Hot Plate. A report of automatic blaster fire sounded from somewhere in the distance. A staccato reply came from another direction, echoing off the buildings and high walls.

Cassius fumbled with a compartment at the base of his seat. He pulled out a subcompact machine blaster and turned it over to read the charge pack. It was green. He primed the weapon and, unable to move from his seat, watched through the open canopy as the blaster fire outside grew louder and nearer.

He waited like that for what seemed like a quarter hour. He didn't bother with the comm, because it had never once relayed the series of requests for status he had anticipated—had hoped for. He told himself that the pain wasn't so bad now. He wondered if the zhee would arrive before a QRF.

There was a crunch outside. Footsteps. Cassius held his breath. Quiet. But the crunch was real. He hadn't imagined it.

The crunching noise sounded again. Moving toward the front shuttle canopy. Cassius held up his machine blaster. It felt so heavy.

And then a thought occurred to him. Those crunching feet might belong to a legionnaire. Perhaps the QRF had arrived already. He had no way of knowing how long he'd been out, though he imagined it had been only a few minutes. But who could say how consciousness worked once you'd lost it?

He decided to call out a warning. Because he didn't want to shoot a friend, and if it wasn't a friend... well, he was dead either way.

"Ha-a-p," he managed. That wasn't what he'd meant to say, but it was what issued forth from his mouth. He didn't know what it meant.

"Don't shoot," came the otherworldly voice of a legionnaire speaking through his helmet.

Cassius lowered his weapon.

The legionnaire seemed to sense the resolved tension, and a pitch-black form appeared at the corner of the shuttle's missing front canopy. Had Cassius not spent many of the last ten years flying Dark Ops from one mission to the next, the sight of the black ghoul standing darker than night would have terrified him. As it was, he felt only moderately scared.

The Dark Ops leej approached. "You okay?"

Cassius was not okay. But the legionnaire knew that. He was really asking, *How bad are you hurt?*

"My leg," Cassius managed, grunting from the very memory of seeing that grotesquely fractured limb.

The legionnaire clambered up to take a look. Outside, another legionnaire limped into view. He held a blaster rifle and seemed to be scanning for zhee.

"We're gonna have to get you out of here," said the legionnaire.

Cassius recognized the voice. Trident. Cassius knew the man well enough; he'd delivered this team more than once in times past. Trident was a good soldier. "Oba, I'm glad to hear your voice."

Trident reached inside and unfastened Cassius from his harness. This caused more of Cassius's weight to sit on his broken leg.

"Agh!"

"Sorry, buddy," Trident said. There was compassion in his voice, but also urgency. He was not so sorry that he was going to stop. "But we've got to get you out now. Zhee are coming." The legionnaire made a motion with his arm, but no words came from his helmet. Probably a discussion over their private L-comm.

The other legionnaire joined Trident half-in and half-out of the shuttle, their legs on the ship's angular, sloping nose. Each man grabbed a handful of Cassius's flight suit at the collar. They looked at each other, then pulled Cassius from his seat and through the window.

Cassius roared in pain all the way out. He was nearly hyperventilating by the time the legionnaires lowered him to the filthy dirt street. Resting, he felt his senses coming back to him. The pain was still intense, but at least he was no longer being jostled and jarred. He never wanted to get picked back up.

He realized he'd dropped his machine blaster inside the shuttle's cockpit. "Weapon," he panted.

"We'll get you one," said the second legionnaire. Revo, Cassius thought he was called. "First we gotta get you to cover. Zhee are coming."

The two legionnaires hoisted Cassius off the ground and fast-walked him into a three-sided shed with a view of the crashed shuttle. The trip hurt, but not as bad. They rested Cassius upright, with his back against the wall. Then the two men left Cassius alone—only to come back the moment Cassius told himself they'd forgotten him.

"Here." Trident handed Cassius an NK-4 rifle and four charge packs.

Cassius took the weapon and primed it. He leaned his head against the wall and felt its cool through his wet scalp and hair. He wanted something to drink. "Others?"

"All dead."

Cassius felt his chest heave with emotion, as though he was about to burst into tears. The sensation passed. Black spots paraded across his vision. He heard the ocean, could see the beach. It was beautiful. The glowing orange sunlight reflecting on the shimmering sea looked like a field of unearthed diamonds.

But then the crashing waves of the ocean morphed from a peaceful respite into the shouts of an angry mob. Cassius heard blaster bolts—close. He shook his head and cleared his vision. A legionnaire was running in his direction. Trident.

"QRF is inbound. We gotta hold out until they get here. I need you to watch our backs." Trident pointed to the wall of the shed opposite where Cassius sat. "An alley runs alongside that wall and empties out by the front of the shed. Anyone comes from down that alley, you kill 'em. Got it?"

Cassius nodded and readied his weapon.

He watched the two legionnaires use the wrecked shuttle for cover as they sent blaster fire into a mob of approaching zhee. Many of them were armed, but not all. It seemed to be a mix of males, females, adults, and children, all wearing their rage on their faces. And every time a zhee shooter would attempt to storm forward, the legionnaires would mow him down. This repeated over and again, until the sight of zhee falling before Dark Ops was almost soothing.

Cassius heard a clatter coming from the alley. A zhee in red robes emerged and ran by, carrying a blaster rifle. Cassius fired several rounds into the zhee's flank, dropping it in a heap. The Dark Ops legionnaires kept up their murderous fire, ignorant of the threat Cassius had just eliminated. The swelling zhee crowd pulsed around the wreckage.

Another zhee fighter ran screaming from the alley. Cassius shot this one dead as well.

The legionnaires were synchronized killing machines, sharing charge packs, reloading in the time it took Cassius to blink, and killing zhee with every pull of the trigger.

Cassius killed a third zhee. Then a fourth. He wondered if they would ever notice the bodies. Ever stop trying to run the gauntlet of death the legionnaires had charged Cassius with overseeing.

Two zhee sprinted together. Cassius killed one and wounded the other. He needed to change charge packs. The legionnaires slew their enemies. He needed to change charge packs.

More zhee ran past him—several this time. He felt a painful burning blast in his arm, accompanied by a flash of blaster fire and the report of a zhee-fired rifle. His arm disobeyed him, dropping helplessly to the earth like the shuttle had before it. The blaster rifle clattered to the dirt.

Cassius watched as the two legionnaires became aware of the new threat to their rear. Aware that Cassius had failed them.

The Dark Ops men sent their fire into the zhee who had gotten by Cassius. They dropped them left and right. But the zhee continued to swarm, getting closer and closer to the armored black knights on the field.

Trident was the first to fall. While he was occupied with a trio of zhee to his rear, another zhee appeared from the opposite side of the wreckage and sent a charge pack's worth of automatic blaster fire into Trident's head and back. Armor works, but too close is too close.

Trident pitched forward and fell hard onto the ground.

Revo brought vengeance, killing the zhee who'd killed his squad mate. Repaying blood for blood. But he was just one man. He fired and killed until his blaster rifle was empty, and then he pulled his service pistol. He fired that too, until it had killed its last zhee.

They shot him down before he could unsheathe his knife.

Cassius waited, slumped half-over with a broken leg and a useless arm. He waited for them to kill him, now that he'd witnessed their victory over the kill team. Everywhere the zhee screeched and celebrated, climbing all over the shuttle and firing their blasters into the night sky. They began to pull the broken bodies from the wreckage. One of them appeared to be taking bites from Hot Plate's legs.

And then a zhee stood above Cassius, its face wrapped in a merlot hood, but its dead eyes visible, staring down. A hoofed foot struck Cassius in the temple, and darkness came again.

13

Legionnaire Captain Jul Besson watched the burning red sun of Ankalor drop into distant western sands. Ahead rose Gibraltaar Rock, towering above a sea of dunes and the broken wastes of the deep desert beyond Ankalor City.

The rock in which the fortress was built was so huge, and so alien to the low broken mountains of heat-beaten granite and the huge expanse of drifting sands, that many wondered whether the massive rock had once been a piece of some greater stellar body that had fallen onto Ankalor long ago.

The small column of legionnaires, leading shuffa beasts and dressed in the flowing black robes of the Guzim Haxadi, maintained a slow but steady crawl toward the westernmost air defense tower beyond the base's invisible deflector shield. The air defense tower was built on a jagged lone spire of rock, high above the burning sands, but much lower than the four-thousand-foot Gibraltaar Rock.

It was just before twilight when the column stopped, a few thousand meters short of the tower, and went through the motions of building a cook fire and settling their beasts for the night. As any band of Guzim Haxadi would. No doubt the zhee had snipers in the tower watching them, but from this distance none of their optics would see anything beyond dark shapes in robes.

That was, if the zhee were even interested. Though fierce warriors, and constant advantage seekers, the average male zhee was quite lazy. When not ululating their bloody war cry and coming at you with gnashing buckteeth and a flashing *kankari* knife shining and ready, they liked to smoke and do nothing but argue. Or plan some new horror to get up to.

L-comm sat and weather told the captain of Shadow Company that the local evening windstorm, known as the *centauro*, was picking up. It would turn quite fierce once the sun went down. Which was all the better to cover their infiltration after they'd jocked up in their scout armor.

The massive bloody sun sank, and sure enough the wind began to skirl, sending sweeping waves of sand across the desert floor. The men of First Platoon, Shadow Company, began to shrug into their armor and assemble their weapons, which they had pulled from the large dirty bundles atop the cantankerous shuff beasts. The beasts paid them no mind; they were content to spit and howl forlornly at the night and the wind.

Though the men would be carrying the scout version of the N-4, they also carried asymmetrical weapons unique to their line of work. This was one of the few units authorized to use silenced slug-throwing pistols; each man carried one in a shoulder holster. You could silence a blaster, but you couldn't make the blast invisible. Slug throwers did both. In addition, the two platoon snipers carried old-school large-caliber sniper rifles.

Captain Besson, in armor now, pulled his silenced pistol with the customized sights and grip—the grip was embossed with a winking cartoon Tennarian beauty and the letters "KTF Baby!"—and made sure he had one round in the pipe.

The platoon sergeant and the platoon leader approached their company commander.

"We're up, sir," whispered the lieutenant, call sign Mustang. The platoon sergeant, Sergeant First Class Jayzo, call sign Warpig, nodded wordlessly.

Captain Besson scanned the night. Drifting sand was beginning to obscure the crescent moon as the storm picked up. They'd been over the ops briefing, and every man had a breakdown of the mission, step-by-step, running on his HUD. They'd done this before—but never with the stakes so high. If that air defense artillery tower wasn't down and hacked by dawn, then a lot of leejes were going to get shot up on the beachhead during the landing in less than twelve hours.

"Time to move then," said Besson.

"Copy that," replied the LT. Warpig was already off and getting the men ready.

For the next hour they ran at the double, crossing the sands in a wide circular pattern as quickly as possible. The howling wind pushed against them, and the sand raking the old-school armor they'd been issued for the job. No more of the cheap shiny silver. This was the good stuff, made back when the Legion had the budget to make armor that protected a leej in a firefight.

The sniper teams, spotter and shooter, were dropped back along the ridges of some of the higher dunes that lay away from the air defense tower. Even though the sand obscured tangos on the watch balconies that climbed along the tower's face, their imaging gear allowed them to see through the storm, tagging as many of the zhee on perimeter watch as they could spot.

"Eyes on targets," reported one of the snipers as the rest of the platoon continued on, using the storm's cover to get as close to the base of the tower as possible. "Got donks on levels two, four, and six. Two apiece, and they don't seem happy about being out here tonight."

Besson tried to listen over his own gasping breath as he pushed himself to continue on through the drifting sand and driving wind. The sand scraped wickedly across his armor.

Check your pistol, he reminded himself, *before you go live. The sand is probably everywhere.* And, like the good officer he was, he reminded himself to remind his men to do the same. But not now. Even for legionnaires, pushing through all this at the double, in full armor and pack, was a feat of extreme strength and endurance. And since the standards for acceptance into the Legion had been relaxed—at the insistence of the House of Reason—many of the younger, newer legionnaires were struggling to keep up. Warpig stayed behind them, encouraging them—negatively—to keep up. None of the NCOs had any problem, of course, but most were old school. As was the platoon leader, who'd been an NCO before taking a commission.

They came to a wide dirt road that had been grated around the tower. Intel indicated there would be sensors along its outer side, but there was an open question as to whether the donks had mined it. Donks loved explosives of all kinds.

"First Team, go," whispered the captain over L-comm.

Two leejes dashed forward at a crouch, gear out without weapons, knowing the rest of the platoon, and the distant snipers, were covering their approach. They quickly set up the gear to disable the nano-sensors embedded in the road. When they had a green light on the data feedback loop, they hustled across the narrow sensor-free lane. They waited to see if any alarms were triggered, but none were. Intermittent light poles along the roads in front of the base and the tower, seen now like waiting gallows in the shifting sandstorm, would have sprung to life if the sensors had been tripped.

"All clear, sir."

The rest of First Platoon, Shadow Company, crossed the road in teams and went to their positions, with the platoon leader moving quickly between the various elements to get them set up for the next objective. Four teams of two would scale the sides of the rock tower and come in just under the balconies. Timed takedowns would happen quickly, and then the platoon as a whole would infiltrate the facility.

That was step one.

Step two was everybody inside got cleaned.

Captain Besson checked his gear one last time, handed his rifle off to the man following him, and checked his sidearm. It was his favorite weapon, and he enjoyed any opportunity he had to employ it. The high-tech pistol had been designed based on the old 1911 platform, though no one in the modern era had any idea what that meant. It had a built-in silencer for "soft work," and it was bored for 9mm so it fired like a child's first air-powered hunting blaster. It was perfect for near-silent cleaning.

He holstered the weapon, then checked his climbing gauntlets and the prevailing conditions. The wind was beginning to die down across the desert floor. The *centauro* hadn't lasted long this evening. That was not good, but it couldn't be helped. Finally, he checked in with the seven other leejes going up with him. They were all pros—as were most of the men in his company. Scout work required a promotion out of the line units.

When all seven were good to go, they set out up the side of the rock.

The climbing gauntlets adhered to any surface, even industrial zero-tension diamond glass. So scaling the rock face was no problem. The only problem might come if the zhee guards decided to have a look over the side of the tower. Then there'd be a problem. But that's why they'd brought sniper teams. The first zhee to look over the side of the tower got his head blown off.

Normally the platoon would have been running drones instead of, or in addition to, the human snipers. But the fortress had a high-tech detection network, and if the zhee hadn't fiddled with much, the base AI was keyed up to look for drones specifically. The mission decision had therefore been to ditch the drone packages. The two sniper teams would be the eyes of the assault team.

The watch balconies were all at different levels and on different faces of the rock, away from the main ground level blast door that faced the road. The door had never been an option; no doubt security feeds were watching that. As it was, the donks would see little beyond the swirling sand, unless they cycled through some of the more advanced imaging modes.

Halfway up to the targets, the sand striking at their armor and visors faded to the flute-like notes of a fading whisper. The storm had passed.

Twenty minutes later, all teams were in place and ready to go up over the sides of their assigned balconies. The move was a one handed pull-up, gyro-assisted by the armor, anchor the boots and eliminate the tangos with a minimum of fire.

Real time feedback on the donks came in from the snipers.

"Balcony four..." said the lead sniper. That was the balcony Besson and Davies hung beneath. "Your tangos are huddled inside the porch. Seem to be yakkin' intently about something. Suggest you come from opposite angles. Take out your facing targets. Signal when in position. Cowboy out."

Besson and Davies, hand over hand, pulled themselves in opposite directions until they'd reached the ends of the guard balcony. Besson gave a two-click ready signal, then waited. The platoon sergeant was running all teams from the snipers' position. Once they were in place they'd get a whispered, "Go!"

When the signal came, Besson heaved himself over the ledge, ignoring the "kill confirmed" tags appearing in his HUD. The other teams were pro and moving fast.

With his boots anchored on the ledge, Besson aimed and fired at the donk facing him. The first and second bullets smashed into the long skull of the jihadi in near-synch with Davies's shots on his donk from across the balcony. Both donks dropped, bodies twitching.

Besson crossed the balcony, covering the small blast door that led into the facility, while Davies put two more slugs into each donk's heart. The suppressed weapons made definite metallic *clacks*, but nothing more. Across all four balconies, Besson could hear the insurance shots being doled out by the second man in each team.

"All teams reporting access points clear," reported Warpig.

"Send 'em up. Move to position two."

Now the rest of the platoon began the climb to the secured balconies. The next ten minutes were tense. There was no time for over-cautious stealth; the men climbed fast like their lives depended on it. Because no one knew how the zhee—notorious for their lack of organization and commitment to chaos in all aspects of their lives, including military operations—ran their guard watch. The men who had taken the balconies waited with fresh mags in and barrels aimed at the door. If some zhee watch commander or replacement guard shift opened any one of those blast door, the leejes would alternate shots until everyone was dead, or they were out of ammo.

It was at these moments that Captain Besson missed his scout N-4. The standard combat load of charge packs gave the option for a near endless supply of fire. The ancient slug throwers, relics from humanity's deep past, though beautiful on levels that approached artisan craftsmanship, still gave you only seven shots. Then it was mag out, and there were only so many mags one could carry amid all the other gear one carried when heading into a combat zone.

First Squad was just coming over the lip of the balcony when everything went to hell. Alarms sounded throughout the base, and in the distance, smoke could be seen rising from the shuttle crash site in the Ankalor City slums.

***

The battle that followed was a series of brutal engagements along the hallways and upper floors of Air Defense Tower Four. Besson and the Shadows found themselves quickly switching from battlefield assassins and intel gatherers to shock troops.

But every legionnaire started out a killer. So they adapted quickly, falling into something that felt as natural as walking to them. In moments they were moving by fire teams, taking key intersections within the complex, and setting up brutal fields of crossfire against the near psychotic zhee. They lobbed fraggers through forced blast doors, or used the breaching charges they'd brought along in the event they would need to crack reinforced blast doors. Massive explosions rocked the lower levels of the tower, and beyond its walls, the cry of energy displacement guns could be heard across the night.

Explosions in the tight corridors, and in the zhee's densely packed firing positions, combined with the co-ordinated fire from the teams, decimated the zhee on the lower levels quickly. Second Squad breached the blast doors that guarded the access to the fire control nexus above. That would provide access to the main batteries that ringed the upper level.

Within moments it became clear that the zhee were determined to hold the line at the top of a wide set of stairs that led up to the control nexus. Except the zhee as a whole had no idea how to actually "hold a line." They excelled in other strategies—strategies that made them something to be feared by all other races in the galaxy. The zhee were definitely a "handle with care" fighting force. They were so unhinged in battle that fear turned quickly to frenzy.

The zhee idea of holding was to charge.

Just as Third Squad was preparing to go up the wide, dimly lit stairs in wedge formation, covered by an over-watch from the remaining squads, the zhee attacked like a torrent of wild zathabulls. In seconds they were in and among the advancing legionnaires, who were firing back at them at point-blank range. N-4 blasters spat out hot wicked blasts of fire that illuminated and strobed the darkness of the rising stairwell.

Second Squad tried to put fire into the advancing wave of zhee, but as quickly as the front rank had been punctured and ventilated by searing bolts of blaster fire, the next rank of zhee were pushing the fallen aside and swooping down into Third Squad with their bright *kankari* knives flashing. Behind these, another rank of zhee carrying heavy blasters fired into anyone in front of them, including their own if they managed to get in the way.

This sudden and devastating zhee counteroffensive was only the second-most jaw-dropping aspect of the assault.

"Donks got armor!" screamed some kid from one of the overmatched squads. And it was true. And that surprised everyone. From within the melee along the stairs, Captain Besson could see that the zhee warriors *were* wearing a type of armor, similar to Legion armor, across their massive chests. Blaster shots that struck the plate were reflected off and away. But the zhee's limbs and their braying donkey heads were uncovered, and well-placed shots cut them off in mid-bucktoothed battle cry.

It was clear to Besson almost immediately that they were not going forward this way. The zhee were raining down hot fire into the attackers.

"Warpig!" shouted Besson over comm as he pinned himself behind a control panel at the bottom of the stairs.

The platoon sergeant came back over L-comm. "Pig here, sir!"

"Set up both N-42 gunners. Interlink fire for the bottom of the stairs. We're pulling back behind that line!"

Fall back, thought Besson to himself. *I never thought I'd order a Legion unit to fall back.*

"Second and Third fall back behind the intersection Fourth is set up on!" he shouted over the comm. He didn't need to tell his leejes to pull the wounded back with them. No legionnaire would ever leave a brother behind.

Besson stepped out into a corridor and filled it with blaster fire, meeting the return fire of the zhee. He laid down as much covering fire as his N-4 would put out. Two legionnaires ran past him, dragging another legionnaire who was bleeding out from a slash that managed to get in under the bucket.

Legionnaires were getting shot down as they tried to pull back.

Third Squad leader came over comm. "Get down! Bang-bang out!"

Besson watched in horror as the junior NCO at the tip of wedge pulled something from his cargo belt while firing his blaster with one hand into the two zhee lunging for him. A third zhee was coming in with two knives, both curving and shining in the darkness, his massive donk buckteeth wide and chomping. The NCO stepped forward and slammed the adhesive explosive breaching charge onto the third donk's chest plate. Then the legionnaire sergeant fired at point blank.

The entire stairway was engulfed in an orange apocalyptic boom that knocked everyone to the ground. Besson was momentarily knocked out, and when he came to he was being dragged behind the already working N-42s. The heavy squad automatic blasters, interlocked and manned by two competent gunners, were near impossible to get past in small-unit tactics.

Besson's head and ears were ringing. And he was getting a text message over L-comm from the commander running all the recon ops in advance of the main assault.

Hurricane had just entered atmo.

14

Most of the Repub Navy personnel who flew the sturdy assault carriers liked working with the Legion. They sympathized with the Legion's grievances and had made the switch to fall in with Article Nineteen.

"We've come out somewhat early, sir," announced Commodore Rist.

No scowl crossed General Hannubal's face. He'd been in enough Legion battles to know that things started going sideways fast once any plan was set in motion.

"Problem, sir!" called out the sensor officer over the chatter of bridge traffic.

Both Rist and Hannubal turned away from the tactical holos in the center of the dark Combat Information Center at the heart of the assault carrier *Hurricane*. Other officers hurried through the darkness. The static wash of traffic between the task force's carriers and units staging within each ship filled the ether.

"What is it?" snapped Rist.

Commodore's never been in a firefight ten feet off a SLIC in an LZ that wasn't supposed to be hot, thought Hannubal as he studied the updating tactical displays. He could already tell what the major problem was. Every Repub military asset on Ankalor was flashing combat ready status. The Legion base was now marked hostile, and her radar and sensors were up and scanning.

Someone's tipped them off.

A moment later Rist was back at his side and looking positively sick.

"I don't know how, General... but they know we're here." Rist looked at the deluge of information coming in. "Oh. Oh, dear. The shuttle containing the Dark Ops team sent to take down the planetary shield was shot down."

"Have they put it up?" demanded the general. Time was of the essence. This was all split-second, and it could cost lives. If there was a chance the carriers could still slip in, Hannubal would take it. But if the shield came up before he could get into atmosphere... they'd all be dead.

"Not yet. It could be any moment. Shall we call off the assault?" Rist looked desperately at the general, who was in full battle rattle.

"Negative, Commodore. Our teams down there still have time to knock out those guns. We're committing. *Before* the shield is up. Not about to abandon those leejes by getting stuck in orbit. Signal *Tornado* and *Sirocco* to stand by to activate the interlocking defensive shield system. Center on us."

Commodore Rist turned away and set a series of orders in motion.

"All legionnaire companies, report to your assault bays," echoed a public address system across the interior spaces of the assault carriers.

Thirty-Third Legion Recon, Shadow Company, First Platoon
Air Defense Tower Four
Ankalor

The deadly crossfire set up by the N-42 blaster teams wasn't enough to dissuade the zhee from relenting in their suicidal counter-assault. As Besson led what remained of First Squad back out onto one of the balconies, one of the team leaders remarked over L-comm, "Them donks don't take the hint, do they, Sergeant?"

Warpig agreed that they did not.

The N-42s continued their high-cycle blare of shrieking fire. Captain Besson was momentarily afraid that one of the N-42s would over-cycle and melt down. Their repeating high-pitched whine indicated the weapons were firing almost non-stop without even pausing to engage individual targets.

"Warpig... blue sky?"

Besson reached a balcony beyond the tower walls and chanced a quick glance upward. If the zhee were smart, they'd be doing what he was about to do. But they weren't.

As what remained of First Squad began to climb upward once more, this time as fast as their arms and legs could haul their armor upward, the platoon sergeant came back with the casualty and ammo report.

Effectively, Shadow was down to half strength.

"Copy that. Keep 'em busy, Sergeant. We'll start our flank shortly," said Besson between gasps as he pulled his armored body up from handhold to handhold along the side of the tower. Above, the eighty-eight displacement gun batteries on their massive concrete spurs were lobbing massive photonic energy shots surrounding a shell in which antimatter was encased. Deflector shields wouldn't hold up against that kind of firepower for long.

Besson turned away from the rock face and stared out across the horizon. He oriented himself between the massive Gibraltaar Rock and the ranges that had been established as the assault force's landing zone out on the desert floor. Lonely roads snaked out through the pre-dawn darkness. Searchlights crossed the night and scanned the desert floor beneath the base. Dawn was just a short time away.

His men passed him along the side of the tower, berating each other over L-comm for weakness or general unworthiness.

Then he saw what he was looking for. The unmistakable flare of the Legion's assault force, inbound and hot, streaking through the lower atmosphere. Three massive Hammer-class assault carriers, wide and squat for most of their length, with massive hammerhead bridges located above the bow, were flying in a tight formation.

For a moment he got a reflection glare from the IDS deflectors that were now engaged, thus making the ships almost invulnerable to forward attacks. Unfortunately, the eighty-eight batteries that ringed Gibraltaar Rock would have firing angles on the ships' sides.

"Move!" he shouted to his men, using a command tone he'd learned from a particularly brutal drill sergeant out of his past. "We got five minutes, Leejes, or this mission is ate up real bad."

His breath came in catching gasps as he pulled for the extended firing positions above his head.

"Once you reach the balconies, go over the top. Team up and KTF! Objective is the fire command center in the control tower above the batteries. Forget our flanking maneuver. We've got to stop those guns now or the assault force is going to get shot up on the LZ."

He got affirmatives, and moments later they were going over the concrete lip of the massive batteries.

Massive shots of displaced energy were hurling themselves away from the quad barrel systems that pumped energy and encased antimatter skyward. Besson could feel the air pressure around his suit contract and expand with each dynamic shot. He had no time to see if any of the shots were finding their range and slamming into the inbound ships; he was already engaging zhee danger close. He wasn't an officer now. He was just a leej, and he moved quickly, killing more than thinking, like it was something he was born to do.

Task Force Whirlwind
Approaching Landing Zone
Ankalor

Aboard the *Sirocco*, *Typhoon*, and *Hurricane*, legionnaires—broken down by battalions, companies, and even platoons and teams—were already in the assault holds that would swing open and forward allowing the first units to hit the ground with enough cover to get clear of the carriers as they sank onto the LZ.

The assault battalions, three from each carrier, would have the hardest job. They had to cross open terrain once they crested the berms that surrounded the LZ. Once they traversed a quarter mile of open terrain under fire—covered by SMAFF rounds lobbed from the assault carrier's top-side artillery batteries while covering fire from the carriers' forward turrets hopefully kept enemy heads down—they would be the first into the extensive trench network that had to be cleared before the main doors to the facility could be breached.

No one was under any delicate illusions here. Drone recon estimated the zhee force inside the trenches numbered fifteen to twenty thousand.

It was going to be a slaughterhouse in there.

Six companies were assigned to protect the HK-PP walkers that would be dropped as the carriers came in through the atmosphere. Even before the ships touched down, the walkers would be unlocking from their drop configurations and approaching the LZ on massive hydraulic articulating legs. Two stories tall, and armed with heavy forward blaster cannons, they would provide critical fire support on trench bunkers and other fortifications once they made it to the forward lines. They could target fire down into key chokepoints the zhee would no doubt try to defend in there. But they were extremely vulnerable to infantry with anti-armor, hence the added company legionnaire protection.

Several platoons mounted in fast-attack ATVs called "mules" were gunning their engines and performing last-minute weapons checks. Armed with N-50s, the mules would act as cavalry; they would swarm from the assault hangars down ramps and attempt to destabilize any flanking attacks the zhee tried that didn't come from the main trenches.

From the aft flight deck of the hangar, shielded by the massive forward-arrayed interlocking deflector system, SLIC dropships would be ready to pull the wounded out, provide more troops to critical points on the battlefield in order to take advantage of any exploitable developments, and make close-air support runs against well-defended targets as long as the anti-air capacities of the zhee were minimized.

Task Force Whirlwind was ready for a fight.

At fifteen hundred feet, all three carriers side by side, six HK-PPs were dropped away. Limited capability repulsor pods fired, cushioning the impact of the landings, as five of the massive walkers touched down on the desert floor. But a round from a nearby air defense tower managed to connect with the sixth falling HK-PP, and the armored walker went up like a sudden fireworks display, raining down equipment and legionnaires across the desert floor in a terrific explosion.

Another round smashed into deck five of the *Sirocco*, tearing away a gun turret and an unoccupied barracks passage. The shot narrowly missed the ship's IDS relay tower, which, had it hit, would have collapsed the power-ful defensive system altogether.

At five hundred feet, the assault doors began to swing out and away from the ships, acting as spoilers to retard the carriers' massive forward motion. The pilots had set throttles to max approach to give the air defenses as lit-tle time as possible to range and target the incoming Legionnaire assault force.

Within the bellies of the massive ships, legionnaires began to whoop and call out to one another as the doors exposed the bays to the fireworks display of incoming fire.

At two hundred and fifty feet, all three carriers re-versed main engines to full and brought in all available power to the repulsors. Lighting flickered across the inte-rior passages and bays as every spare ounce of power was diverted to arrest the sudden drop of the multi-hundred-ton starships.

On *Hurricane*'s bridge, the flight crew stared out the blast-reflective cockpit windows surrounding all three sides of the flight deck. The scene before them was awe-some. And utterly frightening.

Above them loomed the mass of Gibraltaar Rock. The fortress's artillery batteries were lobbing shots that arced like bright falling angels and smashed into the desert floor, creating geysers of sand and flying dirt. Heavy turret fire was already smashing into the ship's forward IDS system. And beyond the massive rock, the sun of Ankalor was just beginning to rise above a range of low broken mountains, dark in the distance at dawn.

Traffic and comm died as the flight captains called out, "Brace for impact!"

And a moment later all three ships slammed into the barren wastes of Ankalor.

"Down and clear!" called out the first officer of the *Hurricane*.

"Commence the assault," ordered Commodore Rist as a signal to all three ships.

General Hannubal was not on the bridge at that moment. He'd gone aft to the hangar deck just as the ships cleared jump. He would direct the battle from an operations-configured SLIC.

Nine thousand legionnaires hit the sands of Ankalor, running to clear the berm that provided forward cover for at least the lower decks of the assault carriers. The massive IDS system that provided deflector cover for the force stopped twenty feet above the ground beyond the berm. Sergeants screamed at their men to move faster than they were moving. Concussive whumps from the top side carrier's artillery batteries prefaced the smoke rounds that arced out and upward before landing across the desert floor, exploding into sudden ghosts of swirling blaster-retardant smoke that obscured ECM and IR targeting.

The Legion companies had just begun to run hard into the smoke when the zhee unexpectedly surged out of the trenches and ran straight for them.

What would happen next would go down in Legion history as the Battle of the Blind.

15

The battle started out as good tactics meeting bad tactics.

General Hannubal had managed to get his force in as close to the zhee-held fortress as possible while still providing enough cover for disembarkation not under direct fire and establishing a forward operations base around the carrier assault group. Good tactics for what was going to be a straight-up fight anyway.

The zhee holding the extensive trench works around the base should have—according to all rational tactical decisions made by any sane commander—held position in the trenches and waited for their foe to come in after them. The trenches were arranged in three concentric rings surrounding the fortress, and each ring was a mass of locks, kill zones, and pillboxes overwatched by larger bunkers. A state-of-the-art monitoring system also ran a vast array of automated defensive systems. Inside these bunkers, pillboxes, and protected staging areas, the zhee could have easily waited out the assault and surrendered each line while exacting heavy casualties on the attacking force.

Which, of course, was the specific purpose for which the base's trench system, and even the base itself, had been constructed.

The Legion had known it was just a matter of time before the zhee declared another holy war and sought to take out their grievances on the Republic. Violent uprisings were an essential part of who they were. And Legion War Planning Theory—which was a term the House of Reason points overseeing the projected hated—argued that instead of fighting that inevitable fight on the zhee's home grounds, in brutal house-to-house combat within the zhee slums, it would be wiser to create a rally point, a target... a military base for the zhee to try and storm.

A base that was really just one big kill zone.

And so, if the zhee had understood the grand scheme underlying the technological wonder that was Fortress Gibraltaar, they would have waited for the Legion to attempt to take the trenches.

But that was not the zhee. It was not their way.

The Legion had dared array itself before the zhee's glorious new "Palace of Kibbel Ba-Ram," as they were now calling Fortress Gibraltaar. And so these outsiders would be met in fierce battle. They would see who the superior fighting force was. They would know the zhee to be the master race destined to enslave the galaxy.

The galaxy would see the might of the noble zhee tribes.

It was thus that the zhee, with numerical and tactical superiority, sacrificed half its numbers in the trenches to go out and meet the Legion in a battle without pity or restraint.

Charlie Company, First Platoon, "Punishers"

Private First Class Lango Huzu ran forward into the electrochemical smoke now drifting across the battlefield. His HUD immediately began to experience distortion and signal drop due to the inherent ECM effects of the refractive "smoke" known as SMAFF. Comm went sideways a moment later, and he looked off to his left and right to check his orientation relative to the rest of the platoon, which had started out in a rough wedge formation on the leftmost flank of the attack.

"Donks are coming out ... st... at us!" someone shouted over comm, their transmission breaking up, the pulse and whine of blaster fire bleeding through. Then a message appeared in Huzu's HUD. *Switch to hand signals.*

He caught sight of his platoon sergeant just ahead, signaling for everyone to continue moving forward. As fast as possible. Double time. Blaster fire came in from overhead, raking the dust and sand about twenty meters ahead of Huzu's position. The donks up along the face of the rock were firing down into the smoke regardless of their ability to target. The sand all around the running legionnaires exploded, throwing grit in concussive blasts that scraped at their armor.

Then the first donks came running in through the foggy SMAFF. And even though the platoon was supposed to have switched over to hand signals and local audio comm, leejes were still attempting to call out targets over comm. The broken chatter was a blare of static and unintelligible targeting locations.

The savage donks came in firing, and before Huzu knew it he had multiple tangos all across his front. He hit the dirt and sent return blaster fire streaking into the smoke all around. Two donks tackled the platoon leader, coming out of the swirling shrouds of smoke all around like nether phantoms from a grave of unquiet rest. PFC Huzu scrambled to his boots and moved in close, taking down both donks with precise fire.

Then a hundred or more donks came at the platoon from an odd angle that didn't seem to be where the attack should have been coming from—they came from what Huzu would have sworn was the right flank and the other attacking assault battalions. But in moments the donks were in and among the platoon, hacking and blasting away in a desperate scrum to see who could shoot each other down first.

One of the donks Huzu had shot down off the platoon leader was getting back to his knees. The jihadi lunged for the prone officer's back with a long curving knife.

Huzu rushed forward, bringing his blaster, which had been pointed at the flank attack, to bear on the donk. But his charge brought him close fast, and instead he delivered a savage kick with his armored combat boot to what he thought would be the donk's unusually swollen belly. Instead of gut, the boot connected with ceramic molded armor, but the donk still went down, through sheer ballistic physics. As he rolled over the sand he brought up a small blaster pistol and fired at Huzu, all his shots missing and flying off into the white smoke that was now choking out everything beyond five meters.

"Iron sights," Huzu reminded himself as per training when engaged in SMAFF conditions.

He drew a bead with the N-4's sight and had just enough time before trigger pull to notice the zhee was wearing some kind of advanced armor system similar to Legion armor. But even Legion armor often did little good if you fired close and knew where to shoot.

With a quick yet precise adjustment of his elbows Huzu, landed the small matte-black sight at the leading edge of the barrel on the donk's wide and comically ridiculous muzzle. Then the PFC pulled the trigger on the combat blaster, smashing the donk's skull with a blaster bolt.

And for good measure he put two more in the ruined chest armor. A stab seemed unnecessary since the donk's gray brains were seeping out onto the sand.

Blaster fire came from out of the smoke, wild and unaimed. It barely missed caressing Huzu's armor. He even felt like he'd dodged each shot at the last second as his reactions flared into some kind of overdrive and the bolts seemed to move almost in slow motion. Maybe an optical trick brought on by the swirling smoke.

The LT was still down on the ground, and when Huzu shouted for the officer to get up, the man didn't move. He was saying something, but there was so much blaster fire and braying and squad chatter over the jammed comm system that he barely heard the man until he bent low, covering the wall of smoke in front of them with his weapon, oriented on where he thought the next zhee attack would come from.

Though honestly, Huzu admitted to himself, it was hard to tell what direction was what direction at the moment.

"I'm cut," whispered the LT hoarsely through gritted teeth. He was obviously in a lot of pain.

"Where?" shouted Huzu. A group of donks came through the smoke, close and crouching. Huzu fired at them. They fired back.

The LT's comm came through on the HUD. "Got me in the gut. If I stand up... it'll all come out."

Huzu was looking at four dead donks in the sand ahead. They'd been firing at someone else, and he'd managed to knock them down with some unseen help from another quarter. "Stay low, sir. Keep pressure on your wound. Use your hands. C'mon..."

Huzu picked up the LT's rifle and shepherded the man to what he thought was the rear. The LT crouched and stumbled ahead of Huzu, who kept watch on their rear, expecting the donks to come out of the shifting fog with knives out at any moment, braying for blood.

A moment later they walked into a full-bore fire fight between two larger elements of zhee and leejes who were both using the fallen dead for the bare cover the bodies provided. A legionnaire sergeant major was pulling wounded men back while returning firing with his blaster pistol.

"LT's hit, Sergeant Major!"

The sergeant major bent down to the wounded LT. "You all right, Lieutenant Vay?"

"Not Vay," muttered the LT. Blood was seeping through his gauntlets as they clasped the wound beneath the chest plate of his armor. "Lorca..." he whispered.

And then the LT died, his body going limp without ceremony. Like some sack of undone laundry, or a thing not needed anymore, cast aside into the gutters and alleys of the galaxy.

"Ah, hell, kid," whined the sergeant major. "Waste of a fine officer. Thought he was Vay. Vay was all ate up. Lorca was okay in my book."

The sergeant major spoke at the top of his lungs. He seemed to like to talk for the sake of talking, and Huzu would find that the man was in love with the sound of his own voice, which was at once wry and hectoring.

Behind them the legionnaires at the front of the battle intensified their fire as more donks surged into the impromptu firefight.

"Look like we're about to be overrun, kid. What unit you with?"

"Two nine!" shouted Huzu over the fusillade of blaster fire.

"Two nine?" cried the sergeant major. "You're lost, son. This is the three sixteen. Either that or we're just as lost as you."

The sergeant major moved forward to the firing legionnaires, and Huzu followed close behind. Out of nowhere, a mule, firing its N-50 on full auto, careened out of the swirling smoke and lit up the advancing wave of zhee, cutting them to shreds in great piles and barely missing a few legionnaires it almost drove over.

"Move forward, boys!" cried the sergeant major. He turned back to Huzu. "Come on, kid. You're with me now. Name's MakRaven. Stay close and don't get lost. We'll fold you into our network on the L-comm once the smoke clears. Looks like we got us a real cantina dance goin' on!"

They'd only moved about twenty meters deeper into the smoke, shooting down any zhee they encountered, when they heard the rise of a chorus of more zhee braying. Above this it sounded like someone was beating pots and pans to create a disturbingly untimed din within the chaotic cacophony of donk war-braying.

"It's a *Zhuzwafa*!" cried Sergeant Major MakRaven. "Form up on me, boys, and use them bodies for cover. They're coming at us in full in about the next two minutes. If you were gonna tell your sweetie you loved her you shoulda done it already, because I doubt most of you are gonna survive this!"

Huzu began to drag the heavy and lifeless bodies of the zhee away from the spot where the sergeant major had positioned himself as though he were some kind of flap pole that could not be moved. The bodies were piled into a rough circle, stacked one on top of the other.

"What's a *Zhuzwafa*, Mak?" asked one of the legionnaires as he dug sand, creating a quick fighting position among the bodies.

"A *Zhuzwafa* is when they get real uptight and swear to kill all o' their enemies of their brothers regardless of pain or injury to themselves. It's their version of a last stand, but it's kinda like a full-bore charge for the most part. Also, they're probably on drugs. They chew up lotus grass to get immune to pain and such. But they still die if you shoot 'em. A couple o' times at least."

He stopped Huzu, who was dragging a particularly large dead zhee warrior across the sand. "Hey," he said. "Gimme that one." The sergeant major bent down and unsheathed a *kankari* knife just like the ones the zhee carried. "Good thing you got me here, boys. This here is one of their big ol' head men. So we might just pull a little trick on 'em."

The sergeant major began to pull back the zhee's armor, exposing the alien's swollen gut. "You are no doubt most likely prone to wonder at I'm doin'," he opined. "Right?"

Huzu didn't respond.

"Here they come!" shouted one of the legionnaires. "KTF!"

Huzu, kneeling next to sergeant major, had no idea from which direction the zhee assault was coming. But the smoke was beginning to clear, and within its drifting depths he could see men and vehicles running or firing at other half-seen shapes in the fog banks. The dead of both sides were like islands in the sandscape. In the distance an artillery strike fell across the sands, and the ground trembled beneath their feet.

Sergeant Major MakRaven paid no regard to the impending assault and surrounding battle. He continued on with his monologue as he dug around inside the donk's guts.

"You may not know it, but I'm the Legion's foremost donk fighter, and though I lack humility, I am at the same time one of the zhee's greatest friends. I know all their tricks, 'cause they taught 'em to me when I was working with group to train insurgent tribes to fight one another. Been fightin' zhee for almost my entire career. What no one bothers to learn, though I have lectured many, is that the zhee have a musk gland..."

Mak stuck half his arm into the zhee's swollen guts and rooted around with his un-gauntled hand. Even through the legionnaire armor's filtration system, the smell was simply awful.

"Good thing we got our buckets on, kid! This don't smell like flowers, do it? But sometimes a little taste'll get through and all. If it do... try not to throw up in your bucket, 'cause that'll make things much worse. Trust me on that one."

The legionnaires continued to defend their impromptu fort of bodies, firing into the charging zhee horde that looked like bloodthirsty demons surging out of some nether pit.

MakRaven pulled out what he had been looking for. A hint of its scent managed to slip through to Huzu, and the young PFC almost gagged.

"This here is their scent gland," said the sergeant major. "It's how they rule one another. The head men and big tribal chiefs have a certain scent that makes the others afraid of 'em. Makes 'em more docile and amenable to what they want 'em to do. And we're gonna need this in about thirty seconds 'cause it's about to turn into a real knife and gun show, boys!"

Even though the legionnaires all around were keeping up a steady stream of fire, dropping the charging zhee in heavy numbers, more appeared through the gaps, stomping their dead pack brothers as they came, firing blasters that struck down some of the legionnaires. The nightmare aliens gnashed their giant buckteeth around their *kankari* knives and charged into the fray, intent on closing for the kill no matter how many times they were shot dead.

Sergeant Major MakRaven stood up and held the swollen musk gland high above his head like he'd just won some bag of candy at a carnival for throwing pins and knocking down enough targets. Then with a whoop and a deft flick of his *kankari* blade, he sliced the fleshy sack and showered the legionnaires beneath him with its putrid contents.

Ten seconds later the zhee line slammed into the small stand of legionnaires on the sand. Except in the last moment they came up short as though suddenly unsure of themselves. They even neighed and snuffled loudly as though their massive sinus cavities had filled with mucous. And as they came to a dead stop, those behind them flew into them, beating and kicking their pack brothers to move forward into the kill.

The legionnaires filled that first rank with intense blaster fire at almost point-blank range.

Whatever objection had come over the following zhee from the smell of what one leej said was like "cat piss gone bad" was overcome within seconds of seeing the gratuitous massacre of the front rank. They stumbled badly, but regained their composure as the scent of blood tried drowned out the overwhelming musk.

Zhee warriors tackled legionnaires, knives flailing and stabbing for the kill. One massive legionnaire deployed his bayonet from the end of his blaster and began hacking and slashing at the zhee who came in close to taste his fury. His squadmates closed in behind and fired into the swarming zhee. Any break in the Legion line meant death for them all.

Huzu dropped to one knee fired into the horde, dropping five zhee who got within two meters of him. Each shot was desperate, close, and tense. He aimed for headshots against these bobbing, weaving monsters that charged like runaway bulls gone mad.

Sergeant Major MakRaven directed the defense, calling out fire concentrations. Every legionnaire fighting from the pile of bodies concluded that the sergeant major's joke about saying goodbye to their sweeties hadn't been so much a joke as a promise. At the height of the chaos, every one of them was completely convinced that they were making their last stand. Taking their last breath. Looking out upon the galaxy one last time here along the edge.

Then, as quickly as the wave had come, the zhee assault broke. And when the last blaster shot whined off into the smoke, the surviving legionnaires were staring at a sand field littered with the dead bodies of the zhee.

And closer at hand... the bodies of their own.

Distant artillery shocked the sky with booming eruptions. Shells whistled overhead through the clearing smoke, promising destruction farther ahead.

***

"All right, boys!" cried Sergeant Major MakRaven. "The L-comm is back up! Follow me. Orders say we're to take the trenches. Drone recon cannot, I say *cannot*, identify their current occupation statues because yes, the zhee actually do have good snipers and they keep takin' our little flying bots out. Of course, I coulda told 'em that, but no one listens to an old zhee fighter like me."

The smoke was now drifting off in large continents at the behest of a light morning breeze, revealing more and more of the battlefield carnage that spread across the quarter mile from the big assault carriers to the trenches. Other units of legionnaires, moving swiftly in wide wedges, raced for the trench works just a few hundred yards ahead.

The batteries and blaster turrets atop Fortress Gibraltaar had ceased firing for the moment, but behind the legionnaires the ground shook in small, regularly timed earthquakes—the result of the four HK-PPs that towered over the battlefield, firing at unseen targets within the trenches. Their forward turrets swiveled and rotated, sending massive blaster shots across the battlefield as their legs articulated forward with each slow step.

"Ooah, boys!" whooped the sergeant major. "Now let's go kill the enemy for darin' to oppose our formidable wrath." Except this was said in a way that didn't seem triumphant. It came off as more matter-of-fact.

Within moments their wedge was moving at a trot, closing on the massive trenches that lay before the giant rising fortress rock.

Fire from the fortress opened up all at once. At first ranged sniper fire, then the massive N-50 gun emplacements, raked the desert, and sand exploded in volcanoes all around the waves of legionnaires as they sprinted the last stretch and took cover behind a defensive wall that wasn't defended.

Huzu, sticking close to the sergeant major and now folded into their L-comm network, shuddered as the brand new duracrete wall at his back shuddered and exploded in sprays of fragments displaced by the high-cycle, high-power fire coming from within the fortress.

"Breaching charges!" wailed the sergeant major as he moved down the line pointing at two specific spots on the wall. "Here and here!"

Two legionnaires rushed to obey. Farther down along the wall on both sides, other leejes did the same, at the direction of their own commanders.

"Stand back, boys. We're goin' through."

A blast from one of the zhee-operated N-50s punched through a wall and gutted a nearby legionnaire in an instant. The man fell over dead. Another legionnaire had his head blown off by a sniper a second later.

When the breaching charges were set and the count was underway, Huzu, down the wall and far enough away from the pending explosion, had a moment to survey the sands they'd come through. The consequence of the blind battle they'd been in. The smoke was gone now. Out in the distance the massive assault carriers were still lobbing shells into the fortress and the trenches. They arced overhead like dark angels being cast down from heaven. And on the sands between the fortress and the carriers lay uncountable dead, both zhee and Legion. Each one was someone's one too many.

Still, there were more living legionnaires than there were out there dead and dying on the wastes.

All up and down the wall, the breaching charges went off, shattering the duracrete and exploding inward in fragmented sprays.

As the first leejes roared and charged through the gaps in the wall, jumping down into the trench eight feet below, the zhee tried to range the breach and kill them with blaster fire. The sergeants pushed their men through.

A flight of three SLICs, gunship-configured, came in over the trenches. They were flying low, their mounted blaster pods spooling out high-cycle blaster fire in adult-sized doses. One fired an AGM that lanced out deeper into the trenches, but Huzu didn't have the time to see where it went. There was a terrific explosion as he landed on the duracrete floor of the trench.

The trench corridor ran the length of the wall they'd been crouched behind, and all along this wall, teams, squads, and companies of legionnaires were spilling down into the trenches, escaping the fire of the zhee, who sprayed them with every weapon they had.

As Huzu dropped down, his armor easily absorbing the impact, he found himself inside a scene of unrealistic carnage. Even though the dead all around him were the enemy—even though the dead were the zhee, the most hated race in the galaxy—the shock and horror of seeing what had been done to them defied his mind's ability to rationalize. Maimed and mangled bodies lay in every position, with the occasional horror show of a donk face staring back at him from amid the bloody carnage.

The entire corridor had apparently been hit by a massive artillery barrage—and within the last few minutes it seemed, because many of the bodies were still smoking. Or rather, *pieces* of the bodies that remained were still smoking. The artillery batteries aboard the assault carriers had prepped the trench works with highly accurate fire, no doubt assisted by drone-enhanced targeting. An entire company of zhee had been stationed here, only to end up mutilated beyond recognition.

"Hey, this one's smilin'," said one of the legionnaires over L-comm.

Sergeant Major MakRaven erupted over the comm. "All right boys, time to form up. Sounds like the other units are already fighting their way through the secondary access routes that lead deeper into the trenches. Our line of attack is being assigned now, and it don't look like no cake walk from what I can see. Though I will say some cake would be good right now."

Distant blaster fire mixed with the sound of fragger explosions. Sniper fire whined. And the turrets atop the rock were still firing into the trenches. Even the artillery from the assault carriers had shifted forward, "walking" across the desert in front of the advancing legionnaires in other sections along the line of assault.

But here, in the trench filled with dead zhee, all was quiet.

Huzu looked at the donk face that stared back at them all with a smile its face. Like that zhee knew some joke about life and death the rest of them hadn't heard yet. But would soon enough.

16

Major Owens knew that, now that he'd been given the position of his former point commander, he would be a lieutenant colonel within two standard cycles. But the prospect—one he'd worked hard to achieve, only to be passed up in favor of point after point—brought him no joy. Not now.

A holoscreen provided a real-time feed of the stealth shuttle's crash site, via an observation bot deployed by the Legion base in the Green Zone. Comms to *Night Stalker* itself were dead, but Owens had made contact with the two surviving legionnaires over the L-comms in their buckets. They were working quickly, getting the ship's pilot free of the wreckage and out of the way, and stockpiling ammunition.

The peeper bot showed swarms of armed zhee traveling down parallel streets, all headed toward the smoking wreck. Other bots flew over the city declaring an immediate curfew and demanding all beings return to their homes. The zhee weren't listening.

"Be advised, Zenith," Owens said calmly, "there are multiple hostile elements heading your way."

"Yeah, we hear 'em coming," replied Trident over the comm. "Sounds like more than we can keep back. Can you provide support?"

"Negative," Owens replied. "We have no destroyers on site, and we haven't managed to obtain fire authority from Camp Rex to provide artillery support."

The point in command of that base was more interested in running the request up the Republic chain, checking in with the House of Reason or whoever, than helping the legionnaires in mortal peril on the ground. Owens let out a sigh. The point had no idea this was a full-scale Legion invasion and not just another zhee uprising—and Owens couldn't set him straight. Because if the point knew the truth, his bureaucratic foot-dragging would probably turn into outright resistance. So for now, the major had no choice but to accept the delay.

For now.

There was no use being sour about the long list of things he *didn't* have. He would make use of the assets available to him, which thankfully included the Legion's observation capabilities, and a loyal force large enough to provide help.

"We've got a QRF mobilizing from the base," he continued. "KTF until they get to you."

"Copy," answered Trident.

Left unsaid was that the base was under the command of another point, and early indicators from *Mercutio* were that this point was keeping the base on lockdown until he could get approval from the House of Reason.

Owens looked to his aide. "Get me Chhun. We need to get that planetary generator down. It's a miracle they haven't put it up, but it can't be much longer, and those legionnaires are going to need the support of the combined fleet once they take the fortress."

"Yes, sir." The staff officer moved away from the command table to call Victory Team over his comm.

Owens pushed up his shades and watched the zhee surge toward the *Night Stalker's* crash site. The first sprinkling rain of blaster fire—indirect—was splashing around the stealth shuttle as the two legionnaires swept for targets.

"Here they come," called one of the leejes, as much to his buddy as to command.

Owens ground his teeth and blew out frustrated breaths through his nose. This was a setup. Stealth shuttles didn't just get shot down. Someone had leaked their arrival, and Owens was going to find out who. Who had done this to his legionnaires.

And then he was going to make them pay.

Task Force Grinder
Camp Rex Legion Base, Green Zone
Ankalor City

The smoke from the crash site was visible out in the zhee slums on the edge of the city, distinct even among the usual haze created by the heaps of burning garbage gathered in the neighborhoods and set ablaze at nightfall. Those stinking fires usually burned all night, and there was never any telling what the patrols assigned to the slums and outskirts would find mixed among the ashes the next morning. You only hoped the bones were all zhee. Any other race triggered an investigation, which meant standing around taking sporadic sniper fire under orders not to return fire. Wouldn't want to upset the apple cart.

Staff Sergeant Arlen Vix hopped from the passenger seat of his combat sled, bucket in one hand and rifle in the other. He *never* let his leejes see him without them until they'd returned to the safety of the wire.

He surveyed the smoke and took a deep, sinus-clearing sniff. Ankalor always reeked. He hocked a thick loogie, depositing it with a splat on the permacrete road leading from Camp Rex to the base's main gate. In the distance, blaster fire buzzed furiously—much more than the typical shots the zhee were always sending up in the air as warnings, target practice, celebrations, or just to disrupt the quiet of the night. And this blaster fire was pitched. A firefight.

Vix was part of the quick reaction force—Task Force Grinder—that was rolling out to the crash site of a Dark Ops stealth shuttle that had crashed right in the heart of the zhee outskirts. Or at least, that's what they were *supposed* to be doing.

He observed the column that sat stalled at the gates. Eight combat sleds equipped with twin heavy blasters. A trio of main battle tanks—MBTs—leading the way. The sight of all that destructive firepower strung out in front of him gave Vix a sense of euphoric pride. "Ooah," he muttered to himself, and then jogged to the front of the column. He could see his Lieutenant, Teller Po—a good man, a real leej—arguing with two other men. One was Captain Noggus, and the other was Major Wiley. Both of them were points.

"Lieutenant," Vix shouted as he approached. He saw two more sergeants converging on this powwow at the front of the column. Evidently Vix wasn't the only one wondering what the holdup was.

The discussion halted as the three officers turned to examine the approaching staff sergeant. Vix could make their features out clearly as the last of the darkness began to recede with the dawn.

"We gotta go, LT," Vix said.

Captain Noggus held out an accusatory finger. "You're not going anywhere, Sergeant. None of you are."

Noggus had at least been in combat before. He'd left the wire, and he wore that confidence like a steel resolve. The major, by comparison, seemed weak-stomached and faint of heart. Like he was afraid of the legionnaires armed to the teeth all around him. As a result, it seemed, despite his junior rank, that Captain Noggus was the one in charge. He was certainly the one doing all the talking for the two points.

"Sir?" Vix asked, genuinely confused. *What the hell? Isn't there a smoking stealth shuttle out there with wounded crew and leejes?* Even if they were all dead, they were supposed to secure a crash site like that and use burners to destroy the tech. *Why wouldn't we be leaving? If not us, who?*

Lieutenant Po held up a hand, asking his sergeants to hold on. "We're going," he insisted.

"The hell you are!" Major Wiley had found his voice. Nothing angered a point more than being questioned. "There is *much* more than this shuttle crash, Lieutenant! Three assault carriers are hitting Fortress Gibraltaar, and we have no idea why. Are they Black Fleet? Something else? We are sitting tight until I receive directives from the House of Reason. Whatever mission this shuttle was on, it was not authorized by us. We are standing down."

"Sir," Po continued, unfazed and bolder than Vix had ever seen him when dealing with a point, "these orders came through the chain from Legion Commander Keller. The Legion commander doesn't owe this base an explanation, but we do owe him our obedience. Delegate Kaar himself could be standing here and it wouldn't change anything. We're going, with or without your approval."

Po turned to face his sergeants, even as Major Wiley shouted, "You are *not* leaving!"

But it was clear they were. And Vix was elated to see what was happening.

"Get in your sleds," Po said. "We'll break the gate down if we have to."

The other sergeants dispersed, but Vix paused a moment longer. This was a thing he wanted to see. Had wanted to see for a very long time.

Captain Noggus exclaimed, "We'll order those drivers to kill engines if *we* have to! The army is still loyal to the Republic!"

Po shook his head. "Not these guys. We stopped riding with the basics who wouldn't leave the wire to save lives a week after our first rotation began."

Po motioned for one of the fearsome main battle tanks to roll forward. The armored behemoth floated forward on repulsors, its tracks not touching the ground, though it could roll on its own in the event its repulsors ever failed. MBTs were a thing of beauty.

As the tank rolled forward, the rest of the column inched behind it. Po moved to the waiting basic driving the tank, his head barely visible above the magnetically sealing hatch.

"Go through 'em if you have to," Po said.

With a nod, the driver rolled forward. The captain and major jumped to the side, and the gate's arms swung up as the tanks, and then the sleds, began leaving the base.

Vix watched the two points. The captain fumed with barely controlled rage, and the major's face held a solemn expression. Probably worrying about the implications this would have on his career.

As he should, thought Vix.

No one had had to brief Vix about the reason for the stealth shuttle. No one had had to tell him about the coming assault. He knew. He just knew. Something like this... it meant a change was coming in the Legion. A change that should have come a long time ago.

***

The QRF column was almost to the edge of the Green Zone, ready to enter the badlands, when the L-comm chatter from the base began.

"Grinder One," came the voice from Camp Rex. Each sled had a Grinder number, and the three tanks were designated Boomers One through Three. "We're uploading a route to you via our observation bots to get you to the crash site as fast as possible."

There was a silence. The voice from Camp Rex must have felt a need to fill it by explaining the sudden change. "Major Wiley, uh, the major hadn't realized a stealth shuttle was down. You are to secure the crash site, retrieve the casualties, and burn the sled."

That was exactly the order that had come from *Mercutio*.

Vix chuckled and announced to the other legionnaires on Grinder Ten, "More like Major Wiley wants to cover his ass now that we've already rolled out."

The sled interior filled with nervous but agreeable chuckles. Going out into the zhee badlands was never a dull experience, and each man knew there was a good chance he might never return to the wire. Especially when the zhee were worked up into a frenzy, like they were now.

"Affirmative," answered Lieutenant Po. "Route received. We have entered the badlands."

The progress and opulence of Ankalor City's Green Zone quickly gave way to a slum of shanties and permacrete huts surrounded by high walls. Nothing was new. Everything was falling apart.

"Hey," called out Boomer Two. "Just rolled by some donks hiding in a west-side alleyway. Looked shady as hell, think I saw a few blaster rifles."

"Just went by," announced Boomer One. "I confirm about six zhee, at least half of them armed. If I had to guess, they're waiting for us to pass by so they can take some shots at the sleds."

The tanks were about fifty meters in front of the sleds, which kept a twenty-five-meter separation in their column. Grinder Six would be the first combat sled to reach the alley. It was a narrow enough road that the whole column could get stopped up by a disabled sled.

"Maintain combat protocol," advised Camp Rex. "Do not fire unless you first come under fire."

"No," said Lieutenant Po. "They're armed and out after being ordered off the streets. Ambush. Grinder Six, KTF."

"Roger, KTF," came the reply form Grinder Six's gunner, LS-818.

"Dammit, no!" called out the point toady working the comms at Camp Rex. "You are *not* cleared to engage. This is a violation of the Fairness in Combat's protocol—"

"Shut that off," Po ordered. "Get me a link with *Mercutio*."

All this happened at once, part of the chaotic nature of combat. There was always so much. Focus was the key. Focus on the right things, and live. Focus on anything else, no matter how important it might be...

Grinder Six moved fluidly toward the intersection. Vix watched the sled through the exterior holocams. "Get ready to dismount," he told his boys. Their buckets were on; they were ready. Vix felt himself pucker as Grinder Six's gunner began a preemptive stream of twin blaster cannon fire.

Dat-dat-dat-dat!

As the gunner chewed up the corners of the stone walls on either side of the alleyway, then swung his twins to fire straight down the alley itself, feeble return fire attempted to take the legionnaire down. He stood defiant in his turret, maintaining fire until his sled had moved safely past the intersection.

There was a brief gap, and then the next sled began to roll by, its gunner opening fire as he went. This time there was no return blaster fire. And so it went, each convoy sending rounds into the alley until Vix's sled was up.

"Vix," called Lieutenant Po. "Dismount and check it out."

The combat sled pulled into the alleyway, and Vix gave the order to drop ramp and disembark. He led two legionnaires along his side of the sled, and his other three men formed a similar column on the other side. They moved into the alley with rifles up.

Grisly burnt and rendered zhee flesh littered the alley. There were pieces of zhee on the street, pieces splattered against the walls, pieces on dumpsters, stoops, and doors.

"Okay, Grinder One," Vix said, deftly toeing aside a torso to reveal a beat-up blaster rifle. "Confirmed seven kills. Armed with blasters and..." Vix looked at a cylindrical tube hidden behind a blaster-riddled dumpster. "At least one RPG. Good call on KTF, LT."

"Check for any signs of the crash. Survivors, intel, whatever. And then mount up and rejoin. Boomer Three is maintaining security. We're waiting about a half click ahead."

"Copy." Vix waded further into the carnage.

"Sergeant Vix," called out LS-660. "Come and see. This is Leej."

Vix hustled over. Behind the same dumpster where the rocket launcher lay half-exposed was an N-5 blaster rifle with an auto-feed frag launcher. Dark Ops gear. A black bag lay next to that, and it looked Dark Ops, too. It still had its webbing partially attached, with frays looking like it was half-cut, half-pulled off of whatever it had been attached to. It appeared moist and sticky. *Blood*, thought Vix.

"Open it up," he said, "look inside, and then let's go. Take the weapons."

"Holy..." The legionnaire didn't finish his sentence.

Vix leaned down and peered into the bag. It was full of det-cord and other explosives. Enough to bring down a building. He triggered his comm. "Grinder One, we have leej blasters and explosives. These zhee must've raided the crash site already."

"Copy, yeah," answered Lieutenant Po. He sounded grave. "Get it back on the sled. I just heard from *Mercutio*. No survivors at the crash site. We're changing course."

"Sir, aren't we supposed to secure and destroy the shuttle?"

"We have a new target."

Vix ordered his men back onto the sled. He carried the bag himself. His bucket blinked a battlefield condition update.

> Staff Sgt. A. Vix: Battlefield Condition Update...
> ...
>
> ...
>
> Planetary Shield Engaged.
> Log Record? Y/N

"No," Vix commanded his bucket's AI. He looked up at the energy field that shimmered high above them like a second atmosphere. Whether it was the zhee who had turned it on or the Republic, Vix had a bad feeling about it. "Sket."

First Expeditionary Legion Fleet
Super-Destroyer *Mercutio*
Ankalor System

The zhee fleet came out of hyperspace closer than expected. Even the veteran destroyer captains, men and women who'd played cat and mouse inside a hundred dangerous wreckage fields and asteroid belts, hadn't expected the zhee to come in so hot after jumping in-system so close.

"Contact!" shouted the CIC officer aboard the *Mercutio.* "Zhee battle group bearing two-eight-zero from forward mark."

"Speed?" said Admiral Ubesk, watching as the real-time near-space holodisplay updated the position of the ten new battle cruisers.

"Attack. Max Impulse. We're detecting power to weapons across all ships."

"Good," replied the admiral. "Hold station. Pattern Alpha. Standard battery fire on turret commander's select engagement targets. But only limited fire. Stand by to slave to Aegis at five hundred kilometers."

The admiral got acknowledgements from all involved section commanders within the CIC.

The sleek state-of-the-art matte-black zhee battle cruisers, with weapon systems the House of Reason had denied for years were in development, opened fire at extreme range. The Legion's ships' deflectors easily handled the first salvos, dissipating the excess energy or, in some of the newer destroyers, transferring it to internal batteries.

"Closing within optimal engagement range," stated the CIC weapons officer calmly. In the background of the busy node, the electronic babble of battle chatter was like an ever-present white noise.

The zhee ships were now looming close and closing hard with no apparent intention of reducing to engagement speed or turning to starboard or port to present at broadsides with the heavier waist turrets. Instead they came on heedlessly, firing from their forward gun systems. Any torpedoes that went live were easily handled by the *Numano*, the fleet's electronic warfare destroyer.

"Torpedo direct fire envelopes opening up now, sir," said the CIC weapons officer.

The admiral ignored this. As did the rest. The man was just doing his job providing the required information in case the initial plan needed to be altered.

"Intensify fire one minute," said the admiral.

"Extreme close engagement. All batteries engaged," relayed a different CIC officer whose job it was to provide that data.

Now it was time to gamble, thought Admiral Ubesk. He'd known all along that the zhee had only a bare understanding of fleet tactics, much less of space warfare and ship-to-ship engagement. They'd come in the same way they did everything: full of sound and fury, firing and cutting, looking for first blood. If they found it, they'd suddenly swarm and concentrate. But they hadn't bothered to put any effort into punching through any shields. Instead they'd just shot at everything, looking for an easy kill.

And here was the gamble: What if they rammed? What if they didn't back off and they just rammed one of his destroyers? That would be catastrophic. But it wouldn't be the battle.

Ubesk was gambling that they wouldn't do this. That they'd had too much fun raiding worlds for plunder with their new House of Reason toys. That at the last minute they'd adjust course and fly by, shooting hard into his shields. And once they did that for long enough, and fast enough, they'd present their aft deflector array—with shields that were weaker than their forward-facing counterparts. Because a battle cruiser attacked. It didn't run.

Except now Ubesk was forcing them to "run" speeding past his fleet. Presenting their rear deflectors. Thinking they would come about like every predator in the world for another pass at an easy, slow-moving kill.

"You may activate the Aegis Fire Control System, Commander," said the admiral as one of the zhee battle cruisers, sleek and wicked, swept in over the *Mercutio*. It was so close that some crewmen on the bridge flinched, and others stopped to stare in wonder.

The zhee were at least holding a tight formation on this pass. Which was exactly what the plan called for them to do.

"All batteries, all ships…. slaved to Aegis Fire Control," announced the CIC weapons officer. "Reporting in ready to fire on your command, sir."

The admiral waited, allowing the zhee to reach maximum safe explosion distance. Yes, there would be debris and some tidal shock from the blast wave if this all worked according to plan. The angle of engagement was critical. There was only a moment in which this plan would work.

That moment presented itself.

"Now!" shouted the admiral. "Target center cruiser. All batteries fire. Target engines and engineering decks."

Every turret in the Legion's expeditionary fleet lanced out and struck the rear engines of one of the massive battle cruisers. That ship went up in a sudden explosion as the engines and all four of her reactors detonated at once. The blast wave struck the other cruisers, destroying another and vaporizing the deflector arrays of those closest to the blast. A few of these were pushed into the outlying cruisers; two collided, and another explosion ensued, sending burning wreckage into a half a dozen others.

Every battle cruiser's deflectors were now down, and the zhee were electronically blind. Close-range explosions did that to delicate sensor systems. But of course the zhee hadn't learned that in their limited experience of raiding near-defenseless worlds.

"Take the Aegis offline. Battery commanders have discretion to fire. Fire at will."

Within five minutes the entire zhee fleet was a field of burning wreckage hovering dangerously close to Ankalor's atmosphere. From the bridge of the *Mercutio*, the admiral saw the first battle cruiser, dead in space, burn in, igniting up along its spine, and then turning into a million flaming little pieces as it reached the planetary shield.

Ship-in-distress messages were coming in from the zhee and their lifeboats. Those messages were ignored as per a directive from the top of the chain of command. The rest of the battle cruisers would follow that first one that had gone in over Ankalor.

Over the next half hour the Legion's fleet held station, and did not conduct rescue operations.

17

Legion Destroyer *Intrepid*
Ankalor System

"Well this is a damn nightmare!" Major Owens pounded his fist on the command console.

"Yes, sir," answered an aide. The fresh-faced lieutenant seemed unsure of even those words. Owens knew the aide only tangentially—he was the non-appointed aide of the man Owens had replaced—but Owens had the sense that he was new to being this close to a command position. Which wasn't surprising—the point Owens had replaced had tended to use non-appointed Legion officers as gofers, caff runners, errand boys.

In the space before them both—the pit, as it was called—Operation Turning Point's progress was projected through a myriad of three-dimensional holos, real-time holoscreen feeds, readouts, status reports, and more. At the heart of this display was a holographic representation of Ankalor. It was a small planet, rotating from day to night much faster than Utopion standard's twenty-four hours. A blue layer, like a stasis field, had lit up around the planet—which meant the planetary shield was up. That was going to completely gum up the ground assault.

Intrepid had been the first destroyer to jump in. Their mission was to retrieve the kill team and launch fighters in the event that the zhee's fancy new fleet showed up mid-battle. And the fighters had indeed been launched, but there was no kill team for them to recover. They were all dead—only their shuttle's pilot remained. And judging by what was happening on the man's live-feed, one hundred cuts in, he wouldn't last much longer either.

There had been a brief powwow among the ship captains, the Legion commander, General Hannubal, and Owens. Priority one was the planetary defense shield. They had jumped into the system far enough away so as not to trigger the automatic defense mechanisms, and yet the shield was already raised when they arrived. A shield that the Republic was supposed to have had control over. Which meant that either the zhee had taken them, or the Republic had gotten word of Article Nineteen and had decided to do something about it.

The latter seemed more likely, given what had happened to Kill Team Zenith.

"Sir," said a white-clad naval officer with bags under her eyes. "Captain Chhun has arrived to see you as ordered, sir."

Owens nodded. "Thank you."

Chhun was in full kit, except for his helmet. He looked stone-faced. All business. And he'd brought the rest of his kill team with him, though Owens had only called for Chhun himself.

"Cohen." Owens gave a quick turn of his head, inviting the legionnaire to approach the command console. "C'mon over. Your team, too."

"This about Zenith?" Chhun asked. He didn't look at Owens for an answer. Instead he studied the various ship alignments and feeds in the pit below them.

Owens popped his gum loudly and pulled off his shades, rubbing his eyes with the tips of his fingers. "You know what happened?"

"Whole galaxy knows what happened," Chhun said, nodding at a newsfeed that kept replaying footage of a naked Dark Ops legionnaire—a man Chhun had met several times—being thrown off of a two-story building. The crowd gave room for him to fall, then scooped the body up and carried it inside to be thrown down again. They were trying to utterly pulverize the man's corpse. "Sir, we need to make the donks pay."

"Yeah, well." Owens punched up his console and brought up the feed of Cassius being tortured. "They don't know about this. Repub has it blocked except for priority classified. That's us."

"Holy strokes," mumbled Masters, watching with a stunned look as the stealth shuttle pilot moaned in agony with each new slice.

Chhun watched dispassionately, then turned to his men. He seemed to reach each legionnaire's eyes. "Sir, Kill Team Victory volunteers to perform a rescue mission."

Owens gave a melancholy smile. Chhun's response was utterly Legion, and the situation was utterly this broken world. Another rescue of another doomed soul who was just trying to do right by the galaxy. Yesterday Herbeer, today Ankalor, tomorrow… who could say?

"I know," Owens said, his voice soft. "I knew you would."

The major hardened his voice and directed Chhun's attention to Ankalor. "But there's a planetary shield standing in your way. I'll be frank. CWO Cassius will be dead by the time boots get on the ground. And that's *if* we can even get them on the ground."

No one from the kill team spoke. Now seemed a time to listen.

Owens continued. "We've got the brains putting together a plan. It involves a modified armored shuttle, a coordinated bombardment of the shield, and a kill team crazy enough to bet their lives on the two-second window we *think* we'll have if everything works out." He looked at Chhun and his team expectantly.

No one spoke, but each man gave a minute, solemn nod.

"How soon?" Chhun asked.

Owens didn't know whether to laugh, cry, or swear. "I don't know. Still waiting."

"Major Owens!" The cry came from a comm officer. "Urgent message from Legion command."

"Send it over." Owens punched up his holoscreen, and the image of Legion Commander Keller's aide-de-camp came up.

"Major Owens, the Legion commander wanted me to inform you that we have assets on the ground who are en route to the shield generator. Keep your kill team standing by in the event this force is unsuccessful."

"Who?" asked Owens, his spirits up.

"*Mercutio* ordered a quick reaction force to disregard the point making things difficult at Camp Rex. They listened."

Task Force Grinder
Badlands, Ankalor City

The streets were thick with zhee as the QRF combat sleds and main battle tanks raced toward their objective. The trouble was, the zhee were never where you could do any damage—except for those few foolhardy donks who found themselves in front of a moving MBT, only to be crushed by the force of repulsors strong enough to keep a one hundred and fifty metric ton war machine floating eighteen inches off the ground.

Boomers One and Two were making a lot of zhee pancakes.

But not enough.

The majority of the zhee flowed around the element like magnets of the same polarity. They just seemed to disappear, pushing down the streets and alleys, and then reappeared behind the column, taking a few shots and then scrambling to avoid the returning blaster cannon fire before repeating the process all over again.

And so it went as the QRF followed the commands coming from *Mercutio*, verified by their own feed from the observation bots. There would be no surviving an ambush of full force, not with the city swarming the way it was. Their only chance at survival was taking down the shield generator and allowing in the destroyers that were lurking somewhere out of orbit.

"Hard turn left," advised the *Mercutio* over L-comm.

Lieutenant Po confirmed that he saw the same. "Hard turn left... then we're a dead run to target."

"Affirmative," said *Mercutio*.

Vix looked to his men. "Get yourselves ready to KTF."

They were ready. He told them anyway. Because telling them made *him* feel like he was ready for what would come next.

The column of vehicles snaked around a turn, and it seemed that every twin blaster cannon opened fire. The tanks boomed with their heavy guns and chopped the air with their coaxial machine blasters.

"Sket, Sarge! It sounds like we just reached the war."

Vix looked at the legionnaire who'd made the comment. LS-01, "Keystroke" Hayes. He was new to the unit, and had taken on the designation of an old leej whose tour had ended. Folks rarely re-upped on Ankalor.

"Keystroke, I tell you what: the war just reached the donks."

Vix stood aside, allowing his men to get a better look at the holoscreen that sat on the dividing wall between the troop transport bay and the driver's cockpit. It was set to forward view, and it showed the zhee that had taken up positions to guard the shield generator. They were being blown to pieces. Utterly destroyed.

"How hard is it to crack one of these generators?" asked a legionnaire.

"Easy for an orbital bombardment, hard for a bombing run," Vix answered. "We'll have to send someone inside to blow it. But once you take down a primary hub, the whole system goes down. All the relays, everything."

Keystroke shook his head. "That's dumb. Why wouldn't they have redundancies on something like that?"

Vix motioned at his reflective armor. He'd been around long enough to know the difference between what he had now and what the Legion used to have. "Why do we have this? Because lives are cheap and the House of Reason only spends top-shelf credits for places they *really* care about. Trust me when I say"—the sled rocked from a nearby explosion—"trust me when I say that Utopion's planetary shield is a whole different story."

"Boomer One," Lieutenant Po called over the comm. "Can you make a hole for us in the generator's exterior housing?"

"Copy that, Grinder One."

There was a sustained volley of booming cannons. The sleds continued to fire, this time swinging their twins around to face the trailing enemy. It must have dawned on them what the QRF's intentions were. Then again, maybe it hadn't. Maybe they just wanted more dead legionnaires.

"Think you can fit through that?" asked Boomer One's tank commander.

Vix looked at the display. A fully extended Raptor could probably fly through the hole they'd left.

"Grinder," called out Lieutenant Po, "assume defense pattern Exodus. Leejes, prepare to dismount."

Vix read his orders through the visor of his bucket. His team would storm the actual generator. They had all the det-cord.

***

The hole provided by the tanks was more than big enough, and when the squad slipped inside, they found themselves in a supply room. Cleaning solvents pooled on the floor, every carton shattered and leaking from the blast. Toppled boxes of spare parts for bots lay partially submerged in the creamy blue pools. Vix heard himself slosh through the mess like a child stomping through a rain puddle.

The leejes stacked up beside the door leading further into the building, and Keystroke swung it open. They stormed into the hallway, looking both directions as overhead lights flickered.

A schematic appeared on Vix's HUD, showing the building's layout and indicating the route they had to take to reach the massive underground power couplings. He motioned for his team to follow him down the hall.

"So there's going to be some sort of security element," he said, moving at the front of his squad. "And they're probably going to want to find out what caused the boom, so..."

As the team moved along their route, more booms sounded from outside. The lights flickered and went out completely, and a soft red emergency light came up in their place. Vix found himself wishing it would go out, too.

It would be easier to just move in the dark, relying on their buckets to see for them.

They moved down a stairwell, the ultrabeams on their buckets and rifles illuminating every corner. Still there was no sign of any security detail—or anyone at all, for that matter. Until they poured out of the door onto the sublevel containing the power couplers. Right next to the stairwell was a speedlift, and Vix could hear a conversation in Standard coming from behind the lift doors. An occasional thump suggested that someone was jumping up and down.

"Looks like someone is stuck in the lift," Keystroke said.

The legionnaires stacked up on either side of it. Vix's voice bellowed from his bucket's external speaker. "Republic legionnaires! What's your situation?"

He braced for blaster fire to rip through the lift doors. Instead he heard a relieved voice.

"Oh, thanks to Oba. We're building security. We were just heading up when the power went out."

The legionnaires pried apart the lift doors, revealing an open car that had traveled up just high enough for them to see two men from the knees down. Both men stepped back upon realizing that the ultrabeams shined up at them were attached to the rails of the legionnaires' N-4s and N-6s.

"Don't shoot, guys," one said.

"Weapons on the floor, then slide out," Vix ordered. "My guys can't hold these doors apart forever."

The security guards did as instructed, sliding themselves out legs first and dropping on the ground. A legionnaire took each man aside while a third jumped up and retrieved their rifles. When the lift was empty, they let the doors close again.

Vix examined the guards. Their body language showed no hostility... and no discomfort at being disarmed by a group of leejes. Vix didn't think these two saw him and his men as enemies.

"You run security on the shields?" he asked.

"Yeah."

"Marines?" It was a guess. They were dressed like Republic marines—tan fatigues with kneepads and combat boots—minus a few key unit patches.

"No," answered the two guards in unison.

One man then spoke for both. "We used to be marines, but we're private contractors now."

"How many more?" Vix asked.

"Just us inside. Twelve-hour shifts split up by six contractors. The other guys are probably stuck in the Green Zone. What's going on out there?"

Vix wasn't ready to answer that question just yet. "What about security outside?"

Now the other contractor spoke. "Oh, dude. Republic farmed that out to the zhee. We watched them bug out hella quick maybe a half hour before you arrived."

"Zhee are fighting the Legion on planet," said Keystroke.

"Stupid donks," grumbled the contractor. "We've been saying for months that they shouldn't be pulling security on places like this. So what's up? Are they trying to take the shield generator?"

"They've already activated it remotely," Vix said, his voice grim. "We're here to shut it down the old-fashioned way so ships in orbit can send relief."

"Guys," Keystroke said, "I know it'll mean becoming unemployed, but can you help a few leejes blow this sket up?"

The contractors looked at each other, grinned, then turned back to face the legionnaires. One of them pulled out a security key card. "Yeah. We can help you out."

***

Vix sat with his back against a low wall, Keystroke by his side. "You think we used enough?"

They'd used the entire satchel of det-cord, wrapping it around everything in the shield generator's housing that a technician aboard the *Mercutio* advised them might be worth blowing up.

"Yeah," Keystroke answered, turning the remote switch in his hands. "So... do we blow it up now?"

Vix shook his head. "I dunno." He hailed Lieutenant Po. "Sir, are we ready to blow this thing? My team is all outside, all accounted for."

The lieutenant was with the sleds and tanks, keeping the surging horde of the Ankalor City slums at bay. They'd already killed a lot of zhee, yet the donks kept coming for more. "How big will the blast be?"

Vix and Keystroke exchanged a look, then Keystroke shrugged.

"Don't know, sir."

Vix heard the Republic Armorworks MBTs send what was probably a coordinated fire on something—probably a few zhee tactical trucks. The booms were followed by a massive secondary explosion. Vix gritted his teeth. The zhee had been loading up trucks with explosives in the hopes of getting close enough to the leej lines to blow them and cause mass casualties. "Everybody okay?" he asked.

"We're good," Po answered. "Donks are hurting themselves more than us. I think they were expecting us to follow the usual rules of engagement. They're getting KTF'd instead."

"Copy," Vix answered. "We've taken cover behind a low wall, about fifteen hundred meters from the target building. Can you call it in to *Mercutio*? Get an explosives guy to tell us if we need to move further?"

Vix had blown up no shortage of weapons caches and vehicles. But he and his team had never blown an entire facility. That was Dark Ops work.

"I can try," Po answered, his voice betraying a less than stellar confidence at the idea. "Response time isn't the greatest. Fleet's engaged in some heavy fighting."

"Dude," Keystroke urged. "Let's blow it. We'll be fine."

"How can you possibly be sure?"

"I've watched holos. We're good, dude."

Vix looked up. He could see flashes and streaks of light from the battle overhead. The distant rumble and roar of combat at Fortress Gibraltaar echoed in his bucket's audio receptors. They wouldn't be able to keep the zhee at bay forever. That was the unspoken reality that had settled over all the leejes. The whole city was out for them, and eventually they'd run black on charge packs.

The mission is what saves lives. Vix recalled the advice of his first platoon sergeant. *Maybe not yours, sure, but I promise you: more legionnaires stay breathing because of a successful mission than in spite of one.*

"Lieutenant," Po said, his mind made up. "We're gonna blow it. The shield has to come down."

After a weighty pause, Po gave his reply. "Okay."

"You do the honors," Vix said to Keystroke.

He could hear the enthusiasm in the young leej's voice. "My pleasure, sir."

Keystroke faced the building and held down the detonation button.

The explosion felt like it was liquefying Vix's insides. The low wall they were covering behind rattled as though in an earthquake, and an instant later the building housing the shield array's primary components collapsed—likely aided by shoddy construction done by cut-rate zhee labor. A cloud of dirt and dust rushed past Vix and Keystroke, engulfing them like some cat-5 storm raging through a desert.

So much dust was in the air that Vix could feel his mouth and nostrils getting coated with it. He blinked his eyes inside his bucket, hoping its fans would draw the irritating particles away. It was like being buried head first in a mound of silt.

The cloud passed, and a relative silence settled over the area. The sounds of the fight at Gibraltaar could still be heard, but the blast and the subsequent building collapse seemed to have halted the local fighting.

A moment later the tanks, combat sleds, and blasters started up again.

Vix looked at Keystroke. "You okay?" He reached out and dusted a patina of grime from the legionnaire's visor.

"I think I found my calling," Keystroke answered.

Vix looked up. The shield was down.

Legion Destroyer *Intrepid*
Ankalor System

The quick reaction force was getting hammered by the enraged zhee. The donks were rabid, mouths literally frothing as they sent in wave after wave toward their position, and the big guns on the main battle tanks had been firing incessantly—so much so that one of them had actually super-heated its cannon, warping the barrel and making it ineffective. It now sat idle, providing only physical cover for the legionnaires to fire at the mass of hostile aliens seeking to swallow them whole.

Attrition was taking a toll. There were only so many near misses, so many fraggers, rocket explosions, and blaster bolts that could be dodged or absorbed. Only so many times the leejes could get knocked down before something failed and they physically couldn't get back up. It had reached a point where there were as many legionnaires lying down on the blood-slicked floors of the combat sleds as there were men still in the fight. And the zhee... they just kept coming.

Chhun studied the battle from the *Intrepid*'s war room. The battle was raging at Gibraltaar, but the leejes on the ground over there would carry the day. Of that Chhun had no doubt. The QRF, on the other hand... These were men who had left the safety of the wire and Camp Rex in an attempt to save the lives of his Dark Ops brothers. Men who re-routed and successfully destroyed the planetary shield. Men who were heroes, worthy of honors and commendations. Those men were stuck there, about to die for a lack of support.

With the zhee fleet engaging the Legion, every laser battery was needed for ship-to-ship combat. The fighters, such as Dax Danns's Reaper Squadron, were out mixing it up with Republic tech. True, it was Republic tech that was manned by an inferior class of pilots—the zhee were no featherheads—but it was Republic tech all the same, and disabling it was taking time. Time the QRF didn't have. General Hannubal's main element had to win the day and send relief down to the planet, quickly. That was Task Force Grinder's only hope.

Unless.

Unless...

"Major Owens, I'm going down there."

Owens had been monitoring the status of numerous Dark Ops teams that were staged to hit the House of Reason where they slept. The time was drawing near. Things were tense.

"Where?" asked Owens. "Utopion?"

"No, sir," Chhun said, giving a look to the rest of his team to let them know he spoke only for himself. "Down there. Ankalor. That QRF needs someone to regain control of the rooftops. The zhee are close to pinning them down. Once those guns stop... that's it. Total team kill."

Owens examined the holos that showed the raging firefight in the zhee slums. He frowned. "Too hot down there. The air defense towers are still at it, and we don't have the bombers available to stop them until the admirals can whip the donks enough to get them running."

"The shields are down," offered Masters. "So we can get in a drop pod and assault that way."

"We'd crash through a roof or land in the middle of the zhee," Bear mumbled. "Gotta be another way down, though. We're all with you, Captain Chhun."

Chhun nodded. He thought of the assets aboard the ship. Of who was feeling the sting of the lost shuttle and crew as much as Dark Ops. The shuttle pilots. They'd lost two of their own, just like Dark Ops had lost their brothers.

"How 'bout the Serpents?" he said.

Owens arched an eyebrow. "They're certainly crazy enough to try. See if you can find a volunteer."

***

Chhun sat with his legs dangling out the side of the stealth shuttle as it soared over the Grodan Wastes toward the zhee slums. An explosion lit up his sensors, not five hundred meters away from him. An unmanned drone, flying in formation with the near-invisible—to instruments, at least—shuttle, went up in a ball of flames and littered itself all over the dry wastes below.

The plan, hastily put together by the Gothic Serpents on board *Intrepid*, was to haul ions down to the planet with a wing of unmanned hunter-killer flight drones. The anti-air defenses would pick up the drones, hopefully shooting them down slowly enough that the shuttle had time to deliver its cargo before the zhee in the towers could manually sight and fire on them.

Anti-air bursts and blaster fire streaked all around the shuttle. Not close enough to hit, but close enough to cause everyone on board to continually pucker and flinch.

"I feel like our legs are gonna get shot off hanging over the sides like this," complained Masters over the comm.

The pilot reminded the legionnaire why this was necessary. "You boys are gonna have to get off my ship *real* quick once we reach a clean building. No time for quick ropes. Sure as hell no time to give you a soft touch."

"We're jumping out and hoping it doesn't suck," said Chhun as he watched the target building approach. A heavy deluge of blaster fire was being exchanged between the QRF and the zhee. It reminded him of Kublar.

"I guess we'll just bill the Legion for our knee replacement surgeries," said Masters.

"Spoiler alert," Fish joked. "We aren't going to live long enough to need 'em."

"The thing I like about you, Fish," Masters said, his tone thoughtful, "is how upbeat you are."

Two more drones exploded in a flash. The shuttle reduced speed for its final approach.

"Here we go," muttered Bear, probably to himself, but it was still discernible over L-comm. Jumps and falls were always harder on the big guys.

The shuttle streaked toward a three-story building at the very edge of the QRF's defensive perimeter. A handful of zhee were sending plunging fire from the rooftop down onto the legionnaires. The shuttle pilot sent a lancing stream of laser blasts down at them, sending the zhee diving for cover or right off the edge.

"Jump time!" the pilot called.

The legionnaires hopped off without hesitation. They crashed onto the roof, rolling and bouncing like spent beer cans tossed from a speeding sled. Chhun watched as his N-18 sniper rifle skidded across the deck. He wasn't worried about the weapon becoming non-functional—they were tough rifles, built by an arms manufacturer that actually *cared* about the men who would use them in combat— but at the speed it was moving, Chhun was concerned that it might clatter over the edge and down into the mob of zhee pressing the streets.

"Bear!" Chhun called out.

The burly legionnaire, who was just now regathering his senses after bouncing into the low parapet wall at the roof's edge, threw out a palm and grabbed the rifle in mid-flight.

"Thanks." Chhun looked around. Masters was already putting his old koob sword to use by finishing off the wounded zhee still on the roof even as they struggled against their wounds in an attempt to fight their new arrivals. Fish was limping badly as he moved to set up his SAB.

"Captain," Masters called. "My bucket's telling me that these zhee are all hopped up on stim-cot. Gonna be tough to kill."

This wasn't unusual for zhee. They often loaded themselves up with enough of the narcotic that it seemed they almost became impervious to pain. Chhun moved to a dead zhee, and his bucket showed the parts-per-million readings in the air around the donk's mouth, which hung open in a grotesque death mask. They were stimmed up, all right. That was probably how they'd been able to even *try* to keep fighting after the way the shuttle's front guns ate up their legs and abdomens.

Chhun motioned for each man to take a position, and then gave a two-word order, more of a reminder, to his men in the event any zhee was able to surge past the quick reaction force and get back into the building. "Head shots."

The four Dark Ops men spread to the four corners of the square roof. As Chhun set up his N-18, Fish sent plunging fire into the vanguard of the mobbing zhee, halting their progress. Masters and Bear engaged the zhee on other nearby rooftops, dropping the surprised aliens and keeping them pinned down.

Chhun hailed the QRF over the L-comm. "Thought you guys could use a little help."

"Damn straight," replied a voice, "even if it does mean that Dark Ops is gonna take all the credit."

Chhun smiled to himself. "Who's this?"

"Sergeant Vix—Grinder Ten."

"Captain Chhun, Victory Squad. You're in charge?"

"Lieutenant Po went down so... yeah."

"You're doing a great job," Chhun said, adjusting his scope. "We're going to start demoralizing this mob of donks. I need you to keep up the KTF, but also to have a man on the twins who can make sure that no zhee gets the chance to come up and pay us a visit."

"Copy, Victory. And... thanks."

"Time to make 'em pay, Grinder."

Chhun searched the crowd for a target. He didn't bother with the front lines sending their ineffective return fire up at the building or toward the QRF. Fish, Masters, and Bear would keep them at bay. The captain looked farther back, amid the crowd, seeking out a particular type of enemy. He spotted what he was looking for.

A male donk stood right in the middle of the sea of aliens, surrounded by women and children. He was armed with a PK-9A blaster rifle, but the weapon wasn't being used; it wasn't even pointed at the Legion. Instead it looked like a prop, slung over a shoulder and pointing into the air. The donk waved his arm to accentuate his shouts, urging other armed zhee—all of them clearly younger by the coloration of their fur—to the front.

This was how it worked. How it always worked.

Chhun lined up the donk's head in his sights, held his breath, and squeezed the trigger. The zhee's head blew apart in a mix of cooked meat from the heat of the blaster bolt and gore from the kinetic force of the super-heated particle striking the target. Three more zhee, standing behind the target, dropped as well, as the shot continued through them. Twenties would have been proud.

The zhee in that section of the mob, their feeling of safety and security violently ripped away, began to surge and panic, pushing and shoving to get clear of the newfound danger. The donks who had been urged forward hesitated. Chhun searched for another target, and repeated the process until the crowd was a boiling mix of rage— as it had already been—and fearful panic.

18

Captain Besson and Corporal Davies took Battery Six at the top of the air defense tower. Once they'd scaled to the top of the first concrete protected battery, they'd found the rest of First Squad covering all the entrances onto the gun platform. The donk crew that had been operating and guarding the weapon lay blasted and dead on the deck. The noise of the blaster fire that had taken them down had been drowned out by the steady, thunderous backbeat of all the guns working across all the other platforms.

"Shadow Actual, this is Pit Fiend," announced an incoming transmission over L-comm. Pit Fiend was the identifier for the Recon Operations commander. "We need your battery offline in the next two minutes. They're firing straight into the *Sirocco*."

"Stand by," said Besson, and sent his men to secure the guns between the platform and the fire control. In the event he failed to knock out the command and control center, he hoped the other teams would at least disable some of the guns currently firing into the nearest assault carrier beached out there on the desert floor.

"I'll hit the fire control room now," he replied. "Davies, you're on me."

He and Davies took the ladders up onto the tower, climbing away from the cacophony of the working guns. As they ascended, he wondered why the donks weren't watching the closed-circuit feeds. If they were, then they'd see they were under direct attack. *Because they're donks*, he reminded himself.

He didn't like that he was having to gamble the whole operation on how stupid and lazy the donks were when it came to any task besides actual front line combat. They did excel at that—to the point of being noted as "capable" in any Legion intel assessment—but when it came to secondary tasks, the zhee merely could not be bothered to put in much effort. Still, everything Besson had learned in Legion OCS had told him never to bet on any opponent's weakness. Never hope to get lucky because the other guy has decided to put in half effort. Expect as good as you give.

But he had no choice. He had to take that gamble, because it was the only way to shut down all the active air defense turrets currently engaging at range with the carrier assault group. He *had* to bet the zhee were too lazy to bother monitoring their perimeter security feeds.

The two legionnaires gained the uppermost catwalk that surrounded the fire control center that ran the entire battery. Above the wide windows of the control center, the targeting and acquisition geodesic dome was the highest point on the tower.

Blaster fire erupted from the control room. The zhee were shooting through the glass at them. Besson ducked; he had no time to see if Davies had done so as well.

"On your six, sir," whispered Davies over L-comm.

"Bangers," replied Besson, using an alternate identifier for ear-poppers popular within his Legion. "On three, then I'll pop up and fire. You go for the access hatch. If I get killed, there's a drive located in my intel pouch. Get that in their system and execute run."

"Affirmative," Davies replied as breezily as though they were just running some sand table walkthrough exercise for an afternoon training session. Never mind all the shattering and fused glass raining down on their armor. Or the battle going on across the desert floor. Or the concussive *whump-whumps* of the displaced energy guns. Over ambient they could hear the muffled braying of the donks working themselves up into a battle froth. L-comm translators gave a read on what was being screamed.

"Defend me, pack-brothers! There are no gods but the Four!"

The two legionnaires popped their bangers and hooked them in through the gaps in the broken glass to land on the fire control center floor. Besson counted off audibly as the armor dimmed and hardened itself against the impending EMP effect of the explosives. A nice detail newer Legion armor had decided to do without. And this action caused Besson to remember that they'd be using iron sights for at least five seconds before the armor rebooted the HUD and L-comm once more.

The bangers went off like the tinkling of distant broken glass. Besson popped up and counted six zhee, every one of them clutching madly at their floppy over-sized ears. Giant buckteeth gnashed in pain. Large baleful eyes almost rolled back into their heads.

Besson remembered another small detail.

The zhee, because of their ears, were highly affected by bangers. But they would recover fast. Not because they could hear again or even stand up straight, but because they were born berserkers. Even in a maddening pain to the point of blindness, they'd just start firing wildly, never mind the consequences. Which, in a way, still made them very, very dangerous.

Six of 'em.

Out of the corner of his eye, he saw Davies bolt forward, pounding down the catwalk just beyond the smashed main window of the fire control station.

Besson began to fire. He hit the nearest one in the chest. These zhee weren't wearing armor. As fast as he could, he pivoted and shot two more while Davies executed a hard left along the catwalk and ran for the access hatch.

Shot discipline and breath control allowed Besson to hit another as the donk began to pivot, readying to fire.

In some distant part of his mind, the captain knew they were still blind and yet somehow, in their weird donk brains, they knew right where the access hatch was. Knew that the attack would come from there. Both the remaining zhee pivoted and began to fire at the hatch as Davies smashed through it, firing.

One shot caught him right in the chest and spun him around into the wall.

Besson blew the head off the nearest firing donk as Davies, back against the wall, ventilated the last donk with a spray of N-4 blaster fire on full auto.

Besson was running now. Running as fast as he could, fearing the wound the other soldier had taken was fatal.

I should have gone through the hatch! he screamed at himself, and he heard that long-lost and most fearsome of drill sergeants tell him, *"Straight up you shoulda, Bay-son."*

That sadistic NCO had always pronounced his name like it was a dirty word. "Bay-son."

"Now you got one of yours killed. You gonna make a real fine officer. A regular point you are, candidate."

In Legion OCS, unlike the military academies, trainees were called candidates.

Besson made it to the downed man.

"Corporal Davies..." His combat medical training had kicked in. Always get the wounded man's attention first. Next ask where he's been hit.

"All good, sir. Got a bounce."

The armor had deflected the shot.

"But it feels like I got hit in the chest with a sledgehammer! Still KTF, sir!"

Waves of relief washed over Besson, and he felt his voice catch in his throat. He hated, above all things, losing men. If you were to ask him what his job as a Legion officer really was, he'd have told you getting everyone home safely was his job. Or at least, the most important one to him. It both was and wasn't his job. But he did it nonetheless.

"KTF, Davies!"

"You sure did, sir!" coughed Davies. "Nice shooting, Captain. Didn't think I was gonna get a chance to contribute. But lookie there... I did," he said, pointing at the blaster-mutilated zhee on the floor of the fire control center.

As Besson helped Davies to his feet, he saw the massive blaster sear on the right side of the man's chest plate.

"What're the odds," said Davies, looking down at the black scorch mark and laughing.

"Million to one, some say. But the manual says one in ten… if you believe that," Besson replied.

"Probably written by some point who never geared up, sir." Davies struggled to get a full breath. Medical diagnostic assessment said the man had two broken ribs.

"Probably."

Besson moved over the master fire control panel for the battery. He found a data input port and plugged in his drive. When he got a single line message asking him if he'd like to execute the file. He confirmed.

The constant cacophonic thunder that had almost faded into the background as some kind of permanent white noise… ceased. Here, at this battery, and at the rest of the air defense towers across the desert floor surrounding the Gibraltaar Rock, their fire missions were suspended. The entire air defense network surrounding Gibraltaar Rock was offline for the foreseeable future.

Of course the donks had never bothered to rewrite their security protocols for fire control. They were too busy waiting around to die gloriously for their four gods.

***

Once the tower had been secured, Captain Besson had assumed all elements of Shadow would be re-tasked. But then he'd seen the massive engagement going down on the sands before the trenches. Or more to the point, he'd listened. And judging by the battle chatter they could access through the L-comm, the battle had quickly devolved into a street brawl between masses of zhee and Legion companies. The Legion units had taken the outer defensive wall that guarded the trenches, and the trench fighting had turned thick and hot.

Besson advised command that they could redeploy forward into the trenches now that the air defense towers were all but useless. Each request was denied with a terse, "Hold position."

And so Besson and his fellow legionnaires could only stand by and watch.

Out there above the burning sands that shimmered between the captured air defense towers and the massive bulk of the rising Fortress Gibraltaar, SLICs made gun runs on targets inside the trench works maze. Falling artillery sent massive plumes of gray dust and smoke into the hot desert sky. To the legionnaires of Shadow, watching from the tower, it was like seeing some distant circus in the night they desperately wanted to be a part of.

The ached for a ticket to ride.

If asked, they would have told you they were more than willing to pay the price of admission.

Finally, five minutes after a coordinated massive artillery barrage from every battery on the assault carriers' upper gun platform decks, the orders for Shadow came in over L-comm.

Detach one squad to guard the tower. The rest of Shadow is going in.

Warpig was being left behind with what remained of Second Squad, which had taken the brunt of the beating on the access stairway. First, Third, and Fourth headed toward the rooftop landing pad to hitch a ride with some inbound SLICs.

On the horizon and headed straight at them—never mind the AA fire coming off the fortress and going after anything airborne—were two SLIC gunships dripping with auto-turret pods and AGMs, and one oversized operations SLIC. The operations SLIC set down on the tower landing pad amid a howl of engine whine and repulsor noise, while the two gunships held station over the tower, circling like lethal birds of prey. The legionnaires hustled from the access stairs below the wide landing pad and heaved themselves and their tactical rucks into the waiting dropship.

The big surprise was who was already on board. In addition to the two door gunners on the cargo deck, there was one other figure. L-comm identified that legionnaire as General Hannubal himself. Or... Warlord.

When Captain Besson was aboard and had his count, he gave a thumbs-up to the crew chief, and the SLIC's thrusters spooled up. The repulsors dropped down into their deep hum liftoff range as the bird departed the pad and pivoted, picking up an inbound course on the trenches.

Warlord was busy distributing charge packs and rations while one of the crew chiefs handed out fragger bandoliers deployed from a drop-down rack.

"Take as much as you want to carry," offered Warlord over the L-comm, talking directly to the whole platoon. "But I advise you to take all the explosives you can get. You're headed for some bunker busting, Leejes."

The SLIC rocked back and forth, dodging incoming fire. The gunship off the port side opened up with a hypnotic stream of blaster pod fire on some ground target.

"Captain Besson." Warlord was now talking via the command channel. "Bit of a mission here for you. Need you to re-form on the ground. We're assigning you a new designation and giving you a reinforced company to take an assault lane appearing on your HUD now."

"Can do, sir!" replied Besson as he studied the map he was seeing on his HUD overlay.

"Two Nine and Three Sixteen were devastated. As were a couple of other battalions. They got hit hard by the donks. At the LZ, you will enter the new grouping as commander of an ad hoc assault team we're designating Dog Company. I need you to bust those bunkers along the lane and set up overwatch on the main entrance. Once you're in position, we're gonna push hard on the main entrance with two full battalions."

"Roger that, sir."

The flight streaked over the smoking ruins of an HK-PP that had gone down nose first into the sand. Most likely hit by one of Gibraltaar's anti-armor batteries.

The crew chief held up one finger, meaning one minute to insertion.

Besson tapped his helmet twice in reply, indicating they were ready.

Every leej on the cargo deck repeated the gesture, signaling they too were ready.

The fire beyond the open cargo doors filled the sky as the dropship jinked left and then right to avoid being hit. They were getting close to the trenches now. Besson could see dead legionnaires lying along the wide concrete paths, sometimes hidden by the late morning shadows, sometimes lying in a patch of sunlight that had found its way down onto a trench floor. He could also see small firefights between Legion companies and entrenched defenders whose bunkers hadn't been overrun yet. And there were, of course, a lot of zhee dead.

The SLIC's thrust-reversers kicked in sharply, and the ship executed a hard turn to port, heeling over and circling the LZ marked out inside the trenches. Red smoke flares indicated where the ship would put down.

"Do your best, Captain," said Warlord. "That's all the Legion ever expects of you."

The dropship flared and descended below the trench works onto a wide concrete pad that might have been some inner parade ground set up within the defensive perimeter. Battered legionnaires lay or sat with their backs against the walls, while others, N-42 teams, watched the entrances for a counter-assault. The crew chief began to shout over L-comm for the legionnaires to "Move! Move! Move!"

Quickly and with perfect order, Besson and the legionnaires dropped off the cargo door and onto the concrete foundation of the LZ within the trenches.

"Assault team L-comm is set up, Captain," continued the general over the comm. "You've got an old sergeant major for your senior NCO. Trust him. He's saved many a worse officer than yourself, and his men, from some fool's folly. I know—he saved me once. But he talks a blue streak."

Besson, hunched and trotting away from the bird, half turned and saluted as the dropship lifted up and out of the trench. It then streaked off and away toward some other errand that needed attending to on some other part of the battlefield.

Besson ran toward a group of NCOs near one of the N-42 positions. Via HUD tag, the sergeant major was made clear. Already the senior NCO was stepping out to meet his new captain.

"Cap'n," said the old sergeant major. "Sergeant Major Julius MakRaven. I hear we need to kill a bunch of donks, sir. Welcome to Dog Company, sir."

19

Cassius felt the sensation of many hands, which were really thick and hairy claws, grabbing at him roughly. Slapping and beating him. More hands pulled him along by his arms and one leg; they let the broken leg drag. He was dimly aware of that much, and thought it odd that he didn't feel anything.

There was no mercy in how he was being handled. No desire to rescue. Just an urgency that felt dangerous. And wild.

He blinked away the darkness of the kick to the head. He was still at the crash site; they hadn't moved him far. The zhee were all around, dancing, twirling, firing their blasters in the air. They jumped up and down and off of the shuttle. They were celebrating. Waving their *kankari* knives. Cutting themselves. And each other. In an ecstasy of violence and blood.

They were celebrating the crash of a ship that killed the Republic personnel on board. They were celebrating even more the two dead legionnaires they'd killed themselves. Several of them were currently beating the corpses, cutting them. Some took large bites out of the exposed flesh once the armor was stripped.

To hear the zhee's huffy snorts and braying ululations, this was like winning some unexpected lottery that had fallen from the sky. It was the joy of the underdog beating a venerated and unstoppable sports team—a cross-town rival. Or celebrating the birth of a long-hoped-for child. Their exuberant celebration was that joyous.

It was not a private moment, either. It was all captured on live streaming digital, and broadcast on social media. Citizen journalists, using their own holocams and drones. Everything was captured and distributed far faster than the Republic could block it from going wide. Republic hackers just weren't that good. They worked for the government, after all. And of course there were so many others that were more than willing to help make the Galactic Republic, and the Legion by default, look bad. The MCR would help, of course. And so there was mass dissemination of this horror show, of the victory taking place on the hot and dusty streets of the zhee slums that surrounded Ankalor City.

The galaxy watched in rapt attention. Knowing that this was important—another Kublar, perhaps?—but not knowing just how significant. They didn't realize that Article Nineteen, the Champion Clause, was about to be proclaimed on the floor of the Senate and House of Reason. It would be proclaimed by a legionnaire who had received the Order of the Centurion. A man who had lost much in the service of the Republic, and was now declaring that his service would not be in vain.

Arrests were in the planning stages. Kill teams were preparing for the three a.m. door-kicker raids.

But the galaxy didn't know about that. Not yet. And they likely didn't see what would come next. They didn't realize that this triumphal zhee celebration was something the Republic might use against the Legion itself. Because for so long now, to most everybody in the galaxy, the Legion and the Republic were one and the same.

Most of the galactic information and entertainment webs focused their streams on Cassius's fate. He was still alive. And the galaxy had to know... what would happen next?

They did cut away to the dead body of a Dark Ops legionnaire whenever something particularly indignant was done to it by the zhee. Those men were dragged by the crowds, sometimes in opposite directions, until their battered and broken bodies tore apart. The zhee wore their armor as trophies. They cut out and ate their eyes. They desecrated those warriors. It wasn't pretty.

What was being done to the pilot wasn't much better. From time to time it seemed that the man with just the first hints of silver in his dark hair would begin to regain consciousness—and then those around him, his honor guard of pain, would beat him savagely until his head fell limp once more. This occurred repeatedly before he was tossed unceremoniously into the back of a repulsor truck.

It was at this point that the feeds all changed to a broadcast sent out directly by the zhee interrogators. Finally, the enrapt viewers could hear what was said; they could hear Cassius's feeble, almost delirious answers.

What they didn't know was that it was a farce of an interrogation—a false search for information his interrogators knew he didn't possess.

After a time, the cameras cut to the Legion base in the Green Zone, though the view was restricted by the no-fly zone. The feed focused on the main gates, which remained closed. The cheering, bloodthirsty crowds parted as if on command, and the sled carrying the pilot inched by. The crowd fired their blasters and danced with each other in joyous gaiety.

In the back of the truck, ten zhee took turns beating the pilot's body. They avoided the head, correctly judging that he couldn't withstand many more blows there.

"Who are you?" brayed a zhee.

Cassius could only croak. "Chief... Warrant... Offic—"

A kick to the stomach. "You are Legion!"

"N-no. No... I'm an officer in the Republic... Army."

A kick to his broken leg caused the useless limb to flop. Caused Cassius to scream in agony. Caused him to slip back into unconsciousness.

"You are Legion! You bring Legion assassins to kill zhee!"

"What is your strength?"

"Who is your general?"

They asked for all kinds of ridiculous information he'd didn't have. All kinds of ridiculous questions he couldn't answer, even had he been conscious.

The zhee worked themselves into a kind of frenzy. They took turns coming in at him to yell and spit in his face and then deliver some savage and unexpected blow with a balled-up claw or the butt of a blaster. And with each blow they got wilder. Their speech raced. At the end they were braying like wild animals.

Yet Cassius didn't emerge from that deep dark place called unconsciousness.

So it was then that they humiliated him.

As was their way.

When the sled arrived deep in the no-go zones of the slums, Cassius was dragged out onto a quiet street that dead-ended in a courtyard of ruined old colonial warehouses. Down the way, two zhee children were throwing small knives at a dead cat in the gutter. They stopped to watch the Repub pilot being dragged into a dark building. The children knew they were never to go near that building. They returned to their game of knives, focusing intently on getting their throws just right. Not minding the screams coming from within the dark warehouse.

For a time, there was nothing more. No feeds from inside the warehouse. No continuation of the important "breaking story" that was a man's life. For two hours, there was nothing for the citizens of the Republic to be entertained by but overhead shots of the braying crowds. Two hours in which drone recon *could* have sent out a team to find the pilot. The Green Zone feeds showed a column of combat sleds and tanks—vehicles that hadn't left the wire—sitting idle. Military experts, most of whom had never seen combat or served in the Legion, postulated about why that was the case. But any leej watching knew. They knew why those vehicles hadn't moved, and they cursed the points and the Republic for it.

Then a new holofeed came through. It starts inside the warehouse. It is a live feed, transmitted by the zhee who hold the pilot's life in their clutches.

The pilot is tied to a chair. One overhead, hot, white light is staring down onto his bloodlessly pale and blood-spattered face. Eye swollen shut. Left cheek caved in.

The video records nothing about who Cassius is. Or was. It does not tell you that he is a husband. A father. A son. A brother. A friend. A neighbor. It does not tell you that he was once a kid who collected that thing we all collected that year when the galaxy didn't seem such a dangerous place. Or that he broke his arm that summer. Or wrote a song once to a girl he loved. Or had hopes and dreams. Or *was* someone's hope, someone's dream.

When the woman who bore him first held him and dreamed of all the things he might be one day.

The camera records none of those things.

It just records a man tied to chair. And it is immediately clear that something bad is about to happen. This is one of those videos that will someday—on whatever site you happen to be surfing, looking to be momentarily entertained and distracted—come with a warning.

Beware. Graphic Content.

Maybe it's even blacked out.

All you have to do is press a button on the screen, and it will allow you to see something you never wanted to. Or at least, that's what you'll think later when you can't get the images out of your mind.

You'll wish you'd never watched.

A large zhee comes into frame. He is wearing a black hood, so his features are hidden. But this zhee is not like all the other zhee. To him, they are inferior. To them, he is a leader. Someone to be admired. To be feared. To be obeyed. That is clear from the moment he walks into frame to stand near the captured pilot tied to the chair. Sitting beneath the glare of a lone hot white light.

He begins to speak the zhee language.

A translation appears at the bottom of the screen.

"I come to you by the will of the Four. Your servant. Your pack leader. By now you will notice, my pack brothers, that the Republic has sent their Legion dogs to shoot and kill us once again. Just before dawn, one of our royal guardsmen shot down a dropship full of assassins come to slay us in silence. *This*"—he gestures to the bound man—"was one of them. He was sent to kill us in our sleep. And we have captured him."

Pause.

The *kankari* knife comes out. This is the part where you should maybe turn the video off. You should stop it. You know the story. You know where this is going. You've seen enough dictators hanged. Or begging for their lives at their pathetic last. The Republic, and really the House of Reason, has a fun little habit of destabilizing petty potentates who end badly. Only to replace them with their own brand of tyrant. One who gives them a bigger slice of the pie.

But don't tell anyone that.

"More are coming. The assassins will meet their deaths," the large zhee says into the camera, in his own language. "In the streets. On the battlefield. In the skies above. Even now our powerful fleet is returning to deal with this menace, raining down fire and fury. And until that time I am asking you to rise up, brothers. Our ponies. Our colts. All zhee of all the tribes worshipping each of the Four are called now to the Whirlwind of the Centauro. It is time for the holiest of wars. *The Centauro.*"

He turns to the pilot, who seems strangely calm given what looks certain to happen. Maybe they have drugged him. Or maybe they have beaten him to such a state that death seems a welcome escape.

Who can say?

When one watches these kind of videos... who really knows?

"We have passed the place of bargaining and peace agreements that mean nothing to you. For you, for the Legion dogs attacking our palace at the rock of Kibbel Ba-Ram, there is only one kind of death that is acceptable. You have violated our ancient laws. Our rights. Our people. And this is your fate. The death of foreigners and thieves."

The hooded zhee says the word that indicates the technique.

But there is no translation on screen.

Long has the House of Reason claimed no such thing exists in such a rich, noble, and diverse culture as the zhee. And though the translation fails, the lie that it does not exist will be revealed. Scholars, and soon everyone who sees the feeds and watches the punditry, will know the word exists. And they'll know its meaning, without needing to be told.

Because they watched.

Death by a Thousand Cuts.

If it is done properly by a zhee of great standing and skilled expertise, the victim will survive each and every single pain-filled cut of the thousand.

It takes hours.

The last is a mercy to the pilot tied to the chair. Screaming and screaming.

He was once someone's dream.

The last cut is the kindest. In a way.

The zhee watching will take to the streets. Ready to spend the lives of others, no matter the cost, in the cause of the Four. They surge out into the maelstrom of the slums, ready to become the Centauro.

The Holiest of Wars has begun.

2Ø

As the battle entered its second phase within the trench system, beneath the mushroom cap of the base's deflectors, First Team of the newly established Dog Company went forward to do their part in cracking the first bunker the unit had been assigned to take—a bunker they needed to take in order to reach the second ring of the trench works. But the ensuing firefight between the bunkered zhee and the leejes in First Team was merely a diversion. PFC Huzu, following Sergeant Major MakRaven and all the other legionnaires grouped into Second Team, were the main assault force. They were staging in an access trench that ran alongside the main passage to the first bunker.

The push to take more than fifteen designated assault lanes had ramped up across the first ring. Legion counter-sniper teams had found positions in and under the base's deflector shield, and were firing up onto the rock itself. Their objective was to knock down blaster turrets and take out any zhee snipers who tried to fire down at the advancing legionnaires in the trenches. Casualty collection points had been set up to the rear of the trenches, and medical SLICs were coming in under fire to pull

271

the wounded out of harm's way. The dead were stacked to wait until hostilities ceased.

From behind the bunker's dark firing slits, three N-50s blared forth in hot bright streams of blaster-dealt death. Legion marksmen carrying N-18s popped out from the Legion-held portions of the trench and tried to put shots through the firing slits. Traffic over the L-comm indicated they were getting kills, but of course the donks were stuffed full in there, and the downloaded base plans the Legion had access to indicated there was an artery resupply corridor that could bring a lot more troops up into the bunker as casualties mounted.

Captain Besson called in a fire support mission and got some artillery dedicated, but it did little more than leave blast marks across the duracrete surface of the trench before the bunker. Further and more extensive fire missions were denied due to the tremendous amount of requests coming in from all across the lines. In the end, there were no two ways about it. The bunker would have to be taken out head-on by breaching teams. One N-50 was more than murderous enough to knock down a company of legionnaires in armor; three was pure overkill.

As the leejes in Second Team waited with their backs to the wall in the smaller trench, a tremendous explosion shook the duracrete all around theme. "Looks like they got theirs," remarked Sergeant Franceschini—one of the scouts from Shadow First Platoon who'd been folded into the new Dog Company. "Must be nice."

"Aw, now don't fret there, young sergeant," said the sergeant major, winding up into one of his long-winded speeches. "You're gonna get yourself a chance to die gloriously for the Legion any moment now. I was once on a defense at Tangor Ridge out along the zhee frontier. Whole place was filled with this plant they call Scotch broom. It's wiry and thick and—"

"Pushing now," announced Captain Besson over the L-comm. Besson was leading First Team forward, broken down into a series of smaller teams, heading up the trench to grab cover and suppress the N-50s as best they could. In about two minutes, Second Team would flat-out rush the bunker from as close as the access trench could get. Then it was close in and lob explosives packs.

While getting shot to pieces.

"Almost time, boys. Say yer prayers," continued the sergeant major without pity or remorse. "Any-who, we was up on the ridge and the zhee was a-comin' out of the broom all night long, tryin' to probe our lines. We weren't much more than a platoon. I was a buck back then—that's how long ago this was, if you young'uns can believe that.

"So about dawn, I had this crazy no-account second lieutenant who was really not good for much when you came right down to it. But that don't mean he was worthless. Because that boy was a stone cold killer. Never should've been an officer. That was just a waste of good shooter. But as I said, he was a straight-up no-holds-barred killer. All night long when we was supposed to be watching our sector, he just slept like he knew they weren't comin' for us. About dark the night before he says to me, 'Sergeant, I'm gonna rack out. Tell me if anything happens.' You know the type. Not a leadership bone in his body.

"So I stand there all night waiting for the zhee to come through the wire and slit our throats, and about dawn they attack in full. 'Cept the attack is way down the line in someone else's sector. And this LT hears the fire, gets up, and says, 'Hey, Sergeant! They're not comin' through this way, so let's counterattack their flank and roll 'em up.' So of course I remind the officer that we're a-'sposed to just hold the line in case they come through this way. Two minutes later he orders me out of the trench and goes running off down into the broom.

"Well, for the next ten minutes it was just the two of us runnin' around in there killin' zhee. They had no idea we was even in among them. Hell, lookin' back at it, we were most liked to get ourselves shot by our own up on the side of the volcano. Anyway, that boy was a *killer*. Killed a whole bunch of 'em. Stopped the whole zhee strike dead in its tracks. And there was a lot of 'em. They got freaked out and ran off after a while. But if they woulda kept pushing, they mighta broke through our line and got at those colonists. So he was right about that. In fact he was right... right up till he got killed in there."

"Killed?" said a legionnaire.

"Thirty seconds, boys. Blasters up. Full tilt and get them bang bangs in close. Once you let 'em go, get down and throw up covering fire. So yeah, the LT... he was kilt deader'n stone. We got surrounded, and the zhee were shootin' into the broom from all around us. Killed the LT and wounded me. They stabbed me real quick on the way outta town but didn't cut nothin' on me but a bit of muscle. We was dry on charge packs by then anyway.

"Couple a minutes later some of our own came in and pulled us out. Thought I was dead that time. Might be today from the look of it, with how big a show the zhee are puttin' on. But I must say: I've lived a good long life, unlike most of you. And so, for those of you about to die... I am much sorrier for you than myself. You have not been afforded the opportunity to die as many times as I have."

MakRaven fell silent. No one said a word.

The order to assault came in from Captain Besson.

Huzu and the other legionnaires leapt into action. They streamed out of the secondary access trench and into the main one that was being guarded by the three murderous N-50s. They ran right toward the bunker, N-4 in one hand, satchel charge in the other.

The corridor was filled with blaster fire from all directions. The N-50s opened up in a hurricane of bright red fire, blasting the duracrete around the legionnaires to chips. Twenty meters ahead of the surging men was a holographic line, visible only in the Legion HUDs, showing the range they had to reach to lob the explosives for effect at the bunkers.

Bolts seared the air around Huzu as his legs pumped hard to take him to the line so he could deploy his explosive. The leej next to him outpaced him, only to be taken down by a blaster bolt. Huzu had no idea if any of the other leejes were even still behind him, and he expected at any second to be hit by fire and meet the same fate as the man who'd just fallen. And that final bolt, the one with his name on it, could come from anywhere; everyone was firing at everyone. From behind him, he knew that First Team and Captain Besson were pouring down as much targeted fire as they could on the slits, even popping up to provide more targets for the zhee to shoot at while the assault team hustled forward under intense N-50 fire.

And in that moment, Huzu felt like a legionnaire. Which was all he'd ever really wanted to be. Every moment up until this one, even when he'd completed Basic, or been in other situations, had felt like a debt incurred. A debt that promised the redeemer he was indeed a legionnaire. And now, in this moment, as scared to death as he was, he knew he was good for the debt.

And to that young boy becoming a man... that was everything the galaxy had to offer.

Huzu stumbled and fell, thinking he must have been hit so badly he didn't even feel it. Thinking maybe an N-50 blaster bolt had gone straight through his armor and severed his spine, denying him the ability to feel his own passing. But he disregarded that thought and crawled forward under the continuing barrage of whining blaster fire.

Someone was screaming unintelligibly over L-comm. They were either hit or directing fire.

Five meters to the range line. Huzu struggled forward, feeling his body become distant and useless. He wasn't hit; it was just the fear of being hit that was trying to carry him off and make him lie down and curl up. He concentrated on working all four limbs. He crawled forward as fast as he could, dragging his battle rifle with him, forcing himself to stay here for just one more moment.

Another leej ran past him and dove for the line, narrowly missing being hit by a concentration of N-50 fire that shifted and raked the front of the trench. The leej pulled the cord on the satchel charge and flung it forward at the bunker.

The throw didn't make it. The charge bounced off and landed in front of the solid bunker wall. Its explosion blew the legionnaire back past Huzu.

Huzu reached the line marked on his HUD. He made ready to hook his own charge into the firing positions within the bunker.

"Not just yet, son!" cried Sergeant Major MakRaven, who had crawled up next to him. Blaster pistol in hand, the NCO reached over and pulled Huzu's arming cord.

"Now!" he yelled.

Huzu flung it.

The charge disappeared behind the dark slits of the firing windows from which the zhee blazed away at Dog Company.

The N-50s stopped at once.

And then an explosion shattered the bunker from within. Duracrete was sent flying in all directions. The explosion was so powerful it knocked Huzu's HUD offline for a moment. Sand and grit washed over him in a powerful wave, lifting his armored body off the floor of the trench. The force seemed to squeeze every cell in his body. Even the air in his lungs, which was guarded by the armor's self-contained breathing system, was compressed beyond reach.

The explosion was like a massive *crack* in time, space, and reality. And then a dull boom that seemed to hover over the world. And Huzu thought...

This is what it feels like to die.

For at least a minute after he picked up his bucketed head from the floor of the trench, all he could see through the HUD was swirling smoke. Light debris rained down on his armor, unfelt and yet distantly a part of him.

Then he heard the sergeant major laughing over the rebooting L-comm. He looked up from the raining grit and swirling dust to see the old leej sitting on his butt next to him. Slapping one knee. And laughing. Shaking with laughter.

"Don't get any closer'n that, does it, son?"

***

First Team, with Captain Besson on point, swept the shattered remains of the destroyed bunker. Its back half looked out onto a maze of trenches running into the second ring of the defenses. Some of the battle along the flanks was visible from here, and for a moment, once Sergeant Major MakRaven had come forward, he just stood in the shadows, observing the other battles out loud over the L-comm, as was his way.

"Looks like Wurzt's boys are having a tough time of it over there. And from what I can see, them zhee got a pretty good crossfire going on that trench it looks like they're supposed to take. Gonna be hell to pay for those losses."

He clung to the wall, deep in the shadows, and observed the other flank. Snipers were still firing down from Gibraltaar Rock into the trenches.

"They're all mixed in over there. Whoever's runnin' that show down there is runnin' it like a ate-up point. No clear lines. Look at that! You got a leej platoon about a hair's-breadth away and firing off at something, and they don't even see the zhee comin' up on their right."

The sergeant major went off Dog Company's L-comm to yell at the tactical overwatch and alert them to whoever it was that was about to get flanked by the zhee.

Besson and two other legionnaires rooted around in the destruction, looking for something. Huzu stood watch near a small staircase that led down into the trenches toward the left flank. If the zhee counterattacked the bunker in order to retake the ground, they'd come from there.

"Found it, sir," announced one of the legionnaires. Besson moved low, avoiding windows of fire that would have allowed the zhee to shoot down into the blasted bunker. Off in the distance, another massive explosion rocked the trenches, and the sergeant major was back over L-comm wondering who that was. He finished off with a "Hope it's one of ours gettin' their objective!"

Besson came over the L-comm. "We've found the access passage that should take us in under the second ring. There's a good chance the zhee didn't have time to figure out the bunker system and these lower tunnels, but that doesn't mean it's unguarded. The original intent of the designers was to build a tunnel system by which some new drones and bots they were developing could be moved forward as the lines collapsed. The idea was to allow the drones to pop up behind the enemy and—"

"Thought war bots were illegal now," interrupted Sergeant Davies.

"They are, son," said the sergeant major, his band saw voice winding up to override further discussion. "But that don't mean the House of Reason and the Legion don't stop playin' around with the idea of 'em. Off-book development and all that spooky stuff. Them big brains do like to invent new Frankenbots to play with all the time, no never mind who has to go out and fight 'em." He turned to address the captain. "Any indications, sir, of what kind of bot we'll be fightin'? Ran into a re-purposed THK once and chewed up half the platoon trying to put the thing down. And can you believe it, it had only one arm. Musta been blown off at the Sayed Massacre and someone left it for junk. Then probably found its way onto the black market."

"None, Sergeant Major," said the captain. "And there's still a chance we might meet some zhee down there. So, men, we're leaving First Team here to watch the assault lane and move forward to hold the line with the elements on our flanks. Reinforcements are coming up through the trenches as we speak. I'll take Second Team down in there, and we'll move forward under the next set of defenses. There's a route map appearing in your HUDs now. Anything happens, stay on mission and reach our objective marked Oscar Whiskey. Tie in on main L-comm and provide cover fire for the assault on the base main entrance. Got it?"

All the leejes in Second tapped their buckets, and Besson set to organizing an order of march while the sergeant major redistributed charge packs and fraggers.

"We'll need all your ear-poppers down there more than the fraggers," MakRaven said. "Bots don't like 'em and neither do the zhee."

Captain Besson switched channels to command and linked direct with the old sergeant major.

"I'd like you to stay with First, Sergeant Major—"

"No, sir," interrupted the sergeant major genially enough. But his tone was clear, and Besson knew that what a senior NCO of the rank of sergeant major suggested wasn't really a suggestion. Good officers took their suggestions as orders. "I think it might be a good idea to go down there with you if you are so inclined," MakRaven continued. "The team leader for First is a platoon sergeant anyway. And he can keep 'em moving alongside the advance line. But it's probably going to get hairy down there, and you seem the type of officer that likes to try to do everything himself. Which is the kind of officer that gets killed a lot—y'know, because he's doing everything. And far be it for me to stand in the way of a fine officer like yourself leadin' by example, but in the more than likely chance you do manage to get yourself kilt, these boys will need my calming influence to keep them on mission down there. Tunnel work, even for leejes, sir, is what separates the crazy from the sane. Different kinda work altogether, and it can make a man crazier faster than a tyrannasquid can drag you down and crush you in the dark. And, I further suspect that if the donks have a clan of Crimson Knives in the mix, well, those slippery little suckers will have found a way down in the dark where they like to work. And they can be a bit tricky, sir, which is about as mild an understatement as this senior NCO is willing to make at this time."

The captain was silent for a moment, weighing the sergeant major's words and reaching a decision. When he knew there was no decision to reach. It had been made the moment the sergeant major had inserted himself into the equation.

"Crimson Knives?" asked Captain Besson.

"Yes, sir. It's a donk secret sect of deadly assassins that specialize in blind fighting. In fact they *are* actually blind. They rely on something the donks mostly forget that makes them far superior to us: sense of smell and hearing. And they got ways to knock our systems and detection out before they attack. So if it's all the same to you, sir, I'd like to attend that little soiree. I feel I might be of substantive use."

Again Besson was silent. Second Team was all stacked and ready. One of the legionnaires, Turnbull, had his cutting torch out, ready to cut the tunnel cover off and reveal the dark depths of the system that ran beneath their feet. A system possibly crawling with deadly bots and murderous zhee.

"I think that's a good idea, Sergeant Major. Thank you for your assistance."

"You're welcome, sir. But if you don't mind the correction, it is in fact a *terrible* idea for one who is most likely to retire after this little conflict, as I was plannin' on doin'. Still, until then, it is my job to keep you boys alive, or at least from unduly hurting yourselves. And I have learned a thing or two, mostly the hard way, in my many years as a hard-chargin' legionnaire."

21

"It's tight down here," said Davies over the Second Team L-comm as they followed the captain into the darkness. Low-light imaging revealed little more than a dark tube of silent gloom. From above their heads came the occasional distant heavy boom of an explosion, reminding them that the tunnel could collapse on them at any time.

"War is dangerous," opined the sergeant major after a particularly loud explosion. "That's why we get paid every month, young troopers."

No one murmured a reply over L-comm, though the sense of impending doom was palpable. Not that anyone, or even Davies, was complaining. But Davies was carrying the N-42. So he grunted a little bit more than the others as they duck-walked forward.

"You let me know if that big ol' blaster gets too heavy for you, young legionnaire," chided the sergeant major from the rear. "I ain't too old to hump the pig."

"What's a pig, Sergeant Major?" asked Davies as the squad hooked to the right to follow a new tunnel into further darkness.

"Pig's what we used to call the N-60. Fine weapon. So good at killin' donks that the House o' Reason reasoned it was an unfair advantage that affected the 'Tribes of Peace'—as they were calling 'em that year—disadvantageously. It was like a lighter version of the N-42. Barrel did have a propensity to melt down though. But if you knew what you were doin', you could make it work."

"Sounds nice," grunted Davies. "Especially the lighter part."

"I say again, young leej, I ain't too tired to carry—"

"Got it, Sergeant Major. Wouldn't want you to throw your back out."

The sergeant major muttered curses and promises, telling Davies once this op was done they would see whose back was out after a nice long run through the desert for some counseling PT. Davies remained silent after that. Every legionnaire had lived long enough to know that however old and broken they thought some NCO was, he could most likely run them into the ground for hours on end and not break a sweat.

"Got two bots ahead," whispered the captain over L-comm.

"Can you identify type, sir?" asked the sergeant major with unusual succinctness.

"Other than that they look like mech versions of thermascorpions... negative. Maybe the tail is some kind of blaster. But my capability assessment doesn't yield much. They're bots. They're probably guards. They're probably nasty."

The captain flashed a sand table overlay across Second Team's HUDs. The tactical map showed a T-intersection ahead. The two bots were guarding the branches of the T.

"Switching to EM sig to see if they're running," whispered the captain from point. He came back a moment later. "Low signature. They might not even be activated."

"Or they're in some kind of hibernation mode," offered one of the legionnaires close behind. "Set parameters might wake 'em up to active engage."

The sergeant major responded over L-comm. He didn't bother to use the whisper tone most legionnaires used during operations that required stealth. Whispering didn't make a difference—the leej bucket covered all internal sound and traffic. Someone could be standing right next to two legionnaires who were shouting at the top of their lungs over L-comm, and as long as ambient audio was squelched, they wouldn't hear a thing. Still, some situations just *felt* like they required a whisper. Even if only to remind the legionnaires that not being detected was a priority.

"I would think," erupted the sergeant major, "that the entire base being under attack would fit any parameters that would alert these stupid machines. So if they were active, then they would be active now. *If* those were the parameters. So I say, sir, take a shot and see if they respond."

There was a pause as Besson considered this. Then he said, "Taking the shot."

He fired. Beyond the loud whine of the sudden blaster shot there came a secondary shot of a twanging ricochet.

Both bots snapped to life, deploying deflector shields from their scorpion tails.

"Reflective armor!" shouted one of the leejes.

The two bots began shooting from small minipods located at the front of their mechanical torsos.

"Guess I was wrong. Dust 'em!" shouted the sergeant major.

"Davies," said the captain matter-of-factly. "Bring the 42 forward."

At the front of the small column, due to the narrowness of the passage, Captain Besson shot at the advancing bots, which were coming side by side down the corridor. The translucent yellow deflector shields emitting from the bots' tails adjusted and deflected each incoming shot, and the corridor was filled with the bots' return blaster fire.

"Ready, sir!" cried Davies behind Captain Besson. "Lay down, sir, and I'll hose 'em!"

Besson fell forward to the deck of the tight corridor. He felt the heavy barrel of the N-42 being rested on the armor that protected his body.

"Eat this!" shouted Davies, and fired a long burst from the powerful heavy blaster. When the firing stopped, both bots had been blown to pieces. "Got 'em, sir," said the leej, without ceremony and with maybe more than a little satisfaction.

Besson decided to let the N-42 take point after that, so Davies was shifted forward. Besson took second, and soon Second Team was back underway, following the map HUD to objective Oscar Whiskey.

A few hundred meters on, they felt another titanic explosion shift the ground all around them. Everyone held their breath and waited for the walls to collapse, or for the low ceiling to cave in.

"They crazy with them explosives today. Ain't takin' no chances," murmured the sergeant major.

They continued on through the darkness, the light levels dropping so low that even their bucket's low-light imaging system had difficulty rendering their surroundings.

"Any tighter in here and we're gonna have to shuck our armor," someone muttered as they crawled on through the blackness.

After a few moments the sergeant major replied, "I worked skin before. It's good for ya. Makes you a better leej, like before we gave you the armor and ruined ya. Like back in Basic. I tell ya, you work an op in skin, you are a real bona fide legionnaire then, boys."

No one doubted this.

And no one wanted, at that very moment, to skin out of their armor in order to add a new bragging right to the hardcore resume every leej seemed bent on perpetually building. Working "skin" in the middle of a major battle just didn't seem wise at this moment.

Davies whispered, "Open area in the tunnel ahead. It's lit. Fifty meters."

The sensation of relief was palpable.

After what seemed like forever, Davies crawled close to the widening of the tunnel and relayed that it was some kind of chamber. "High and open," he said.

"Surface access?" Besson asked.

"No, it's covered. It's clear, too. No bots."

Besson gave the order to move into the chamber, which showed on the HUD as some sort of air-exchange processor. The legionnaires entered the chamber, which was bathed in a bluish light. High above, the undulating blades of the venting system moved laconically, sifting the shadows within the room. In the distance they could hear the shrieking pulse of blaster fire.

"Map says there's supposed to be some kind of maintenance access halfway up the wall," Besson said. He pointed to a section of the chamber. "There. Let's—"

He was interrupted by the loud wail of a klaxon, and the soft blue lighting shifted at once to emergency-hull-breach red. The ceiling irised in to place at the same time that the portal through which they'd come guillotined shut with a tiny blast door that came out of the wall.

"Well, this doesn't look good," remarked the sergeant major.

Plumes of yellowish gas filled the chamber from small vents in the walls.

"Don't panic," shouted Besson. "Armor's identifying it as a nerve agent. We're good inside the armor. As long as no one's got a breach, we're—"

One of the legionnaires fell over, his body thrashing. Immediately the sergeant major was down and pinning the man, shouting, "Find the breach in his armor and therma-patch it!"

Huzu dropped to one knee. He let his rifle go as he searched the thrashing leej's armor for any rents or punctures, or any tears in the synthprene they wore underneath. But he found none. And within a violent minute the man was dead. His body twitched a bit longer, then fell still.

The sergeant major crawled off the dead legionnaire, swearing softly.

Huzu recovered his rifle.

A hidden analysis laser array swept the room in a sudden special effects display.

"System's trying to find out if the gas worked," said Besson. "Come on—find the hatch out of here and cut it. Quickly, people!"

The spider bots came out of the ceiling, unfolding themselves from the wall panels they'd been stored in. Imaging, despite the shifting yellowish gas, picked up the spindly-legged bots articulating down the walls.

The bots didn't fire blasters, but instead jumped down savagely at the legionnaires. The agile legionnaires avoided the first three, backpedaling and firing short bursts from their blasters, knocking the spiders down in a flurry of exploding parts. But the fourth landed on a legionnaire, and an unbelievable second later it had deftly sliced through the man's armor, exposing him to the deadly nerve gas still swirling in the chamber.

Huzu blasted the spider off the man, who was already thrashing on the floor, seconds from death.

Captain Besson and another legionnaire, both with climbing gauntlets, managed to get halfway up the wall next to where the HUD overlay marked their route. More spiders raced along the curving walls to get at the two men trying to find a way out of this chamber of death.

"Keep them things off the captain!" shouted the sergeant major. He fired his blaster pistol, nailing one and sending up a huge spray of sparks. The thing exploded, its components raining down across the chamber floor.

Besson spiked his armor's hydraulic assist to full and tore the security hatch from the wall with one massive heave. He swung into the darkness beyond, heedless of what might await him there, and shouted over the L-comm, "Follow me!"

Forming a tight phalanx, the legionnaires covered and egressed the chamber as more and more spiders, an endless stream of them, issued from the ceiling. The sergeant major was the last one through, and told Huzu to hold up.

"Gimme your bando, son! And don't attempt this at home—it ain't in the book!"

Huzu shucked the bandolier of fraggers from around his torso and handed it to the senior NCO. The sergeant major took it, ran a piece of paracord through the trigger spools of all twelve fraggers, then pulled the two ends of the cord away from each other in a sudden jerk. All twelve fraggers were now armed. The sergeant major tossed the bando into the chamber behind them and shouted, "Run for your lives, boys! She's gonna blow!"

But the legionnaires were already engaged fifteen meters ahead with more bot sentries coming out of the darkness.

***

The blast pushed the running sergeant major into Huzu. As they both hit the deck, the subbasement ceiling of the gas-filled chamber collapsed, crushing the bots and blocking the tunnel.

"Well... I do believe we will not be going back the way we came any time soon, son!" said the sergeant major.

Their HUDs switched over to IR. Up ahead was some sort of underground warehouse, where Second Team was locked in a fierce firefight with strangely shaped human-oid bots. Not full-scale war bots—more like souped-up protocol bots that had been given blasters. They moved a bit more agilely than the average bot of that type.

Besson was tossing the remaining fraggers into the stores area where the bots had taken up defensive positions, but the explosives were doing little good. The bots weathered the damage even when parts of themselves were blown clean off. As long as they could fire their blasters, they continued to select targets and engage—and by sheer volume of their numbers, the return fire was enough to keep the legionnaires' heads down.

"You, you, and you," said the crouching sergeant major to three nearby legionnaires. "Deploy your bangers on three. That ought to discombobulate them infernal bots. The rest of you, pop up and put all the fire you got on 'em. One... two... three!"

The three legionnaires did as they were instructed, and the rest of Second Team popped up from their various positions and fired at what should have been stunned bots. But the bots fired right back at them as though they'd shaken off the EMP effects of the bangers in a mere picosecond.

Thankfully, no one got shot, but the bots continued to pour fire into the legionnaires' ad hoc defensive positions. They inched forward a step at a time as though they had all the time in the world

"Well, sir," said the old NCO humbly. "I, unlike many officers I have served under, do not claim to know everything. Those things must be hardened. In other words, I'm outta tricks. How we doin' on charge packs?"

The leejes sounded off with what they had.

"Well, we at least got the ability to defend ourselves goin' for us at this moment in the game."

"Sir," piped up a leej tagged as Stacey. "I did some time in combat engineers on my first enlistment. I'm looking at the ceiling, and these here load-bearing pylons that're probably holding the whole thing up. Trenches might be right above that. I could bring all that down on 'em."

Sergeant Major MakRaven practically swore in disgust at the thought. "Stacey! Then what? Drop the ceiling on the rest of us. Hell, boy, what good is that? Armor can only take so much. And I'm pretty sure it ain't gonna take no ceiling."

Stacey waited for the senior NCO's tirade to blow itself out.

"I think I can drop most of it on them, Sergeant Major. We can squeeze back in that tunnel a bit and we'll be fine."

"You *think*!" shouted the NCO. "That's all you got, son. A thought that you *might not* crush us all with the roof! And of course I suppose you're carrying non-infantry-designated det-cord with which to accomplish your hare-brained scheme?"

Beyond the blaster fire they could hear the servo-assisted joints of the bots closing in. It sounded like a lot of them.

"Looks like it's all we have, Sergeant Major," remarked Captain Besson.

"Well that is indeed a sad state of affairs, sir. This is a classic last stand. I prefer to shoot my way out of such predicaments than be crushed by a falling ceiling like a bug, or trapped in a tunnel by a wall of debris. But… seein' as how you are the captain… I will allow that you may decide to seal our fates with this here young legionnaire's bold yet foolish plan to prevent a bunch of tough-as-nails war fighters gettin' killed by *bots*." He spat this last out, the word "bots," with a certain amount of disgust. It seemed he had a particular hatred for bots.

"Wrap it," said Besson to Stacey, indicating the nearest support pylon. "The rest of you fall back into the tunnel." After a pause, he added to Stacey, "You do know what you're doing?"

"I got this, sir. I could make a pole fall and hit a credit anywhere I placed it within the radius of drop. I'll bring that half of the room down on them for sure." Stacey said all this while rooting around in his tactical ruck and pulling out the cord and necessary supplies he would need. In a minute and change, he had the pylon wrapped at the base. Wider loops on one side. Tighter loops on another. Then he nodded to the captain and fell back to the tunnel.

"Well, no use waiting," said the sergeant major.

Besson nodded. "Blow it."

Stacey brought the entire ceiling down on the advancing bots.

Which didn't surprise anyone as much as what came down *with* the ceiling. The zhee who'd been in the trench above were now spilling out into the ruins of the sub-basement. Fortunately, most had been injured in the fall. But their pack brothers still up in the trench above looked down in stunned belief.

"Navs up… Got a re-route!" shouted Besson. "Up along that trench and we're almost there. Turtle and follow me!"

With Besson at the tip of the spear, and each legionnaire falling into the much-practiced basic movement-to-contact-in-tight-quarters "turtle" formation, everyone watching their sectors and the sergeant major barking commands from the center, Second Team advanced out into the swirling dust of the collapsed storage room. They ascended part of the collapsed ceiling that had also been the floor of the trench, shooting down zhee as they moved quickly upward.

Within seconds they were in the trench and firing into the flank of the zhee line at point blank. The action was so close that the sergeant major was firing his blaster pistol over the head of a crouched Captain Besson while the lead team members deployed their bayonets and stabbed at the zhee—who throwing down their weapons either in surrender or in favor of their wicked *kankari* knives. Huzu, in the rear, kept the zhee on the far side of the sinkhole busy with high-cycle blaster fire, while Davies hosed the rest with the N-42.

The zhee were quickly routed, and those who still could fled to the far end of the trench, leaving a corridor of their dead blasted and bleeding out.

When the trench was clear, Besson raised his left hand indicating a halt, while keeping his barrel on the trench and the dying zhee.

As charge packs were swapped out, the sergeant major levered his head over the side of the trench facing the assault. "Well, lookee there. We made good progress, sir.

We made such good progress, in fact, that we are well in front of the line of assault."

Which was true. They were now inside the third ring of the defenses.

"Which means—technically, sir—that we are indeed surrounded."

Task Force Whirlwind
Assault Carrier *Hurricane*
Landing Zone Near Fortress Gibraltaar
Ankalor

"Commodore," said the CIC officer aboard the *Hurricane*. "Problem, sir."

The CIC officer looked grave. He unfolded a flexy and showed the commodore exactly what the cause for concern was.

"They're coming out of the desert, and out of Ankalor City. On fast-attack speeders. All indications are it's a light force and our defenses should be more than enough to handle them. But…"

Within the real-time scrolling tactical display images on the flexy, the map showed the Legion forces down before the mass of Gibraltaar Rock. It even showed major asset groups engaged in the battle within the trenches and the near-invulnerable IDS range at the front of all three carriers. But what drew the commodore's attention was at the rear. Hundreds of unidentified red-tagged tangos, inbound on the carrier group's position.

The zhee were actually counterattacking.

"Go to battle stations," said Commodore Rist. "And let's divert our air cover to screen. Get me the general."

A moment later General Hannubal appeared on a display. He was still in the back of his operations SLIC, somewhere over the thick of the battle above the trenches, directing troop movements and providing fire support and emergency medevac.

"Hannubal…" began the commodore. "We've got inbound zhee marauders trying to attack the carriers. We should be able to handle it, but we're going to need to divert close air support to see if we can break up the attack. We'll leave the indirect fire in place for your units to continue the assault."

Hannubal nodded. "Roger that, Commodore. Let me know if it gets too hot, and I can divert some resources to reinforce. We're close to cracking the front door."

The commodore nodded, and the link was broken.

Across the bridge, the alarm for battle stations began to whoop. The situation was detailed over the ship's address system and the crew were told to reorient to meet the incoming counterattack.

22

To their credit, the zhee did not retreat in the face of Second Team's assault along the trenches, effectively flanking the defenders. But that didn't mean that they effectively counterattacked against the insurgent legionnaires within their lines, either. Instead the zhee's zeal conspired to work against them as they trampled, and occasionally shot or even knifed, their own as they surged to meet the attacking legionnaires.

At a small mortar pit, at a place where the trench opened out into a small square meant to accommodate an indirect fire crew, Besson moved Davies forward while the rest shifted into an active defense. Suddenly the zhee were facing the murderous onslaught of the powerful N-42 workhorse heavy blaster, which blasted the zhee to pieces without mercy. The deadly weapon system required little thought; it needed only to be fed with a continuous supply of linked charge packs.

A couple of the zhee attempted to use the jump jets on the armor they'd been issued, but that merely brought them to the attention of the Legion's ranged snipers, who were set up back along the first ring, hidden in the shadows and waiting for just such an opportunity. What the snipers failed to hit, the squad-designated marksmen in the other advancing units managed to take care of, for the most part. And when one zhee did manage to set down with a flare of jets right in the midst of Second Team, the sergeant major shot the donk without ceremony, blowing the zhee's brains all over the trench wall.

"Don't get me wrong," MakRaven said. "I'm a good friend to many a zhee. But the only good donk is a dead donk. That's a fact, boys." The sergeant major pronounced this despite the volume of return fire on the pit.

Stacey got hit, the shot destroying his arm guard and breaking his arm. As Huzu and the sergeant major stabilized him, the NCO asked Stacey, "You done, kid? Or you wanna fight a little more today?"

Stacey, who looked pale and shaken, got to his feet with a groan.

"That arm's gonna be okay," Mak said. "And if not, the Repub can grow you a new one. Here—take my sidearm. I'll play with your rifle for a while."

And with that they swapped weapons.

A few minutes later, the battle quieted. The zhee had either been slaughtered to the point of zero viability, or they'd decided to cede the trench and fall back to their bunker. Still, Besson didn't let the team move forward until he'd shot every last zhee that was still twitching along the length of the trench. Finally, he gave the hand signal to form up into a wedge and follow him forward.

"You want me on point, Cap'n?" asked Davies.

"Negative. Let the forty-two rest for a few minutes," Besson replied.

"She all right," Davies said. "She just got a taste for the work. And frankly, she hopes there's a bit more of it."

They advanced down the trench, following the route to target in their HUDs. At the next passage through the defensive line they'd hook left and take a side trench up to a bunker that overwatched the main gate.

A furious exchange of blaster fire could be heard in a nearby trench, indicating two sides had met each other for battle. This was quickly followed by a series of explosions that indicated the use of fraggers.

"Most likely us," commented the sergeant major.

Besson hustled down the trench, stepping over the zhee dead as cautiously as possible, knowing that at any moment one could wake up from playing dead and start firing, or worse, detonate a suicide vest. If that happened, they'd never reach Oscar Whiskey, and the Legion would charge into certain death.

Sergeant Major MakRaven had lectured at length on the fun little trick of zhee suicide vests.

"The zhee aren't as dumb as everyone thinks they are. I mean they *are* dumb... after a fashion. But they're also some of the craftiest devils you'll ever face. It's not uncommon, as I have encountered this particular little tactic myself on occasion, for them to lose a small engagement and put what they call a 'sacrifice' in with the dead. So we got to watch ourselves in here, boys. A sacrifice can turn a victory into a loss in a heartbreak moment.

"Had that happen at Watti Sharah with the Tenth back when I was staff sergeant. Just me and three others survived a two-hundred-mile trek, on foot I might add, back to the forward operations base after a sacrifice took out the ops ship the point was in. We'd set up an ambush, and the point wanted to come in and assist after we'd killed 'em all. Problem was, they'd put that sacrifice in with the company we shot up. He just laid there and played dead until the ship came in, and then he detonated one when our ride home touched down. Killed almost all the platoon except us three. Other two died on the way back to base."

"Sergeant Major..." said one of the leejes.

"Yeah?"

"Do you have any stories where everyone lived happily ever after?"

"Not many. But there are some. And I am indeed hoping this is one of them. If not for your sake, then it might as well be for mine, son."

The trench that Second Team was following ended, intersecting with the main passage that led toward the gate. According to their schematics, they had to follow this wide passage— wide enough for mobile artillery and even heavy cargo sleds—for about twenty meters before ducking into another side passage on the opposite side. But in doing so, they'd be walking directly into a nest of entrenched zhee.

Poking his scout rifle around the corner, Captain Besson was rewarded with a feed from off the weapon's barrel. The zhee had stacked mobile barriers all up the trench and had dug in, apparently anticipating an assault of this kind. There were no zhee between Second Team's location and the trench they needed to reach—but the barriers started only about ten meters beyond that.

Besson fed the picture to everyone in Second Team.

For a moment, with everyone stacked against the wall, there was nothing but silence.

"Well…" said the sergeant major as he watched the feed. "That's a sure enough way to get us killed."

No one replied. And Captain Besson seemed to be on another channel. After a moment he came back.

"Negative on close air or fire missions. Seems the zhee are counterattacking the carriers. Also, the two companies that are going in on the main door are in their staging locations, but they can't move until we engage the defenses around the door and buy them enough time to get close with breaching charges. If we don't go in the next fifteen minutes, they're going to be ordered to take the doors without overwatch support fire. And casualties will be much higher."

"Well, sir," remarked the sergeant major, "we ain't going to be any position to help anyone if we have to make twenty meters over open ground while getting drilled dead on like ducks in a shootin' gallery. I have no doubt they got snipers too, a ways back watching that passage. Just waitin' to shoot poor old Davies right through the eyes. Heavy gunner is considered a zhee target of honor. Why, if we all get killed and they can get a hold of our bodies, they'll make a meal of Davies's liver like you ain't never tasted. They are savages, but they can cook a touch."

Pause.

"I hear you, Sergeant Major. But this is what we do."

Which meant, to everyone in Second Team, that they were about to do something dangerous. Something like charge head-on into enemy fire, hoping someone *might* make it to the side passage. Hoping that side passage wasn't mined with IEDs, or filled with more zhee waiting to kill.

"You are, unfortunately, right, sir," crooned the sergeant major. "Well, boys, this is where we leej up and do all the things we ever dreamed of. Which is, to put not too fine a point on it, die gloriously and leave good-lookin' corpses behind. Some of you are excepted from that last part. Sad that it has to be the donks bein' the ones to do it, but who says you get to pick your death.

"Drop your rucks and shuck any excess gear here. You're gonna need to move faster than you ever thought possible, despite how tired you might think you are. How many bangers we got left?"

A quick count revealed there were four.

"That'll have to be enough then. Who's got a good arm?"

Everyone agreed that Turnbull did.

"All right, Bull," said Mak. "You are gonna lob, catty-corner, while I feed 'em to you. Then we all go for the rush."

Captain Besson softly added a condition. "The win is, we get the forty-two up to the bunker."

"Hey hey! Did you hear that, Sergeant Major?" laughed Davies. "I gotta make it no matter what."

"So if Davies gets killed," said the sergeant major, "see if you can grab the pig—I mean the forty-two. Sorry, Davies, but you will most likely die. Carryin' that, you're gonna move slow, son. But I will be sure to tell your mother that you were a saint and you died with her name on your lips, despite the obvious miscreant I suspect you to be."

The legionnaires, including Captain Besson, shrugged out of their tactical rucks and shed any gear that would slow them down. One of them was whispering "twenty meters" over and over again until the sergeant major gently reminded him that they all understood.

"We got that, son. You'll be fine. Things often turn out better than I suspect they will. You might not know it, but I am considered to be a bit of a pessimist by some."

A moment later the captain gave the green light. There would be no special plan, no sneak attack, no help from another quarter. There was simply just this. A push forward into the face of the enemy with the odds stacked against you. Why? Because other legionnaires were depending on you to be there when it came hit time. Because you were the one percent of the one percent of the one percent. And occasionally that bill needed to be paid.

"Now," whispered Captain Besson, his voice dry and hoarse.

Turnbull armed the first ear-popper and tossed it over the corner of the trench, down toward the emplacements. The sergeant handed him two more, deciding to save one for later, just in case. He called out "Last one" over the L-comm, then, "Go, go, go!"

Besson was out first. He'd barely turned the corner when he got hit right in the chest. A distant sniper, unaffected by the deafening bang and blinding flash, had known they'd charge directly from that point.

Besson stumbled over to the far side of the trench, firing, and then sat down, or rather was knocked down onto his butt. He motioned with his hand for the others to keep moving forward past him, then he unloaded on the zhee behind the barriers. Firing to keep the heads of the defenders down while his men ran forward, legs pumping hard. The sergeant major sprinted past the mortally wounded captain knowing the wound was just that. And knowing what the captain was doing.

The zhee returned fire, targeting Besson, who kept firing at them despite the world inside his vision irising down to a tiny black circle.

Sergeant Major MakRaven, the last in the rushing line, had just made the side trench when the zhee decided to switch targets and go for the rushing legionnaires. By that time, Captain Besson was gone.

Task Force Whirlwind
Assault Carrier *Hurricane*
Landing Zone Near Fortress Gibraltaar

The zhee marauders came out of the desert wastes of Ankalor on light mobile technical speeders. Souped-up hyperchargers, covered in zhee graffiti, allowed them to move fast and get in close on the carriers' defenders. Some of the speeders were configured to bring irregular infantry in close, while others carried mounted Night Market–acquired heavy blasters or missile packs.

The loadmasters and crew chiefs of the assault carriers were all trained to repel boarders, and each carrier had emplaced swing-mounted guns on either side of their massive ramps. Indirect fire from the top side artillery fell out on the drifting desert sands, and the speeders raced through the plumes of artillery strikes to get their troops close. Within moments a firefight had erupted in front of the rear cargo loading deck of the *Hurricane*, the center anchor of the three carriers.

One of the HK-PPs had been recalled from the battle inside the trenches to defend the carriers, but it was still a long way off. At extreme range it began to lob heavy blaster fire into the swarming zhee, to little effect. One shot might kill dozens, but there were thousands streaming toward the rear bay, braying and ululating their war cries.

Within the assault carrier's lower decks, crew chiefs— now turned into heavy gunners—dealt out a steady stream of blaster fire. Zhee speeders were hit and went flying off or exploded in bright showers of fireworks. Sometimes a cacophonic explosion indicated heavier ordnance had been on board that particular transport. But the zhee moved forward in coordinated teams, alternating their fire with their rushes. The situation at the rear decks was deteriorating quickly.

One of the carriers' support SLICs came in low, blasters spooling up high-cycle fire and chewing a line of sand volcanoes across the ragged advancing zhee front, when a missile sidewindered in from off-site, coming from behind some low hills in the distance. It struck the SLIC, which nosed over and exploded in the sand, killing the crew in addition to several zhee on the ground. A shock wave of sand and destruction raced out across the swarming line.

"Direct the artillery to triangulate and switch to counter-battery fire!" shouted Commodore Rist inside the *Hurricane*'s CIC. The zhee were now within two hundred meters of the rear main loading ramp and firing as they advanced. "Bring our engines online and tell *Sirocco* and *Tornado* we may have to execute an emergency lift-off. I want engines at standby in two minutes."

23

"Follow the trench, and watch for bad guys!" shouted the sergeant major over the L-comm. "Traffic from ops says a Legion company is coming down the trench after us to at least keep the zhee pinned while we take Oscar Whiskey. Run and gun, boys!"

The few remaining legionnaires of Second Team followed the trench along a series of angled turns most likely developed to allow small teams, supported by squad-designated marksmen, to bleed off zhee assaulting the main trench. The trench was essentially a series of straightaways that abruptly cornered, and it was from these corners that the marksmen would reduce the zhee. Fortunately, the zhee hadn't bothered to capitalize on this design feature, and instead seemed to be more interested in hunkering down inside the impressive squat bunkers that watched over the trench lanes, or kills zones, throughout the base.

Davies turned one of these corners and saw the access stairs leading up to the second level of what looked to be a four-level bunker. He also saw three zhee with N-20s and armor. Without thinking, he stopped and hosed them from the hip with the N-42. Zhee blood painted the wide clean surfaces of the bunker. Davies was incredibly accurate even when hip-firing. He would have told you it was a calling of his.

"Stack on the door, boys!" cried the sergeant major wildly, as the rushing legionnaires took the stairs two at a time. "I'm first in. We got six minutes until they order the assault. This is do-or-do-not time."

The leejes stacked quickly. On the second floor they got a brief view of the battle going on all across the trenches. Squads and platoons of legionnaires were everywhere and pushing forward all at once. Cascades of explosions ripped across the soundscape as leejes flung grenades into fortified bunkers or rocketed heavy blaster emplacements. And the zhee were fighting back for all they were worth, not going gently into the paradise of pleasures they'd been promised.

"Go!" yelled the sergeant major.

Huzu kicked the door with his armored boot, landing the kick just where he'd been taught to in basic. The locking mechanism smashed and the door gave way with a sudden burst. Huzu danced backward while the sergeant major raced through the gap, following the barrel of his N-4. Stacey reached out and balanced Huzu with one hand while at the same time following Davies through into the darkness.

As they entered the bunker, all of their HUDs started to fritz in washes of static like waves rolling on shore. Three slow rolls of white static in which signal and telemetry returned and then disappeared once more. Then they went offline altogether.

There wasn't even a boot message.

"Quick!" shouted the sergeant major, his band saw shout cutting through the muffled dead silence of the buckets in order to be heard through their helmets. "Buckets off!"

But it was too late. The first assassin came in from the ceiling. He planted an industrial diamond-forged blade right in Davies's back. It slid through the hardened legionnaire armor like it was cutting butter.

Huzu pulled off his helmet and stared at the pitch-black darkness all around him. He heard the rustling of cloth, then a hoof smashed into his face and sent him reeling into a wall. Stars exploded, and it felt like he'd just broken his nose.

"We got blind assassins, boys!" shouted the sergeant major somewhere off in the darkness. Davies moaned. Stacey shouted, "Weapons don't work!"

In the darkness all around was a near silence. Near because there was something soft moving all about them.

Someone got hit. Went flying. Smashed into something.

The sergeant major muttered through gritted teeth, "Gotcha!" and a horrible crack followed—the distinct sound of a bone snapping.

"That's one, but there's another in here. Don't use your eyes, boys. Listen and smell and that's—"

Something knocked the wind out of the sergeant major. The sound of his boots shuffling across the floor indicated he was hit but not down. He grunted something

inaudible, then came back over the soundscape, his hectoring and ragged old voice breathy and labored.

"That's when you can tell they're close." He coughed
and spit. In the near silence Huzu might have heard a tooth
go skittering off into the dark.

Stacey let out an involuntary grunt. Not like he was being hit, but like he was suddenly swinging a bat. The sound
of air being displaced could be heard.

"Thought I felt one," he gasped.

"Probably did," replied the sergeant major. "He's close,
this one. I broke his brother's neck, so he won't let this go."

Huzu levered himself up the side of the wall in the dark.

Stacey got hit next. And whatever hit him knocked
him out cold, because nothing was heard from him again.
Except now someone was gurgling.

A moment later Huzu got kicked in the head for the
second time. As he fought not to go down into the unconsciousness that was trying to take him, he heard the sergeant major swear and say, "All right, boys, one last trick,
and this ain't gonna be fun! Banger out!"

Three seconds later the world exploded in a sudden
concussion of noise and light. For a brief, star-stunned moment Huzu saw a malformed albino zhee, almost a runt,
hanging upside down from the ceiling like some kind of
nightmare mutant vampire bat, the whites of its eyes rolled
back in its head, its donkey ears pinned and listening. And
then, as the negative image faded to black, the last thing
he saw before he blacked out was the sergeant major, his
old face hard-set and angry, white hair standing out like a

ghost, long mustache flowing like some ancient gunfighter, charging in at where the stunned zhee was.

And then the darkness took the young private. His last thought was that he didn't want to fail... not now... not as a leej. The thing he'd always wanted to be. He couldn't ever fail at that.

He was sure he hadn't been out long when the sergeant shook him awake. "PFC, you got to get up! Now!"

Huzu immediately pushed forward, up off his back, driven to alertness by the urgency in the senior NCO's voice.

The lights in the guardroom were on now. Two dead zhee were on the floor. Stacey was bleeding out from a slashed throat, and Davies had a knife sticking out of his back. Turnbull was out cold.

"I disabled their EMP generator," said the sergeant major to Huzu as though giving a sitrep. "But I got to deal with these two men before they die. So I need you to get mobile and get that forty-two up to Oscar Whiskey overwatch. Lay down all the cover fire you can on the door so our boys can get good and close. They go in three minutes."

Huzu shook his head to clear the double images. Then he nodded.

"They're depending on us, boy. Gotta move now."

Huzu got to his feet, forgetting his bucket. He staggered over the N-42 and hefted it up. For a moment the room swam. He shook his head once more, and it cleared. He grabbed his bucket and fitted it back onto his head.

The sergeant major was already working on Stacey. Pulling out skinpacks and trying to get the ragged wound on the man's throat closed.

"You good, boy?" shouted the sergeant major at Huzu. "I can't leave these or they'll die. But I will if it's what I have to do to save those other men. So you got to go now, son, if you can."

"I got this," said Huzu, and he staggered off toward the tight stairwell that led up to the turret's top.

Warlord One
Above the Battle

The SLIC lurched to the side as the pilot threw it into a hard bank. Out the down-side cargo door, the door gunner raked a zhee trench. The zhee were counterattacking into one of the pincers staged to take the base's main door.

"Traffic from Hurricane Actual," noted the command operations officer over General Hannubal's L-comm channel. "Situation at the *Hurricane* deteriorating. Zhee are at the main cargo deck and they've knocked out one of the engines with an anti-armor rocket. They're about to be overrun, General."

"Acknowledged," replied Hannubal tersely. "Reply inbound to stabilize the situation."

"Sir," responded the ops officer. His tone was definitely not just cautionary, but downright urgent. "Counterbattery fire has not located the surface-to-air enemy asset. We advise you not to enter range. We've lost three SLICs."

Hannubal disregarded and switched over to the Ops SLIC's inter-ship channel. "We need to fall back and clear the donks off our carriers. We got anti-air. Any problems with that, Captain?"

"Negative, sir. Thrusters full, inbound and over in thirty seconds."

The door gunner facing the general grabbed the cargo doorframe as the ship powered up and shot off from the battle over the trenches.

Dog Company
Fortress Gibraltaar
Trenches

Huzu made it up to the fourth floor of the overwatch bunker that had been designed to provide flanking fire on any direct assaults on the main blast doors at the base of Gibraltaar Rock. From here, he could see the entire battle as it unfolded below.

Across the wide central ramp that led down into the base, artillery craters had left their mark in the hardened duracrete, but no single strike had managed to knock out either of the two main bunkers. The legionnaires would have to take those bunkers with a direct assault, getting close enough to use explosives and blast their way through the main door.

Assault teams were already moving down the feeding trenches, firing and engaging the zhee defenders before the main gate. Most of the zhee were centered around the bunkers, both reinforced and sturdy. From out of these, at least two N-50s, among other weapons, were firing at the legionnaires, who were headed right into the teeth of the blaster hurricane. And they had at least fifty meters of open ground to cross before they would even get close

enough to use fraggers. Fifty meters in which to be casually murdered by the working N-50s with excellent fields of
fire on every approach.

Huzu raised the blast covers that guarded the firing
positions, hoisted the N-42 into a firing slit, and began to
fire down into the bunkers.

First he shot up the zhee who had taken up firing positions behind barriers. Then he fired directly into the bunkers' firing slits.

The two groups of legionnaire assault teams seized
the opportunity. Both rushed the central ramp to the door.
Huzu burned through an entire charge pack on high cycle
before the N-50s began to fire on him.

He pulled the N-42 out of the slit, dropped down
onto the floor, and swapped out charge packs. Blaster fire
smashed into the bunker all around him, and hot fused duracrete rained down. As solidly built as the bunker was,
even it came to pieces under the high-power settings of
the N-50s.

Charge pack in, he stood to fire once more.

In the last moment of his life he saw his brothers closing hard and fast to get within range to either put fire on
the bunker up close and personal, or to use explosives and
bust their way into the hardened emplacements. But they
still had a few meters to go. The N-50s, plus countless light
blasters, were firing directly into the legionnaires, with
devastating effect. Killing some outright. Knocking others
down. Stalling the assault.

Huzu heaved the N-42 into the slit and fired. He unloaded on the bunker firing at the legionnaires instead of the one firing at him.

The first shot that hit him should have knocked him down, but he held on for all he was worth and kept firing back. He managed to burn through the entire charge pack, killing the defenders inside one enemy bunker while keeping the zhee in the other bunker busy shooting at him, even as he took two more direct hits.

It was the fourth shot that killed him. He had just enough awareness of this life to know that he'd fired the N-42 dry before he died. The weapon clattered to the floor as he fell to his knees and slumped against the wall beneath the slit he'd been firing from.

***

As soon as the two assault teams had taken the remaining bunker, they set up charges on the main blast door. They blew it wide open, and stormed inside in search of their high-value target: Karshak Bum Kali, Grand War Leader of the zhee tribes.

There was little resistance within the fortress itself. Holing up inside a rock wasn't the zhee way. Not when there was blood to be spilled. But there were a few defenders, and the legionnaires even managed to take most of them alive. One of these captured zhee prisoners finally gave them what they wanted.

It wasn't what they were expecting.

Karshak Bum Kali wasn't at Fortress Gibraltaar.

He was deep inside the slums. Slums that were now on fire and rioting. A place where their grand war leader would never be found.

Where he would never be taken alive.

Warlord One
Above the Battle

The SLIC came in fast, thrust reversers kicking in and screaming bloody murder. The door gunners opened up on the zhee swarming *Hurricane*'s rear cargo deck. Marines were fighting hand to hand and lobbing explosives into the nearby zhee. A thin ribbon of smoke trailed away from one of the *Hurricane*'s main engines where it had been hit by an anti-armor round.

The general stood up and grabbed onto the frame of the dropship, calling out concentrations of fire for the door gunners to target. The battle at the rear cargo deck was just seconds from being turned into a complete rout of the zhee. The SLIC had broken the zhee drive on the massive rear ramps of the assault carrier.

But that's when tragedy happened.

General Hannubal spotted it. Inbound and burning like a banshee across the desert sands. Not a sidewindering missile, lancing in to knock the SLIC out of the sky, but a heavy speeder with one driver.

Over the L-comm he shouted to the gunners and the pilot of his ship. "Got a bomb jockey inbound. Tagging him in your HUDs now. Do not let him reach the carrier. Repeat. Do not!"

The SLIC pivoted, allowing one gunner a full sight picture to knock down the inbound speeder. From far too close and fast, the speeder came in across sands filled with ruined and dead zhee. The look on the driver's face confirmed the general's worst fears. It was otherworldly, as though the donk was praying to his one of his four gods to see his sacrifice through.

The gunner ranged short, missing the swerving speeder and sending up plumes of sand.

"Take it out!" shouted the general with bare seconds to go.

The pilot, a killer who'd flown through hell the entire day and didn't seem to mind much, dropped the speeder down to hover just off the ground. Whether he did this on purpose to give the gunner better stability, or because he knew this was the only way to stop the inbound suicide bomber, was never known.

The last words of General Hannubal were, "Good man. He's not getting through."

The speeder hit the dropship and exploded.

24

The House of Reason's audience chamber was less of a chamber and more of a long hallway, lined with fifty columns on both sides, each rising from the floor and seeming to disappear into the night sky—into the universe itself, thanks to an ingenious holographic painting overlaid on the ceiling. The hall had been built in honor of the one hundredth planet to join the Galactic Republic, and the idea was that each planet had its own column, and together they "upheld" the galaxy itself. Polished marble, imported from no less than forty quarries on thirteen planets, gave the place a stately, almost regal feel.

Many planets had joined the Republic since the time of the initial construction, and even after a millennium of hyperspace travel, there were still unknown or forgotten regions of space. Still places waiting to be explored or rediscovered. Cut-off branches of humanity waiting to be grafted back in. New species... potential answers to ancient mysteries. The hall evoked thoughts of all of this. It represented everything the Republic was to be. And though the Republic seemed to have sometimes lost the excitement that followed the Exploration, an excitement that even the

Savage Wars hadn't eradicated, sitting in the hall brought forth a reverence of everything that was and still could be.

It was filled with reporters now, seated in opulent chairs fit for kings and queens. Here was every species the galaxy had to offer, with journobots wearing a patina of holographic skin to represent the species that couldn't be bothered. The cameras wouldn't know the difference. They spoke in whispers, none daring to violate the sanctity of the audience chamber. Their words of speculation, attempts to gain an edge over the competition, idle gossip, and earnest arguments all mixed and blended up to the holographic heavens, creating a sound like a thousand hourglasses spilling onto the marble floor.

In front of the seats was an elegant, hand-carved podium on which sat an ornate lectern draped with the flag of the Galactic Republic. To the left and right of the podium sat lesser delegates of the House of Reason and Senate. They were unimportant. Their names had been recorded for the sake of the record, but no one seated in the gallery of reporters cared for what *they* might have to say.

Call me when you become something, kid.

No, the eyes were fixed beyond all that, at the far end of the hall. The distant double doors from which the speaker would emerge—that was what the Utopion insiders watched. Call it a conference, briefing, press release... the reality of the situation was that it was happening with no preceding leaks. Try as they might, no one invited had discovered anything. Sources weren't being tight-lipped, they actually went on record to say they had no idea. None of the reporters knew what to expect. Still, whoever walked out of those doors would say volumes before they could utter a word.

And then the doors opened, and the gallery of reporters erupted into buzzing voices as Delegate Orrin Kaar strode into the audience chamber. On one side of him was a Legion general; on the other was a yellow-skinned and horned kimbrin immediately recognizable as Loran Quall, the firebrand who had recently assumed control of the Mid-Core Rebellion. Quall walked as a free man.

Behind this trio followed several zhee senators and the members of the House of Reason Security Council.

Orrin Kaar arrived at the lectern, leaving the politically powerful entourage behind the podium, their faces still visible for the holocams as he began to speak.

"Good evening." His voice sounded weary, sympathetic, but firm and strong. There was no one in the House of Reason more suited to the task now being undertaken. "Tonight I am informing the Republic and the entire galaxy that a rogue element of the Legion has attacked, unprovoked, the Republic planet of Ankalor. They have dispatched Legion assassins to kill the members of the House of Reason. These assassins have been intercepted and detained, though not before some of their dark work was completed."

Kaar waited for the worried hum among those gathered to rise, just long enough to capture the sense of wonder while not losing control of the room. "Legion Commander Keller and a cadre of a treasonous elements inside our very government have revealed themselves through these actions and are now seeking to cover this unconscionable offense to the people of the Republic by invoking Article Nineteen.

"The House of Reason and Senate will not be cowed by this poor faith attempt to justify the actions of some in the Legion. Murderers and traitors have no place in the Galactic Republic! For that reason, an emergency vote was held to remove Legion Commander Keller from his position as head of the Legion, replacing him with Legion General Washam, who was appointed by Delegate Nisa Flood more than fifteen years ago, and who has served the Republic faithfully ever since."

That the House of Reason had no authority to place or remove a Legion commander went unmentioned. This was to be the start of a new order.

"Legion Commander Washam will oversee the purging of the Legion, and will coordinate with the Seventh Fleet to protect those planets threatened by the double-headed serpent of the treasonous soldiers inside the Legion and the Black Fleet, who we believe to be in league with one another."

Kaar's face flooded with emotion, as though he were momentarily overcome. He turned and looked at the MCR leader, Quall, and nodded. The kimbrin nodded back.

"Tonight, I don't just bring tidings of war—I also bring news of peace. The decade-long rebellion against the Republic by members of the mid-core worlds has ended. The House of Reason has for months been in secret and extensive talks with representatives of the Mid-Core Rebellion. We found many of their complaints to be valid, grounded in the excesses of the Legion against the will of the House and Senate.

"It is, I think, symbolic that only hours after a peace accord was reached, the rogue Legion sought to overthrow the Republic. Long have they grown fat on the trimmings of war, always eager for more appropriations through taxes levied against the Republic. Taxes that they collected with intense zeal, as our citizens in the mid-core and at galaxy's edge know all too well. The MCR will be folded back into the Republic, and will commit its resources as a new branch of our military to resist those who would destroy our freedoms."

Kaar paused. The audience chamber was still, perfectly quiet. The tap of notes on datapads, the rustling in chairs, the whispered comments, had all ceased. Everyone in the chamber was sitting in rapt attention, and Kaar knew that the same was true of the rest of the galaxy.

"To the galaxy I say this: The Republic will fight to halt this naked grab for power. We will stand for the principles of our Constitution. Together. There are those in the galaxy who believe that because they have power, because they have might, that frees them to do whatever they may desire. That it frees them to attack the citizens of Tarrago while they sleep. Frees them to invade a planet to and commit genocide against its native species, simply because they are not human."

Kaar shook his head. "The Republic says no. No to the Savage marines who sought to conquer the galaxy. No to the parade of lawless dictators who attempted to seize power for themselves at the expense of their citizens after the Savage Wars. No to the treasonous members of the Legion and their Black Fleet allies."

A spontaneous eruption of applause came from the gallery of reporters, politicians, guests, and aides. Kaar stepped back, feigning surprise at what was in actuality an unheard-of response on such an occasion. Of course, Kaar had known this would happen. Had positioned the right people to clap at the right time. He had them, as always, eating from the palm of his hand.

"To our allies and citizens now feeling the hateful and wicked wrath of these enemies: You are not alone. Relief is already coming, and victory will be ours. Hold fast. Persevere. Resist the invaders. Protect your families, your loved ones, your fellow citizens, your homes. And, in so doing... the Republic itself.

"The Republic does not relish the thought of war. *Reason* is the bright shining star that guides our pursuit of liberty." Kaar paused and clenched his jaw. "But we are facing *unreasonable* men. I fear they have irrevocably set a course of bloodshed that those who love decency, equality, and peace in the galaxy must now follow.

"Nevertheless, I have a glimmering hope. A hope in the basic decency found in all sentient species, from the windswept plains of Kublar at galaxy's edge, to the shimmering crystals of Luthia in the mid-core, to the bright shining jewel that is Utopion. I hope that whoever we are, and wherever we are, a spark of compassion remains. Even among the Legion.

"The Republic acts out of a compassion for the lives of *all* beings in the galaxy. We know too well the dreadful cost of war. Innocents will die, *have* died. To those legion-naires finding themselves under the treasonous command of former Legion Commander Keller, and to those oppressing their fellow citizens in labor camps at Tarrago, I say: Stand up to the tyranny inside your own ranks. Stand up! Stand for the Republic! Its Constitution, and the liberties of a free, *united* Galactic Republic!"

The applause, not only inside the audience chamber, but in the House and Senate chambers where the speech was being simulcast, was deafening.

***

X watched the speech from the comfort of his office on Utopion. So much had happened since his conversation with Legion Commander Keller and their subsequent meeting on the *Mercutio*—all properly clandestine. Such *remarkable* times.

And Delegate Kaar was simply superb. X could appreciate a skilled politician. He hadn't always been that way. During his time in the Legion, he had been of the opinion that politicians were good for nothing but the exhalation of hot air. That, coupled with their penchant for getting your men killed and maimed, had led him to despise that particular class of beings.

But time and experience had proved to X the usefulness of the politician. Kaar's speech was one such an example. Legion Commander Keller would be hard-pressed to top *that.* A Legion commander, or any general, really, was an instrument. A mind molded for battle. A lightning rod for *military* inspiration… but rarely did any of that translate to the public at large. The life of a career soldier was as far removed from that of the average citizen as Pusar was from its ninth moon.

So now the galaxy would react to the information before it. The Black Fleet. The Republic. The Legion.

And they would continue to react. The die was cast… but the game was still being played. And X… he would do what he'd always done. The dark, hard, nasty things that needed doing.

"For the greater good," muttered X before downing the last of his scotch.

Bed seemed inviting—or at least, the sofa in his office that so often passed for one. He needed sleep. He hoped it would be dreamless.

If it mattered anywhere in the cosmic scheme of things, X hoped the Legion would be successful. And everything he had done thus far, he believed, would help them. The galaxy needed to hear Kaar's words. It was essential that those words be fresh in everyone's minds—so that the truth the Legion would bring to light would come as a jolting surprise. Smelling salts to a sleeping Republic. The truth would win out. In time.

But there would not have been enough time for Kaar's words to come first had X not… *delayed* the assault on Ankalor. In the end, he'd saved more lives than he'd sacrificed to the zhee by warning Kaar of the pending attack. The Legion owed him a debt of gratitude. But X was no fool. He knew he'd be a dead man if they ever found out what he'd done.

He stood up, sauntered to a window, and held open the blinds to look up at the sky, the stars. "Best of luck, old boys. It was for the greater good."

25

Admiral Ubesk got both messages at almost the same time. The base had been breached and legionnaires were commencing the search for Karshak Bum Kali—and General Hannubal's dropship had gone down over the battlefield.

An hour later CIC had a confirmed KIA on the general, and the Legion was interrogating a senior zhee HVT who was indicating the Grand War Leader wasn't even on site.

Legion Commander Keller was in on all of these conversations, but instead of taking immediate command as the senior-most official, he had elected to allow operations to continue along normal channels as he and his aide watched from the sidelines.

Admiral Ubesk approached the two men. Colonel Speich stepped back a short distance but maintained his focus on the conversation that was about to happen next.

"Sir," began the admiral to the highest-ranking military officer in the Legion. "Here is the situation at present. Operations against Gibraltaar Base were successful, with fewer casualties than expected. But it's looking like our target escaped—either during the battle, or shortly before. And, as you are aware, General Hannubal was killed during the operation when the zhee counterattacked the landing group."

There was a brief pause.

Both men were offering not the full moment of silence they could give for all the dead, but at least a few seconds. It wasn't that they didn't respect their sacrifice, but at this moment, there just wasn't time for any more. The dead would have known this too. The situation was developing, and events were about to get seriously out of hand.

"Our most currently sourced intel believes our target is within the zhee slums that surround Ankalor City."

The CIC continued to hum and update all around them. There wasn't a sense of accomplishment here—not with all the death, and even the loss of a general, a thing that did not happen every day—but there was a sense of success. The zhee had been smacked down. The base retaken.

"There is also the matter of prisoners. We have..." The admiral consulted his tactical pad. "A few thousand captured zhee. Many of whom are wounded."

Still the Legion commander remained silent, watching the tactical maps. Waiting.

"So..." continued the admiral. "I'm not the senior tactical commander here, nor am I suited to that work, sir. And in my opinion, we have accomplished at least half of our mission. We took the base. But we did not get our hands on the high-value target. We don't have the resources to go after him into the slums, which are currently in full-scale revolt against the local Republic government. In other words... I'm a naval officer, sir. I take legionnaires to their targets so they can kill those targets. What do we do next? Sir."

Keller cleared his throat and stepped forward to a specific display showing the ground game around Ankalor City. He pursed his lips and rubbed his jaw.

"I'm in command now, Admiral. I expect the zhee raiding fleet to return at any time, as do you. I'll leave that section of the battle to you, but I'll need the fleet to help pick up the legionnaires who went in on *Hurricane*, *Sirocco*, and *Typhoon*. If we can't get them out of the sand and under their own power, then we'll scuttle them where they lie."

"Yes, sir," Ubesk replied. He sighed. "Today is the very definition of bad gone worse."

The Legion commander paused for a long minute. He watched the satellite real-time update of Ankalor City. The zhee were everywhere. Rioting in the streets. Burning vehicles. Storming police stations. Repub marines were under fire at the edges of the Green Zone.

Finally, he spoke. "The day isn't over yet, Admiral. We've got our best kill team on the ground. We'll secure our objective."

Victory Kill Team
Ankalor Slums

The sun was bidding its farewell to Ankalor City, and Chhun and his men were still fighting. Nothing as intense as when they'd first arrived. The streets were considerably emptier now, and it was mostly a matter of taking and returning fire on pockets of zhee hunkered down under cover. This was when accidents happened. The blaster fire becomes mundane, your body grows tired, the adrenaline is blunted... this was when accidents happened if you didn't force yourself to keep your attention on your surroundings and the task at hand.

"Keep sharp," Chhun advised the team. "We're almost done here."

Major Owens had checked in to provide the occasional status update. The primary Legion force was making progress and expected the fortress and its subsequent anti-air to fall before much longer. It had been a hell of a tough scrap, though.

"Why don't you let me take the long gun?" Masters was standing up from a blaster-scorched housing that led to the stairs. The team had been taking mandatory rests—one man at a time—in between zhee charges.

All except for Chhun. He had remained glued in place, only ducking when the fire got so thick that his team had to wait for the big guns from the tanks and combat sleds to clear the streets of enemy combatants. Until the next charge. It seemed like the zhee were determined to stop the Legion, or die to the last trying.

That was fine by Chhun.

But he still needed rest. He could feel the strain on his eyes and on his mind from constantly looking, surveying. The relentless grind that came from too much time in the red zone, trying to keep himself and his team left of bang. He could play the badass. Mumble some line about sleeping when he was dead. But that was the sort of thing that *made* you dead.

"Yeah," he said, motioning Masters over with a tip of his head. "Sounds good."

The leej who had fought by Chhun's side for years— who had been a kid when they'd first met, would *always* seem to be a kid to Chhun—hustled over, low and hard to kill. He flopped down and assumed the overwatch position, his hands checking the N-18 like a father inspecting a child returning from a long trip out of system. *Let me have a look at you.*

Chhun moved to the covered position of the stairwell and slumped down, his back against the door. It felt so good to just... rest. To let his legs lie at ease, to relax his neck and aching shoulder muscles. To let his arms hang and stretch out his fingers.

"Hey, Fish," Chhun called. One last thing before he allowed himself to sleep. "How's your ankle?"

"Probably jacked up, but I took a narco-shot to cut off the pain receptors. If it still hurts, I won't know until tomorrow."

"Roger." Chhun closed his eyes. *I could probably fall asleep right now*, he thought to himself.

And then the crack of the sniper rifle sounded, and Chhun's mind, which had been slipping along the current to some tropical island, was violently brought back to the here and now.

"That was quick," Masters said as he fiddled with the scope's range.

The HUD in Chhun's helmet showed a black dot where Masters had made the kill. Just around the corner of a building several hundred meters to the east. "There's probably more with him," Chhun said. "Watch the area."

"Oooh, good idea, Cap," said Masters mockingly. "Guys, listen to Cap. Apparently the donks are working together to kill us. Whatever you do, don't kill one and then strip your weapon and call it quits. *Guys*... there are *more* of them."

Chhun rolled the back of his bucket against the door on which he sat propped. As Bear and Fish laughed, he felt a profound thanks that the fighting here in the slums had slowed enough to allow for such a moment. The leejes down below from the quick reaction force were probably feeling the same way. It had been a while since they'd communicated. Chhun decided to check in with Sergeant Vix.

"How's your lieutenant?" he asked, not bothering with call signs.

"Stable, thanks," replied Vix. "We're thinking of making a push for Camp Rex. What do you think?"

Chhun considered a moment before responding. "It's gotten quieter, yeah. Streets home are probably hiding a few more IEDs than when you first came."

Vix paused, considering as well. "Thing is," he finally replied, "we're pretty much all black on charge packs. Twins are pretty good, but even the tanks only have a few blast canisters left."

Chhun could empathize with the sergeant who found himself stuck in an ambush he'd never asked for, tasked with assuming a command he also hadn't requested. The leej was probably second-guessing himself between every trigger pull.

"We could use a resupply ourselves," Chhun said. Victory Team had jumped down loaded with everything they'd need for the fight, but nothing lasts forever. "Tell you what. We're not exactly high priority right now, but the fight is winding down. I'll see if I can pull some Dark Ops strings."

The truth was that Dark Ops didn't have any magical ability to get things done. But the image of an elite, if not pampered and privileged, class of legionnaires persisted among the rank and file. Chhun used to think it himself when he first joined the Legion.

Vix seemed upbeat upon hearing the words. "That would be great," he said.

Chhun hailed Major Owens over his comm, vaguely aware that he wasn't getting the rest he was supposed to be enjoying. Oh well. No one to blame but himself.

"I was just about to call you, Captain," Owens said.

"Oh yeah?" Chhun went right into a sitrep brief. "Things are quieting down here. Most of the zhee have fled the streets. A few armed elements rally enough to try a charge, but they're paying for it. Buy stock in Republic Robotics because this planet is gonna need some serious sanitation bots out in force to clean up all the dead."

"Okay," Owens said, sounding just distracted enough that Chhun figured maybe the call he'd mentioned wasn't to get an update. "Listen, the guy we wanted, Bum Kali, he's not where he was supposed to be."

And that's why you send Dark Ops in to make the grab before you invade the planet. But Chhun kept that thought to himself. Keller had his reasons, and they were usually correct.

"Is he on planet?" he asked.

"He is. I made contact with some of the zhee from off-world—you know how much they hate each other. One of the shared contacts we have with Andien Broxin sold us some intel: the location where the shuttle pilot was killed. We compared our aerial measurements of the building with interior readings taken from the footage of the execution. It's a match."

A map snaking from Chhun's position to a warehouse in the middle of the slums appeared on his HUD. The report of the sniper rifle split the silence, and Masters let out a quiet whoop into his squad comm.

Chhun studied the map—and the holo of the target, a nasty-looking zhee with a pompous air that made him want to jump in and punch the donk in the face. Chhun's team could get this done. He was sure of it. But something else nagged at him.

"Sir," he said. "About the source. I'm not sure that Andien Broxin's contacts should be on the white list."

"Because of the thing with Captain Ford?" Owens let a sigh escape into the comm. "Look, I know you two go way back, and he led us to Nero. But I still have *major* issues with how he's choosing to deal with this situation. If you're asking me to trust Ford, I'm *telling* you to trust this intel."

"Yes, sir." Chhun looked around at the darkening sky. Fires were lit in the streets, whether to prevent or spot movement or to keep warm, he didn't know, but their localized glow made the badlands of Ankalor City pulse and throb with malice. "We can go now, but the QRF is hoping for a way home."

"They can try it," Owens replied, "but I only have limited assets on hand, and those are to support you. Most of what we've got is either out cleaning up or held in reserve."

Chhun squeezed his eyes shut, then blinked away a sudden fatigue. "Can you get us a minor orbital and some buzz ships?"

"I can…" Owens's reply seemed stuffed with unspoken caveats. "What did you have in mind?"

***

Sergeant Vix had the wounded loaded in sleds. He mixed them with combat-effective leejes so that they could fight back no matter where the donks might strike the column on its way back to Camp Rex. He'd had the dead tied to the tanks, trusting that the warriors being borne on those hulking war machines would somehow understand that Vix was only doing what he had to do to get them all out of there. Doing what needed to happen so that no leej was left behind.

"We all set?" he asked over company comm.

The beat up Grinders and Reapers of the QRF gave an affirmative just as the low drone of the incoming Republic—no, *Legion*—buzz ships approached from the Grodan Wastes. Vix smiled. These ships were as ugly as a Ffajan warthog, but Oba could they dust everything in their path.

Through his bucket's visor, Vix watched the buzz ships assume a holding pattern out over the wastes, free of any care of being shot down now that the Legion recon team had disabled or destroyed the anti-air defense network. Vix hopped into the open maw of his waiting combat sled, not wanting to be outside for what was coming next. He thought of the kill team, probably still on that roof, and gave a quick prayer that the operators who'd risked their own lives to save his would be all right.

No sooner had he sat down on a jump seat next to Keystroke—whose right sleeve of armor was stripped away, the blaster-burnt flesh covered in skinpacks—than the ground rattled from the orbital bombardment.

"Turn on holofeed," Vix ordered, wanting a glimpse of the very fist of god as it crashed down on the buildings surrounding what had once been a legionnaire last stand.

Massive blaster battery shots streaked down like meteors, obliterating buildings, gutting them, causing them to collapse and crumble until the forward holoscreen was useless to relay anything but a massive cloud of dust.

The thunderous assault stopped, and the buzz ships began to settle in above. As the dust settled, and the drivers reported in sufficient visibility to get going, Vix gave the order for the caravan to begin its winding trail back to Camp Rex. A tank driver called out zhee targets in the open, fleeing from the wreckage of the orbital strike that had laid waste to this part of the badlands. The buzz ships swooped ahead slowly, their heavy chain blasters methodically sending pieces of zhee and permacrete misting into the ether, paving a path of absolute ruin for the depleted QRF to follow.

Vix knew his men would reach the safety of Camp Rex without having to fire another shot in anger. His thoughts shifted to Captain Chhun and the Victory Kill Team.

Their night was just beginning.

***

Chhun stood motionless in the shadows at the base of the building his team had defended for so much of the day. His leejes were unseen ghosts hiding in the black of night. A chrono in his bucket counted down from five hundred as he looked through his visor at the unequivocal ruin that spanned for what passed as four city blocks before him.

Dust hung heavy in the air, as though the blast had freed it from the shackles of gravity, allowing it to just hover like a fog. Small fires burned among piles of rubble—the toppled buildings from the orbital strike. Exposed power conduits sparked and popped, their raw energy calling out portents of death to any who would touch them. The strike had cut power from the neighborhoods. All was dark.

A slight breeze sent paper and other debris gently sweeping down the rubble-strewn streets. Dead zhee from the day's combat lay covered beneath fallen stones and dirt, the dust stanching their blood, making everything look like it rested under a layer of volcanic ash. It seemed as though the entire galaxy had died, and all that remained was the dark and those who operated within that darkness: the black-armored Dark Ops legionnaires.

The counter reached zero. No sounds. No movement. No survivors.

"Let's go," Chhun whispered over L-comm. "We stay unseen. Ooah?"

The three other members of the team grunted their assent and followed Chhun into the darkness. Their feet made soft crunching sounds in the loamy streets as they followed the pathway superimposed on their HUD, trusting their night vision, thermal, and IR to expose any zhee before they themselves could be seen.

As they moved to the edge of the flattened sections of neighborhood and into the intact streets—the place where the zhee might not all be dead—they encountered a lone fifty-five-gallon drum burning excrement and scrap wood in the middle of the street. One by one, each legionnaire of Victory Squad moved swiftly past it, weapon shouldered and ready to fire, so that the soldiers needed only to lock eyes on a target before pulling the trigger. Chhun crossed first, then Masters, Fish, and Bear. Each man covering their exposed brother. Each man's shadow appearing as an inhuman giant as the orange light from the fire flickered before an abandoned building.

Safely returned to the dark, the team moved through trash-ridden alleys and narrow streets like avenging angels—visitors from the spirit realm.

When they reached a crudely constructed eight-foot-high wood fence that blocked off an alley, Chhun motioned for Bear to come forward, and the two of them held out their hands to providing footing for Masters to use to boost himself over.

Masters put his food in the makeshift stirrup and peeked his head over the fence before slowly lowering himself back down. "Big group of zhee coming this way," he whispered into his comm.

The legionnaires pressed themselves against the walls, sinking into the liquid ink of the blackest shadows, as a company-sized element of zhee marched down the street, waving their battle flag and screaming some unified battle psalm. They were headed toward the retreating column, no doubt hoping to kill just a few more legionnaires before they had the chance to reach the Green Zone and Camp Rex. This was by Chhun's own design—what he had hoped for. That the noisy departure, coupled with the buzz ships and word of a battered force running, would bring the zhee out, leaving Victory Squad room to operate freely.

A few zhee paused and stared with their soulless eyes through knotholes in the fence, looking directly at the Dark Ops legionnaires that hid only meters away, but not seeing them in the shadows. Soon the entire element was gone. This time Masters and Fish formed the boost, intending to get the biggest legionnaire over first.

From the opposite end of the alley, Chhun heard a crunch of broken glass. He raised his rifle and watched as a lone zhee turned a corner and began walking in their direction. The donk stopped, and it was clear that it could see Chhun... or at least see his form in the darkness.

On a thousand other worlds, Chhun would have put a finger to his bucket's mouth, telling the interloper to keep quiet. Then he and his team would disappear. But this was Ankalor. Chhun aimed down his sights and sent a suppressed shot into the zhee's forehead, dropping the alien in a crumpled heap in the middle of the alley. He lowered his rifle, letting it hang on the sling, then boosted up to the top of the fence with Masters's help, straddling the top and holding out his hand for Masters to pull himself up after.

The team moved quietly toward the target warehouse. The building was just a few blocks away, but if the intel was accurate, the threat factor would rise exponentially. Chhun halted the squad before a street lined with dented and beat-up speeders parked on either side. He knew that Owens likely had an observation bot watching from overhead.

"Does the peeper have a clue on what our optimal approach looks like?" Chhun asked.

"Don't have one nearby," Owens replied. "Your idea was a good one, and we're running with it. So not only are the buzz ships, QRF, and other assets moving out of the city to the Green Zone, we've pulled all observation bots. Don't want to risk Bum Kali getting paranoid and thinking we know where he's hiding by spotting a peeper overhead."

That made sense. Chhun wasn't crazy about it though. "Acknowledged." He motioned for his team to cross the road, moving in pairs, each man covering the next.

"Okay," Chhun said on reaching the darkened shadow of a building on the other side. "We've got no observation bots in the sky."

"That sucks," moaned Bear.

"For real," whispered Masters. "There's, like, an entire fleet up there in open warfare, and we're running around like this is another off-slate grab on a friendly planet."

"They don't want to spook the target," said Chhun, peering around a corner to spy farther up the street. He could see the corner prow of the warehouse, but his bucket didn't detect any beings on the ground or in the lone visible window. "And we don't want that either. If we miss him here, we may not get another chance."

"That," Fish added, "or someone else is gonna have to go in and finish the job. Always tougher the second time."

"Exactly," Chhun agreed. "We're almost at target, so let's keep frosty and quiet. We don't want 'em to know we're even in the room with them until out boots are on their donk necks."

The three legionnaires nodded.

Chhun moved along the shadows, leading the team through the quiet of the night to the warehouse perimeter. Somewhere in the distance, an animal gave a bark, probably guarding the place. Victory Squad moved to the warehouse terminal, passing bay after bay, looking for an unrolled door that would provide them entry. The place was huge. They needed to get inside without alerting anyone—making their big push only when they could be sure the target was in range.

"All these doors are shut," said Bear, "but I can probably tear one of 'em open. Don't look strong."

Chhun looked up at a high window just above a corrugated metal awning that protected a double-sized terminal door. The window had a protective cage that was bent and twisted enough that it no longer served its purpose. They would be able to make it through. "Let's get in through there," he said, pointing at the breach. "Masters, you first."

"Yep." Masters slung his rifle over his shoulder and moved to the awning, jumping to grab the ledge with both hands and pulling himself up. He made the most minuscule of clattering noises, then crept to the window's opening and peered inside. "Bit of a drop, but I don't see anyone."

"You two stay here," Chhun said to Fish and Bear. "I'll go in with Masters and we'll let you in."

Chhun followed Masters's route and unspooled a length of synth-rope while Masters kept his blaster ready, scanning for trouble. But just as he'd gotten one end of the rope tied around the security bar as an anchor, a sudden squealing from below indicated that the door beneath him was abruptly rolling up.

Chhun and Masters were unable to see anything below them.

"Two zhee," reported Fish. "One of 'em is squatting to take a leak, the other is lighting a joint."

Bear's voice bespoke an obvious portent. "We slipped into the shadows, more or less, but if they look this way..."

"C'mon," Chhun ordered Masters.

The two men took hold of the synth ropes and quietly lowered themselves into the warehouse, ending up directly behind the zhee. The aliens, each of whom had a PK-9A blaster rifle slung around his shoulders, were talking quietly to one another, passing the joint between them.

Chhun pulled a thin stretch of impervisteel cable from his gauntlet armor and nodded at Masters, who did the same.

Bathed in the shadows, the two Dark Ops legionnaires threw the cables around the necks of the zhee in tandem. They pulled tight and twisted.

The zhee clutched and clawed instinctively at their long necks, their vocal patterns completely silenced by the attack. Chhun and Masters pulled harder, helping the dying aliens to their knees as their claws scraped away the flesh from their throats in panicked attempts to resume the flow of air.

When the struggling stopped, the legionnaires released their death grips. Bear and Fish peeled themselves off the wall and hopped up onto the dock plate to enter the warehouse. Bear drew a knife from his webbing and slit the zhee's throats.

"Just in case," he said as pools of blood formed beneath the two dead sentries, spilling in rapid drips off the terminal dock.

The terminal entry point they'd breached was an open area, probably used for staging or unloading freight. Farther in was row after row of racking that towered up to the ceiling, most of them bare. To the team's left was a sort of open break area with dilapidated tables and toppled lockers. Behind that was a walled-off area.

"Let's clear the warehouse first," said Chhun. "Don't shoot unless you ID the target or you have to."

Rifles up, the team crept through the warehouse, their visors scanning for heat signatures or any other sign of where the target might be. Each man moved down an aisle that on closer inspection revealed terrible clues about what this warehouse had been used for.

"Dude, there's a pile of decapitated heads here," said Masters.

Chhun saw much the same. Zhee heads fixed in grotesque death stares, along with some humans and a few other species. His gaze rested on a simple handheld boring drill with sticky-looking spots of blood on the handle. Pieces of flesh and hair filled the grooves of the drill bit.

"Lights ahead," Fish called out.

"Go in slow," Chhun reminded his team.

They emerged from their aisles and gathered outside of a walled partition built within the warehouse. Its door stood slightly ajar—probably where the two zhee they'd dispatched had left from.

This might be it. Chhun adjusted his rifle to his shoulder and fought to push the butterflies in his stomach all the way down. Calculating, relying on his training, he positioned himself to take the point position.

"It'd be nice to have a crawler bot that could look first," Fish said as Chhun stood poised at the door.

Masters and Bear were taking care to lift the door as they opened it further, so as not to allow any squeaky hinges to give them away.

"Or toss in some ear-poppers first," added Masters.

The door was open.

"Neither of those are an option," Chhun said. They had taken no bots when they'd gone down to relieve the QRF, and they couldn't risk any premature noise. "On me."

He burst into the room.

It was dingy, with splattered walls and silt-like dust everywhere. A drop cloth was suspended at one end of the room, with portable lighting shining on the black background. In its center, the zhee war crest—a *kankari* dagger encircled by their alphabet—was prominent. A holocam was set up on a tripod, with no indicator light suggesting it was recording, and was pointed at a chair.

In the chair was the Republic pilot—the one who had been beaten and carried through the violent mobs at the start of the day. He was dead. Covered in lacerations with a great pool of blood beneath his feet, spilling down from the chair, staining it, making what remained of his tattered flight uniform a sopping brown rag.

A single zhee, not the target, looked up from his macabre work in surprise. He had been sawing away the pilot's head.

Nanoseconds turned into infinities. The target was not here, but this was certainly the place. Chhun's first instinct was to shoot. A quick double-tap that would drop the donk. Stop it from desecrating Chhun's fallen brother. But... the noise.

In a fluid motion, Chhun let his rifle fall to his side, resting on its sling. He reached behind his back to feel for his Kublaren tomahawk—the gift from Masters—and sent the weapon spinning end over end toward the zhee butcher. The blade sank directly between the alien's eyes, nearly cleaving its head in two. The rest of the kill team surged into the room as the donk fell to the floor dead.

A questioning phrase in the language of the zhee came from an adjoining room. An aged zhee peered through a doorway to look inside. Its eyes went wide with shock. It looked stunned. Afraid.

Victory Squad's HUDs identified a positive match to the VIP.

Bum Kali brayed in terror as he turned and ran.

"That's our guy!" shouted Fish. He ran headlong after the fleeing zhee.

Chhun and the team followed, chasing Bum Kali through a series of rooms. The target was running in front of two armed zhee warriors, who used their backs as shields and fired blindly at the pursuing Dark Ops team over their shoulders. Blaster bolts sizzled between the pursuing legionnaires, kissing the walls with black scorch marks and sending overhead lights into showers of glass and sparks.

The maze of partitioned halls and rooms ultimately led back into the main warehouse. One of the two zhee stopped to turn and send direct fire at the kill team. Fish dropped him almost immediately, then bolted ahead. In the cavern of the warehouse, new sounds came to the legionnaires over their buckets' audio receptors. Movement and running and the wild, vicious screams of more zhee.

Masters got a clear shot at Bum Kali's remaining guard and took him down. But a new force of zhee was seeking to intercept. About ten armed donks were running to place themselves between their great leader and the kill team that sought him.

Victory Squad fired on the pack, killing most before they could effectively aim. But one kept running, holding something in its clawed hand the legionnaire HUDs identified as a detonator.

Fish was closest. He let his weapon fall to his side and ran full speed at the zhee, spearing him with an open field tackle. Fish and the zhee disappeared in an explosion that threatened to cave in chests and sent every being in the room hurtling to the ground.

Chhun was the first to stagger to his feet. He pursued Bum Kali, teetering from side to side like a cantina drunk participating in a foot race. The zhee were all caught up in the blast, and what was left of Fish lay on the ground for Chhun to sprint over and past. Kali, though stunned, was far enough from the localized suicide vest's detonation to avoid being physically injured.

Kali wasn't screaming now. He was only running. Trying to reach the outside. To find a place, a home, to disappear to. A safe house or tunnel where he could escape. Chhun's body was reorienting. He was running in a straight line again. His vision narrowed so that Kali was all he could see.

He sprinted, leapt, and came crashing down on top of the zhee warlord. Placing a knee on the donk's neck, he roughly pulled his arms back and secured them with synth-wire before Bum Kali had a chance to grab for his knife—or a detonator switch of his own.

Masters and Bear arrived. They hauled the protesting, vitriolic Bum Kali up, and promptly silenced him with an isolation hood—but not before Bear sent a massive fist into the zhee's gut. "Lousy zhee bastard."

Chhun panted for air, breathing in the oxygen-enriched supply his bucket now fed him. He looked back at the carnage. At the horrible, violent remains of his brother.

He looked at what was left of Fish and he felt... nothing. And it terrified him.

"Major Owens," he called over the comm, still somewhat breathless. "Target acquired. Requesting shuttle exfiltration."

26

The main engine of the *Hurricane* was still smoking high above the aft cargo deck ramp of the assault carrier. Repair crews were up there with firefighting equipment, attempting to repair and control the damage at the same time. Beneath the massive sprawl of the carrier, within the forgiving shade of that long hot day, the bodies of the dead were being laid out. Wounded, critical supplies, weapons, and secure items were being offloaded and carried across the sands to the two sister carriers.

In the distance, across the sands, lay a burnt-out drop ship. Men still stood around it, looking at it, or perhaps just making sure nothing of value was left.

Sergeant Major MakRaven arrived at the body collection point aboard a small sled he had commandeered. Driving the sled was a legionnaire from a platoon that had been all but wiped out. The man had taken off his bucket, or it had been lost in the fighting. The sergeant major had his own bucket resting on his knee. The cool late afternoon wind that came out of the Ankalor wastes tossed his white hair and made his long drooping mustache flutter in the breeze. His eyes were tired, and his jaw was set firmly. He looked old. Old like some statue carved long ago, and forgotten in all the years since.

On the back of the sled lay bodies. Among them PFC Huzu and Captain Besson.

The driver pulled in close. Row upon row of dead legionnaires—shot, stabbed, or blown up—had been laid out the sands, hands folded over their chest plates, helmets, when they had them, staring skyward.

A duty officer approached the sled, and the sergeant major stepped tiredly out of it.

"Who you got, Sergeant Major?"

MakRaven walked around the sled and handed the duty officer a tablet. "Here's their pertinents, Staff Sergeant. Or at least all the info and records as far as I could pull off their buckets' microchips. Some of it was compromised due to the condition of their bodies. But there's enough for the count and the records."

The sergeant major and the driver unloaded the bodies and laid them down in a line next to all the others.

From out across the desert another detail was coming in from the wounded bird down on the sands out there. They were carrying the general. As they got closer, the sergeant major heard the whispers of who it was they were bringing in, and he called everyone to attention. They saluted as the legionnaires laid the general down next to Huzu. Besson was on the other side of the private.

For a long moment the sergeant major held the salute. And then, suddenly, with a quick snap, he dropped his hand. The rest of the legionnaires did the same, and resumed their work.

"Ah, hell," said the sergeant major, staring at the face of the dead general. It was the face of a young captain he'd once known. "I'm too old for this anymore," he sighed to no one in particular.

The wind picked up, blowing sand across the dead, and the sun continued its slow burn down behind cruel and jagged mountains.

The sergeant major stood there. Remembering everything that had once been. When he was young. And a legionnaire.

"Private First Class Huzu?" said a voice from behind the sergeant major. "Is that one Huzu?"

The sergeant major turned, seeing another legionnaire NCO.

"It was," he said.

"I just got a ping on his armor. I was his platoon sergeant over with the Two-Nine. We lost him during the battle."

"Well," said the sergeant major tiredly, "I found him. Don't worry, Sergeant. He gave a good account of himself. You trained him well. He didn't forget nothin'. KTF all the way."

"Good," said the man softly. And then bent down on one knee to touch Huzu's bucket. "Good," he said again to himself.

The sergeant major could tell that the platoon sergeant, a creature as tough as nails, and a kind of father all at once, was hurting. But the two of them said nothing, and the wind continued its efforts to bury the dead in the sand. As though it, too, were sorry for all that had ever happened. As though it were offering the only grace it could provide.

"Who was PFC Huzu, Sergeant?" asked MakRaven.

The kneeling man just shook his head, and when he spoke his voice was hoarse and husky.

"Just some kid who wanted to be a legionnaire," he whispered.

MakRaven heard that. Knew it. Had seen it more times than he could remember. Some kid from all the worlds of the galaxy, showing up scared and determined to be the one percent of the one percent of the one percent. Something honorable. A warrior without peer. He himself must have been that kid. Long ago.

Then the old man he had become, who had seen all the things he had seen, spoke.

"Well..." he said. "He definitely was that. He definitely was a legionnaire."

***

Aboard the *Mercutio*, Karshak Bum Kali, Grand Warlord of the Tribes, Most High Servant of the Four, Defender of the Pack, and Devout Disciple of the Thousand Cuts, was brought in under guard, shackled by ener-chains.

There was a confident sneer on his lips. His zhee eyes, normally baleful and soulless, burned with a fierce anger and naked contempt. Even though he was in chains, and captured, it was clear to all he was in command. *He* was great in a galaxy full of less than average.

He was brought into a large room deep in the belly of the *Mercutio*. Possibly close to the reactor. Or the hangar decks. Bum Kali didn't know much about the inner workings of a Republic super-destroyer, but it was clear this was not the bridge.

There was nothing but a chair. Most of the deck was cloaked in darkness.

"Sit," ordered one of the legionnaires over the armor's audio. It was like listening to a soulless ghost calling from somewhere in hell. Even so, these men were much less fearsome than the monsters who had captured him and killed his honor guard. He did not fear, now that he was aboard the ship.

Bum Kali gazed about as though he'd heard nothing from anyone. He had no intention of sitting. Or doing anything he was ordered to do by lesser beings. He knew exactly how to play this game. He'd been a prisoner of the Republic before. For many years in fact. And he had powerful friends.

The legionnaire struck him savagely in his bulbous gut with the butt of his N-4. It was quick and powerful, like an automatic jackhammer springing to sudden and impressive life.

Other legionnaires walked forward and helped the struggling Grand Prince of the Pavilion of Heaven into the simple chair within the belly of the *Mercutio*.

Out of the darkness two figures walked into the bare blue light thrown from overhead.

Legion Commander Keller, still in his dress uniform, unshaven. He looked tired. And cold. Dead cold. The man next to the Legion commander was a colonel. Bum Kali did not recognize him, but standing beside the Legion commander, the colonel seemed the event horizon of warmth and mercy.

For a long moment Keller stared at the gasping Glorious Hunter of the Grodan Wastes. Master of a Hundred Thousand Suns, and the Inheritor of the Eternal Vigilance of the Zhee Herds. His look seemed unaware of all the titles Karshak Bum Kali had acquired during his long and violent rise to power. Or perhaps he simply did not care.

Bum Kali collected himself. He remembered who he was and how much power he really possessed. Remembered all the influence he had acquired within the House of Reason. Far more than this pathetic soldier—no, *civil servant*—he was being forced to deal with.

"Let me tell you, Legionnaire," he spat with huffy disgust, "what exactly happens to me next. First... I am a *political* prisoner. And in accordance with the Sharlay Conventions established by the House of Reason, you are to treat me with kindness and respect due all species in the galaxy. I am to be afforded *good* food, *clean* water, a bed, safety, and access to counsel and the holo-webs without constraint or overwatch. Section 590.003.03 defined within the Sharlay Conventions grants me these rights. I am no longer an enemy combatant. I am a prisoner of conscience. And I wish to invoke sanctuary. Meaning... you should set me free now or face years in court and loss of rank. These, of course, are all enforced vigorously by the House of Reason. Even against the Legion. But you know this well, don't you, you pig dog?"

Keller showed no response to this. In fact, no one moved. Not the Legion guard. Not the colonel. And definitely not Keller.

Bum Kali continued. He had cowed them, and now he warmed to the next phase of his demands.

"But, Legionnaire, I am not finished with you. Of course I am not so foolish as to think you will release me now. You will *in time*, yes. And of course I will return to the battlefield. I promise to kill you *all* once I am set free."

Bum Kali smiled, knowing that this statement could not be used against him in trial. Because of the situation. Because he was under duress. And even then, he did not believe even a trial would happen.

"This angers you, does it not?" he said. "It is destined. The House of Reason will save me from you, Legionnaire. And someday I will repay this insult by personally administering the thousand cuts to one of your brothers."

Bum Kali awaited a response. When none came, he pushed further, almost dreaming of some breakdown that he could boast and laugh about in years to come. "You see what has happened? You won today. Yes. But did you really, Legionnaire? Did you really? No. You did not."

Bum Kali shifted in his chair. Leaning forward to express just how much he was enjoying this. This, too, was a kind of thousand cuts for him to give to his new victims, his captors.

A pleasant cruelty.

"You will have your way. You will make my home a military district. And... do you know what that will do? Do you, Legionnaire? Well, we will shoot you from buildings. Blow you up alongside roads. Blow up your citizens inside the Green Zones. You will die trying to keep our martyrdom sleds out of your bases. We will take your lives, your limbs, your very souls. We will make your children orphans, and your widows will lament that there ever was a Legion."

Bum Kali laughed. "And all that is until the Republic comes. For they *will* come... for *us*. Do not suppose me to be a fool and think that *this* is what the House of Reason desired for Ankalor. You have sealed your fate. *You*, Legion Commander, have ended the Legion.

"In time, they will become our slaves. Some may even find a way into the lesser harems. And all the while the House of Reason will paint you as the oppressors, and us as the victims. That is what's coming your way, Legionnaire. You will regret today. I promise you that. Every death. Every report. Twenty legionnaires killed by suicide bomber. A convoy of sleds shattered along the road during a night patrol. For years to come, you will read the reports of your little brothers being killed. And I want you to know now... It's all your fault, Commander."

Abruptly Bum Kali leaned back in his chair, enjoying the seat now. It felt to him like a throne.

"My pack brothers will rise from their chains. The House of Reason will see to it. We are a noble and ancient culture that needs to be protected... from you, Legionnaire. Our contribution to the galaxy is immeasurable. What have you given but pain and suffering to the races of the galaxy? You might find this hard to believe, but *you* are more hated than the zhee. To all the lesser races, you are the ones everyone hates. Do you believe that? Because it is the truth."

Bum Kali stopped, satisfied that his last attack had somehow been the cruelest.

Keller stepped forward now. In the cold light of the ship's belly, his face looked like the face of a serial killer who didn't care about anything or anyone. It was the face of reality. Looking down on the zhee, he spoke.

"There is no House of Reason. The House of Reason was dissolved this morning. The Legion is in control of the galaxy now. And no, you're not special. You are, in fact, nothing. The zhee are a blight on galactic civilization. You take. You exploit. You kill. Those are your contributions. That's your rich and diverse heritage. You're like wild animals. You're dangerous. And your time is up. Now the galaxy will have to do without your murder and mayhem. Because there is no House of Reason anymore to protect you from the consequences of your stupidity.

"After Gibraltaar was taken, there were three thousand, four hundred, and thirty-six zhee taken prisoner. I ordered them all executed. Your bases deep in the desert are, as we speak, being struck from orbit, by this fleet. The *Legion's* fleet. And as for the slums that have terrorized the Green Zone and the rest of the planet, the so-called 'badlands'... I ordered them firebombed the moment the last legionnaire was pulled out."

The look on Bum Kali's face was... pure shock. And horror. Horror because the man in front of him meant what he said. Even an old thief like Bum Kali knew the cold, hard, brutal truth when it was told to him.

This man was reality.

"I don't care if you believe me," Keller said. "I just wanted you to hear me say it. Show him anyway, Colonel."

Colonel Speich leaned down with a tablet and displayed a series holovids and images. They showed that everything the Legion commander had just said was true. Zhee being executed by firing squad on the desert sands. Satellite images of orbital strikes on bases Bum Kali thought to be well hidden. The slums on fire, cordoned off by the Legion and the loyal marines. Heavy armor guarding the routes out. Ponies and younglings burning. Pack brothers being shot down without quarter or mercy.

Speich clicked off the tablet and stepped away officiously.

"I wanted you to see this," said Keller, "because you brought it on yourself. You, like most every other race within the galaxy, could have played along and joined the team. But you've always been an enemy to a Republic too stupid to recognize that fact. We both know this. And even when we tried to treat you as friends, you stabbed us. Blew us up. Shot at us.

"There's a maniac with delusions of grandeur calling himself the emperor. And we're at war with him, too. The Republic, the *true* Republic, does not have time to send you to prison camps or re-education centers. Hoping that this time you won't pop back out, a problem just as bad as before. It does not have time to watch our backs. To watch *you*, waiting to see when—not if, *when*—you'll next try to plunge in the knife or send another explosive-stuffed corvette into a population center. The zhee of Ankalor are done. And we both know that once word of what's happened reaches the other zhee worlds, it all stops. They won't make the mistake of Ankalor. You, Bum Kali... you did this."

Keller pulled out his sidearm and shot Karshak Bum Kali in the face. The zhee's head flopped to one side. Blood and brains quietly drooled out onto the deck.

A holocam had recorded the entire incident. *This* was Keller's speech to the galaxy. His response to the House of Reason and anyone else determined to stand in the Legion's way.

And then there were only the steps of the commander and his legionnaires moving off, heading toward the next crisis that needed to be handled in order to protect the galaxy, and save it from itself.

COMING SOON...

GALAXY'S EDGE

MESSAGE FOR THE DEAD

Honor Roll

We would like to give our most sincere thanks and recognition to those who supported the creation of Galaxy's Edge: Turning Point by subscribing as a Galaxy's Edge Insider at GalacticOutlaws.com

Janet Anderson

Robert Anspach

Sean Averill

Russell Barker

Steven Beaulieu

WJ Blood

Christopher Boore

Aaron Brooks

Marion Buehring

Alex Collins-Gauweiler

Robert Cosler

Andrew Craig

Peter Davies

Nathan Davis

Karol Doliński

Noah Doyle

Dalton Ferrari

Mark Franceschini

Richard Gallo

Kyle Gannon

Michael Gardner

John Giorgi

Gordon Green

Shawn Greene

Michael Greenhill

Joshua Hayes

Jason Henderson

Bernard Howell

Wendy Jacobson

James Jeffers

Kenny Johnson

Noah Kelly

Mathijs Kooij

Byl Kravetz

Clay Lambert

Grant Lambert

Richard Long

Kyle Macarthur

Richard Maier

Brian Mansur

Pawel Martin

Tao Mason

Simon Mayeski

Joshua McMaster

Jim Mern

Alex Morstadt

Daniel Mullen

Eric Pastorek

Jeremiah Popp

Chris Pourteau

Walt Robillard

David Sanford

Andrew Schmidt

Ryan Shaw

Glenn Shotton

Daniel Smith

Joel Stacey

Maggie Stewart-Grant

Kevin G. Summers

Ernest Sumner

Beverly Tierney

Scott Tucker

Eric Turnbull

John Tuttle

Christopher Valin

Nathan Zoss

Jason Anspach and Nick Cole are a pair of west coast authors teaming up to write their science fiction dream series, Galaxy's Edge.

Jason Anspach is a best selling author living in Tacoma, Washington with his wife and their own legionnaire squad of seven (not a typo) children. In addition to science fiction, Jason is the author of the hit comedy-paranormal-historical-detective series, *'til Death*. Jason loves his family as well as hiking and camping throughout the beautiful Pacific Northwest. And Star Wars. He named as many of his kids after Obi Wan as possible, and knows that Han shot first.

Nick Cole is a dragon award winning author best known for *The Old Man and the Wasteland, CTRL ALT Revolt!,* and the Wyrd Saga. After serving in the United States Army, Nick moved to Hollywood to pursue a career in acting and writing. (Mostly) retired from the stage and screen, he resides with his wife, a professional opera singer, in Los Angeles, California.

Made in the USA
Middletown, DE
07 February 2020